Oliver had be... looking at it. ... Maria Elena what Puig knew of their affair in Montevideo. It would be stupid. The question was absurd. Of course Puig had known. What could Oliver ask? How did Puig like their having an affair?

Oliver signaled to a waiter in a mulberry jacket with black lapels. When the waiter left, Oliver leaned forward. "You said there was something important—"

"I thought you might be interested," she said, letting her dark lashes close softly several times over her blue eyes. "They are going to kill you because of Freddie. . . ."

Also by John Horton
Published by Ivy Books:

THE HOTEL AT TARASCO

A BLACK LEGEND

John Horton

IVY BOOKS • NEW YORK

Ivy Books
Published by Ballantine Books
Copyright © 1989 by John Horton

All rights reserved under International and Pan-American Copyright Conventions. Published in the United States by Ballantine Books, a division of Random House, Inc., New York, and simultaneously in Canada by Random House of Canada Limited, Toronto.

Library of Congress Catalog Card Number: 89-91245

ISBN 0-8041-0265-1

Manufactured in the United States of America

First Edition: October 1989

To all those who climb the volcanoes.

To Colin:

Inspired by your heated bias, there is a ptatomic slap at the week on p.22.

Yours in peak detection. John
Sept '89

Chapter 1

The young policeman stood over the body, not looking at the half-open blue eyes of a dead man no older than he was. That young man had been, a few minutes before, as alive as the policeman, his feet swift on the muddy ground on which the young policeman now stood heavily. The policeman shifted from one black-booted foot, damp on the wet earth, to the other, his feet growing cold with the cooling body on the ground. He looked away from the body to the line of gray saplings growing at the side of the red-tiled farmhouse. The landscape behind the trees was a monochrome of purple field, fallow, the land running flat and lavender to where it met the gray sky. The policeman's eyes continued to blink from the smart of the tear gas that hung about the yard. He put his head down to cough quietly.

He came quickly to attention, grabbing with one hand the submachine gun that swung from a shoulder sling, saluting with the other. The older of two police officers touched a black-gloved hand to his blue helmet, and the younger officer, his upper lip matted by a squared military mustache, frowned at the body on the ground. The three of them, the policeman as well as the two officers, wore the blue-gray uniform of the Montevideo police. The older officer took off his helmet, ran a gloved hand over wavy gray hair, and put the helmet back on. "There's no doubt. See what you can find."

The younger officer said, "Yes, comandante," and

went down on one knee beside the body, peeling the tweed jacket from the bloody, gray-flannel shirt. He was careful to keep his gloves from the blood. He began to go through the jacket pockets, drawing from an inside pocket a blue notebook the size of a pack of cards, half as thick, passing it up to his senior. The comandante took it, turning at the same time to stare toward the vehicles at roadside. The radio in the command car was raucous with its piercing squelch. The corporal driver hurried to the car, looking toward the comandante as he reached through the window to turn the volume down, but the comandante, head down, was letting the pages in the small book flip through his fingers.

Helmeted police were putting their feet onto the rear steps of the heavy blue trucks, passing weapons up to reaching hands, swinging up out of sight into the dark under canvas covers as the engines started with a rumble and the trucks began to shake with a roar. A booted trooper craned his neck to glance behind him as he paced backward off the pavement onto the matted grass in the farmyard, flapping two gloved hands at the khaki-colored ambulance that lurched back off the shoulder to his signals. Some three car lengths from where they stood at the body, the trooper shouted once, held up a hand, and the ambulance bounced to a stop. The trooper went to the road to stamp mud from his boots and to light a cigarette, hunching his shoulders against the small, cold wind of the July winter.

The wind chased the trucks, snatching at the sound of their engines with its passing. The trooper called something to the ambulance driver, his guttural remark, heavy with the Rio Platense accent, riding the same draft of air that stirred the blond hair on the dead young head, the same raw air that carried the first spatter of that evening's rain.

The young policeman had pulled his mouth to one side of his face, turned his head half away from the body. When the kneeling officer started to roll the limp body over to get at the muddied, hind pockets the young policeman gulped. The comandante glanced at him and told him to walk to the road to stand by at the command car. He added, to the officer searching the body, "This is amusing, a cipher, a transposition system using as a key, of all things, *The Purple Land*. In English, I mean. They regard us as being without culture, you see. The analysts will be happy fussing over it."

"Nothing else, offhand," said the officer as he rolled the body back. "Labels, laundry marks. Does it matter? They'll check the fingerprints. We'll know if we got the right one. And if we did not? What then?"

The comandante did not comment on the younger officer's tone. "Do you know the full title the Englishman gave his book?"

The other did not answer. He was bringing the lapels of the jacket back together, arranging them neatly over the rumpled shirt to cover the wounds.

"I thought not," said the comandante to himself. Out loud he said: "*The Purple Land that England Lost.*"

The kneeling officer came to his feet, not looking at his superior. The comandante handed him the cipher book. "The fingerprints will serve only to complete the record. It's he, all right. You must have seen him playing rugby. I came to know him from his visits to the *jefatura* He was arrested a lot in the old days. Well, too bad, but he chose this end for himself."

The comandante had begun to turn away when the other officer spoke. He was unable to keep his voice even. "It appears to me that the procedure here was irregular." His voice faded at the end and his eyes fell to the collar of the blue-gray overcoat the comandante was pulling up about his ears.

"Irregular?" The comandante's voice was benign. "I would say, rather: necessary. Timely, even. He and his friends killed a good man Tuesday. A man with a family." He paused to look down at the body. "No one made him take this path, you know. *Un niño bien*. Advantages that one of ours never had. You know how we've been working on this, the priority we've given it. You must have surmised that we had good intelligence when we came directly here. There's no mistake."

The comandante's gray eyes went to the whitewashed walls of the farmhouse, the brick underneath pitted with scars of the bullets, the smashed windows, the dark behind the half-open door. For the comandante the precise time had come to start the return, to reach back to the ordinary, to let the house age its fresh bitterness alone. The smell of fear was lost in the reek of tear gas, but the instant of young death would hang on here.

Only the morbid linger about such places. The incident should quickly be reduced to the standard vocabulary of the report form and filed away.

The comandante could see that the young officer did not want to leave it like that. He had come recommended for just this sort of small, precise operation: quick, discreet, intelligent, brave. With all that you must also be capable of foreseeing the consequences of your own actions. It's not a game, not at all—not an adventure. The blood is on one's own hands, not conveniently on someone else's. There are those who cannot accept that.

The comandante observed of the dead young man: "Think of it this way. He is to be preferred as a dead martyr." When the other officer turned away without speaking, the comandante spoke in a tone only slightly less mild. "Perhaps you would like to go in my place to visit the family of him who died on Tuesday."

Immediately he wished he had not indulged himself in that remark. He half turned to look once more at the body on the ground and was not surprised to find himself regarding the dead young man with sympathy. That was, if anything, a relief, a pleasant emotion, not unfamiliar in the circumstance. The comandante was not pronouncing a benediction but rather setting the record straight between them when he said: "No one else will die because of you."

The comandante flicked a finger at the ambulance crew waiting in their dark raincoats and their black berets. As he drove off, they bent to collect the dead young man.

Chapter 2

Some years after that incident in Uruguay—a sparse record of which can be found in the files of the Montevido police—the chief of the CIA station in Mexico found himself losing an argument with a colleague.

"Don't go to France, Harley. Stick around. This'll work itself out." Theodore Oliver had been afraid of how Harley Drew would take rejection, but he hadn't thought it would be that bad. Oliver looked up from the piece of paper Drew had placed on Oliver's desk, keeping his eyes on Drew as he walked quickly to his favorite chair, the largest one in the room. Drew moved nimbly, with the bouncing grace of the fat man. "France is full of Frenchmen," Oliver added.

"I like the French, Ted. I know it's not fashionable." Harley Drew settled in the chair, laced his fingers across his shirtfront, a white expanse the grander for his wearing a bow tie, and crossed one heavy thigh over the other.

"What about the menagerie? No one else can take that on."

"True enough, although you play on my vanity, Ted." Drew waggled a thick finger at Oliver. Drew was hiding his hurt well, keeping his dignity but not fooling Oliver either. "And," Drew frowned, still waving the admonitory finger, "*please* don't call it my 'menagerie.' You know how the wrong person reacts to that."

Oliver was having to handle the situation carefully. Drew's pride had been bruised badly. The paper on Oliver's desk was Drew's request for early retirement. CIA headquarters had refused to accept Oliver's nomination of Drew to be his deputy in the CIA station in Mexico. Not only once refused, but turned him down a second time when Oliver lowered himself to using the high-and-mighty tone, the haughty argument of prerogative of the chief of station.

Having inventoried Drew's virtues in his first cable, Oliver had wagered that headquarters would see his point and give in to his insistent argument in the second: custom gave you one objection to a displeasing decision. The station chief should have a voice in choosing who would serve in the position of special trust and intimacy, in deciding who would take over the station in the chief's absence—that was the gist of it. Oliver muttered, as he pecked out the draft of the second cable, "Headquarters types forget how you need someone to talk to, out here at the end of the line. Someone you can trust. Can't go home every night, unload on your wife. If you can't trust your deputy," Oliver said to the machine, as he paused in composition, "who the hell *can* you trust?"

Oliver was himself at least thrice scarred by headquarters' refusal: first, by not getting Drew into the deputy job, as he wanted; then, at being turned down when he put his own prestige on the line; and still more on being told he would have to make do with someone he didn't know, Nicholas Van Schaik, a name he had heard but not one he could put a face or a career to.

Hindsight told Oliver that he should not have told Drew that he was being nominated for the job. But that would have been foolish. Drew was one of those officers who pretend to scorn administrative duties. Oliver had been surprised when Drew had agreed immediately to be his deputy. Now, Oliver had lost not only the skirmish with headquarters but was having to struggle to keep from losing Drew. That was serious—they got on well together, and Mexico would be lonely without him.

Drew was saying that he would retire to the beige, stucco house in the walled garden in the south of France.

Oliver interrupted him. "People who give it up cold turkey, they're unhappy. You know. Always hungry for news: 'How things going?' You'll be kicking yourself all over the south of France after about three months of it. You've done something pretty unique here, the mena—your project, your work. Thing'll fall apart without you. You know that as well as I do."

"Headquarters may not think so. Or, more likely, not care. Anyway, none of us is indispensable. Isn't that the motto sewn on our battle streamers?"

"Look how fast you settled in here, Harley. The artists—painters, musicians, writers—eating out of your hand. Didn't I hear you've laid on a poetry reading in your garden?"

"You would find that amusing, of course." Drew paused and looked Oliver in the eyes. "Seriously, Ted, maybe I'm getting tired. Tired of having to fight for what I'm doing. Was there ever an outfit like this—like the Agency in this? Having to prove oneself over and over? Every time there's a change in command it's as though we have to start over again, demonstrating the worth of what we're doing."

Oliver wanted to keep the discussion specific. "Well, phooey, Harley. I mean, who will do your work? The boys in the green eyeshades will grab on to your shoving off as an excuse to phase it out."

"Let your new deputy pick it up."

"Van Shaik. With no Spanish?"

"I believe it's Van Schaik, as in 'shrike.' "

"So?" Oliver got up to pace around on the worn blue rug in his office. He had the beginnings of a pot belly, but compared to Drew, he was lean and trim. He was fair, blond, the hair graying at the temples, thick on the back of his head, growing bald in front. Drew, the same age, was pale, dark-haired, balding pink on top, damp-skinned, breathing through his mouth. Drew said nothing now, letting his head rest against the chair back, his eyes half closed. He had put a slight smile on his face. He fluttered the fingers twined on his shirtfront and blinked as Oliver continued talking.

"You'll go nuts in a nasty, little, French village," said Oliver, walking around Drew's chair, watching Drew's face as he spoke. "What will you do all day?"

"Where to begin? I shall rise, late." The smile flickered on his prim lips. Drew used to come to work a good hour or more later than Oliver did in the morning. Irritated, Oliver had told Drew that they might both be happier if Drew worked at home, a suggestion Drew quickly accepted. "After fruit, roll, and coffee, I shall play the piano, on the ordinary day, until noontime. On the odd day I shall write. I shall step out into the garden to go over the gardener's work before he leaves. We shall discuss the next morning's work. No doubt he'll be the one to decide what needs to be done, not I. That will not displease me. The results will justify him. In the village, across the stone-paved square from the church—or did I tell you? There is—"

"Play the piano. Crap, Harley! And write? Everyone's going to *write*. And garden? I see you creeping about with your little watering can." Oliver let out his breath, shaking his head. "I'm not kidding about the menagerie, what headquarters will do, you know, Harley."

Drew again grunted his disapproval of the term. He could not seem to keep others from calling his project "the menagerie," short for Mexico's Marxist Menagerie. He had heard the other silly names, the adolescent humor: Drew's Oh-So-Social Democrats, the Third Degree International. Drew spoke, eyes closed: "You will protect the work. I am confident. Another chief of station might not—not understand the importance of it. You shall not let them destroy it."

Drew sought out Latin American intellectuals wherever he served, for pleasure and for professional purposes. His detractors emphasized the former. His few defenders—possibly Oliver was the only one of them now—recognized his acquaintances with exiles and refugees from repressive Latin American regimes as operationally useful.

In Mexico City Drew moved and was taken in these circles unusual for a North American official. "You are not like the others," the Latin Americans would tell him. Drew would deny that while knowing well that there was some truth in what they said. He was embarrassed by the observation and annoyed at the criticism of his fellow officials, no matter that it was justified. He was consistent in this. On principle he refused to ingratiate himself by agreeing with the attacks of Latin American intellectuals on the United States. Let the visiting academic people, down in Mexico on their foundation grants, play that game for their own advantage. Rather it was Drew's loyalty that gained the respect of the Latins who disagreed with the United States. And his calm replies led some of them quietly to question the fashionable opinions they had been told since childhood.

"Think of Mexico as a vast salon," insisted Drew to Oliver one time. "Here you have politicians, intellectuals, of every ideological flavor, sharing only the melancholy distinction of being unwelcome at home. Out of power, without position, languishing in their Mexican asylum. What a rich brew of ideas!"

When Drew became so inflated as to be in danger of drifting away on the wind of his own oratory, Oliver was the anchor. "Sure, Harley. But let's bring a few into focus. You've got to take aim, even with a shotgun."

"I do, I will, I am, Ted," Drew would agree immediately, to distract Oliver's criticism.

Drew would hurry back to his Paraguayans and Cubans, their democratic ambitions for their own lands withering year by year, despairing ever of going home; the Chileans, more cheerful for reason to expect a change; the moderate Central Americans with their sad hopes, uncomfortably trapped between the extremes in their torn lands.

Drew knew others, too, those afraid to speak to a North American official: Marxist-Leninist internationalists on the lam for kidnappings or killings, thin-lipped Tupamaros, their hands too bloody to let them go home to Uruguay; the stray hard-eyed Argentine Montonero—these sorts living on the Cuban dole. There were Guatemalans with cruel faces, running ratlines into the Quiché, bringing out the wounded, recruiting in the refugee camps inside the Mexican border; clever Salvadorans grinding the propaganda mills for pliant collaborators in the United States; the odd, lonely Grenadian struggling to speak Spanish.

The community was not a unit. Rather there were circles, some openly intersecting others, some being connected only by the secret penetration of one group by others. For Drew was not alone in moving in emigré circles in Mexico. When he had gained the first appreciation of the circles that he considered satisfactory, if tentative—this was after his first few months in Mexico—he had sat before Oliver's desk to report.

"A précis of my findings." Drew had leaned forward on that occasion to slide some typewritten pages across Oliver's desktop. He had grinned, too, at Oliver, a tacit recognition that he had let the deadline for decision slip. "I've been to a number of get-togethers now. At every one, I can say with confidence, I run into at least one dark-browed fellow who gives me a dirty look and turns on his heel. Or I'll sense his watching me from across the room, scowling, not meeting my eyes, asking someone else who I am, what I'm doing there. Doesn't like it, my being there, a North American, you see. Sometimes he's a Cuban. Sometimes a Nicaraguan. Maybe he doesn't like my finding him there. Or a Soviet, not so openly hostile, but not pleased, either, to see me. Or an East German, a Czech." Drew had spread his hands and signaled his conclusion with a fat man's gasp. "And who is not there? The North Americans aren't there, that's who. We're leaving the game to the others."

"Go to it, Harley," Oliver had said at that time. "Let's be there."

Drew's fluent Spanish, the sympathy that charmed Latins who would turn away from the stiff North European or boring North American, his wide reading in politics and literature, admitted him to these circles. But it was his unfeigned interest in these people and his insistence on the need for the CIA to be there, since no one else was, that made him—as Oliver thought him to be—indispensable.

Oliver had come back now to sit down in the chair behind his desk. Drew was not to be taken by the obvious arguments. "So," Oliver said with a sigh. "Well, what the hell, Harley?"

Drew changed the subject. Speaking of the CIA officer headquarters was sending to Mexico as Oliver's deputy to replace him, Drew said, "I suppose you know that Nick Van Schaik is Oates' brother-in-law?"

"No! Who says so?" A wasted question—Drew knew all the CIA gossip. He attributed his sprightly late bulletins to CIA people passing through Mexico to and from posts to the south. Oliver suspected that Drew regularly broke regulations by exchanging news in personal letters with those in CIA headquarters and in posts abroad who, like him, were guiltily scratching the exquisite itch to know who was up and who down, who promoted and who not, who having an affair and with whom, who was assigned where and why. "I don't believe it," said Oliver.

Drew smiled.

Oliver believed it. He turned in his chair to open the blinds at the window behind his desk, looking down at the street, contemplating the people striding below him, presenting the tops of their heads to him, their feet splaying out on the concrete. Walking seen from above came across as a difficult acrobatic feat. Whitney Oates, the chief of the South American Division, was quite capable of appointing his own brother-in-law to the post of deputy in Mexico. First, it would take care of an incompetent ass of a brother-in-law, quieting Oates's sister or wife—to whomever the silly fellow pertained—and second, it would give Oates a way of keeping his eye on

Oliver. Or, by golly, of moving the cretin into Oliver's job. That would be Oates all over.

Oliver watched a wide-brimmed sombrero dance along the walk below him. It stopped, pirouetted, bowed, and began dancing across the sidewalk again. Two, scuffed boot toes and then a pair of tight blue pant legs appeared below it; the occupant was revealed as the sombrero moved from the perpendicular.

Three laborers from the construction work down Rio Danubio scuffled along the walk below Oliver. One had a sledgehammer on his shoulder and the other two circled, mocking him. Above the noise of traffic and the morning stir, in a high tenor, from his throat rose the popular obscenity of Mexico streets: "*Pen-DE-jo*," he sang. As Oliver turned back in his chair to face Drew, the word drifted again from the street, more faintly now, but clear and apart from the noise around it.

"Listen," Oliver said. "He's not going to get away with it, putting his ass of a brother-in-law down here. We can call him on that one. That's a conflict, nepotism. I'm going to send something—"

Drew held up a hand. "I wouldn't, if I were you. After all, you don't know Van Schaik. For all you know, he may have a good file—"

"Highly unlikely if he's Oates's brother-in-law."

"—and they'd fire that back at you. And, anyway, he's on his way, isn't he?" Drew stopped and maneuvered a thick arm in front of him to look at the gold watch on his wrist. "Also, aren't you having lunch?"

Oliver leapt to his feet. "It's your Uruguayan, Pooch, isn't it?" Drew had run into Señor Puig at some boring meeting on economic development at the Colegio de Mexico. "And at that spiv restaurant too."

"Your Uruguayan now," said Drew, smiling. "With my leaving—after all, Uruguay was your beat, not mine."

Chapter 3

Oliver had to dodge through the crowds of aimless, midday strollers, doddering, elderly tourists, rude vendors putting their faces at his. Stepping off the slow sidewalk of the Zona Rosa, he had to weave his way through the automobiles stacked honking in narrow Calle Amberes to get to Delmonico's on time to meet Puig. Oliver was irritated at Drew's having arranged for lunch at Delmonico's. Drew had defended the choice, pointing out that the flossy restaurant catered to businessmen, well-off tourists, politicians; to the expense-account, lobbying, fixer trade: "Spivs—if you want to sweep your net so ungenerously wide—yes. Doubtful that anyone of the other ilk will be there to report having seen Puig with you." Drew was right about that. Delmonico's was no place for the impecunious exile.

When Drew used the surname Puig rather than the familiar nickname Pooch—although the difference in the pronunciation of Puig and the word "pooch" was hardly discernible to the untrained ear—he was reproving Oliver for the childish North American way of slapping these mocking nicknames on foreigners. But Drew was wrong about Oliver in this case. Whoever it was—he could just as well have been British as North American—who had first referred to Puig as Pooch, it was not Oliver. But everyone had picked it up. There was always some doubt whether Puig realized that his surname had been anglicized in that friendly derogatory way or whether he assumed that the Catalan name was too exotic for a foreigner to get quite right.

"Hey, Pooch. *Qué tal?*" On the red, clay courts at the Carrasco Lawn Tennis Club, short-legged, intent at mid-match in his sweaty tennis whites, belt bulging and his jowls red where he was putting on weight, Puig would finish the point before turning to find who had called out to him, peering through the vines on the netting to see who was walking under the eucalyptus trees. He would wave his racket and laugh before turning to crouch, ready for the next point. He was a popular partner for the better tennis players, a good sport, courtly with the women at mixed doubles. He spoke good English. He had gone to "the British," meaning the British School, as had many Uruguayans of his sort, that jumble of families, genteel or striving to be seen so, given to describing themselves as middle class.

Puig was to be seen at all the embassy parties in Montevideo, so notably that someone once suggested that Puig was furnished by the caterers. He himself might make a joke of his presence. At a Soviet Embassy reception, Puig would turn up at Oliver's elbow, half a head shorter, grinning and showing the whites of his eyes at the idea of the two of them being under that particular roof. Or it might be with the Rumanians or, for that matter, at the Spanish or the British embassies.

He was often at the residence of the ambassador of the United States when visitors were in town. With his good English, he could explain the complex politics of Uruguay. "We may be a small country," Oliver more than once heard Puig holding forth, "but our national anthem is longer than yours. In the same way, our politics are more baroque than yours." Having spent time on an *estancia* in the country, Puig could talk knowingly of cows and sheep, gauchos and ostriches. Visitors to Uruguay assumed him to be a country gentleman dabbling in politics. Dazed travelers, confused by having darted from one Latin American country to another, appreciated his crisp way of setting Uruguay apart from the rest. Puig would lightly recount the history of Uruguay, the Banda Oriental, why Uruguayans called themselves Orientales, how the British came to invent Uruguay, the shabby way the Uruguayans had treated their great patriot, José Artigas. And just at the right moment, before he became a bore, "Did you know that until recently," he would ask a visiting diplomat or congressman solemnly, standing at a closer Latin social distance than the North American expected: "Did you know that until our regrettable economic decline we Uruguayans had the distinction of enjoying the world's highest *per capita*—" Here he would pause and raise his tumbler, grinning to warn his listener, "—consumption of Scotch whiskey?"

Puig had stood for election on one of those obscure party lists and thanks to proportional representation was once elected to the chamber of deputies. That was after Puig and his wife broke up, Oliver recalled as he went around the corner in Calle Londres, sneezing in Mexico City's yellow-brown haze. In a few weeks the April rains would do their little bit to clean the air, heavy now with dust and ozone.

Partway down the block was Delmonico's, the passage into the restaurant so dark that Oliver came to an abrupt stop to feel his way. Ahead, up a few steps, a line of waiters in persimmon waistcoats, napkins over their arms, standing in the soft light, inspected him. As he moved toward them the maître d', looking more like the conductor of a symphony orchestra than do most conductors, moved up behind the waiters, preparing to raise his eyebrows at Oliver.

Oliver raised his own at the maître d', looking past him to find Puig rising from behind the white linen of a table for two along the wall. The maître d' walked Oliver over to Puig—probably Puig had impressed him. "I'm a good five minutes late and you early," said Oliver. "You put me to shame."

"*Hora inglesa*," said Puig, smiling. "I run on English time." His eyes were examining Oliver's face as Oliver did his. Puig's colorless straight hair was thinly slicked over a visible ruddy scalp, his jowls heavier, wrinkles running deeper down either side of his nose past his long upper lip and his wide and thick-lipped mouth. His nose was blobbier than Oliver remembered. It had been some years, after all. Puig's head was large for his height. It was the short legs that brought him low. Were he a foot taller, he would be an impressive figure. His narrow, sloping shoulders still looked powerful, his torso filling the jacket snugly, his belly neatly buttoned out of sight. Puig had a tumbler in front of him, Scotch over ice. They sat down and Oliver ordered a Scotch.

"How is the consumption in Uruguay, *per capita*, these days?" asked Oliver, glancing at Puig's glass.

Puig laughed. "You remember." Then his face took on an earnest look. "Not so good, I hear. I haven't been back, you know. But I'm going."

"Oh? I thought . . . well, I don't know what I thought."

"When the Tupamaros—it became much worse after you left, you know? I did my duty as a citizen, you know?"

"What do you mean?"

The Scotch arrived and Puig raised his glass to Oliver's. "Old times," he said. "What do I mean? We could not stand to one side and leave it to the police. They needed help. One had to take a role. Were there excesses? Yes. But now people forget about the Tupamaros who caused the violence in the first place, and put the blame on those of us who tried to put a stop to it.

"All the left has been welcomed back," Puig went on to say, "and they hold a grudge against the rest of us. Try to make trouble over the past." Oliver tried in vain to remember just where Puig had sat on the wide spectrum of Uruguayan politics. Puig was not the only politician better known for seeking office than for his firm positions. Oliver could remember nothing of his group's principles or even if they claimed any.

"So," Puig was saying, "I have been forced to go about arranging my return with some care. My soundings-out have been rewarded. No problem. I shall be welcomed in the circles that matter." Puig here gave Oliver a significant glance but immediately turned to listen intently to the waiter's recommendations for lunch.

And during lunch he gave close attention to eating. Oliver, with a sentimental curiosity about Uruguay, asked questions of Puig that drew short answers, generalities. Oliver tried to ask about people, straining to remember names. Puig replied briefly. So-and-so had been in prison, another had been assassinated in Argentina, another had returned from exile in France, another was now a minister of government. Puig ate seriously, gulping wine, looking at the level in the glasses, filling Oliver's glass and then his own, pausing to praise the wine and to suggest they share another bottle. When they had finished their plates, Oliver asked if Puig would have dessert. Puig suggested instead they both have the brandy and Oliver refused, indicating his wineglass, Puig ordered one for himself and, leaning back against the wall, began to speak.

"You people will need friends in Uruguay now, more than ever," said Puig, looking solemnly at Oliver, "after all that happened—the memory of the military regime. There is suspicion, hostility toward you people. Some blame you." Puig shrugged and rolled the brandy about in the snifter. "Friends of your country—and you count me as one, I know—the sophisticated Uruguayan understands the exigencies of those times." Here Oliver felt the beginning of the twinge that pricks the experienced intelligence officer when he senses that the person speaking to him is about to suggest a step imperative for the good of the United States. It was as though a friendly parasite had taken up residence somewhere in Oliver's lower chest, near the diaphragm, lying dormant until the particular signal came: "Watch out! Here it comes," the little beast would warn, thus paying its rent.

From tentative, Puig turned frank. His scheme was simple. He had a good reputation, unstained, unlike so many politicians who were willing to sell out to the high bidder. His devotion to the United States was well known to Oliver—next to Uruguay, and so on. The United States needed friends these days, and needed a party favorable to United States interests, not hostile or suspicious, not out for their own welfare, as so many are. Oliver would understand with his knowledge of the world that Puig's faction or party—the difference would be defined by the amount of help they got—at the start, anyway, could not blatantly support the United States. Oliver, having lived in Uruguay, knowing the country, "been one of us, in a sense," would see the importance of this where the ordinary North American bureaucrat, knowing only Europe or Asia—short-sighted, petty, lacking Oliver's insight—would be *antipático*, unsympathetic. There was so much more of this, that Oliver's alert parasite began rudely to yawn and then went back to sleep, deciding that Oliver had been sufficiently warned and could be left to operate on his own.

Puig finally paused to let Oliver respond. Oliver was brief: as much as he admired Puig and appreciated his generous offer, he felt sure that the United States would not want to enter politics in Uruguay in the direct way Puig suggested. Puig's face grew limp with disappointment. He repeated his argument in different words but to the same end, suggesting that they have another Scotch each for old times' sake. Oliver tried to hide his annoyance at having to sacrifice the best part of the afternoon to Puig and having it end in a fuzz of alcohol.

Puig had a fallback suggestion. He would go back to Uruguay to serve as a source on the machinations of the *politiqueros*—the cheap politicians—and on the maneuvers of the far left. A less significant contribution than what he had first offered, it would not cost as much—a brief flash of resentment there—but would still be important, perhaps a trial period leading up to something more significant. He would need some help with entertainment expenses, an office, that sort of thing.

Oliver shifted about impatiently, restless and at the same time embarrassed for Puig. The role of supplicant came more easily to Puig than did the opposite role to Oliver, Oliver taking no pleasure in the power either to please Puig or to withhold his favor from him. He began to suspect, the more Puig spoke, that Puig was far out of the Uruguayan political picture. Puig might be able to go back, but hardly to be as welcome in leading circles in Uruguay as he claimed. Hardly a good source on anything that mattered.

What Oliver said, rather, was: "Look, Pooch, I really appreciate your coming forward and offering to help us out. But under the present circumstances"—whatever that meant—"our people won't want to get involved quite like that in Uruguayan politics. We weren't, you know, in the old days."

It was a way of trying to extricate himself from Puig without having Puig lose face. But it was no use. Puig would not gracefully fall back. "I've heard there are some Tupamaros hiding out here in Mexico, you know?" Oliver was sad as Puig went down what he fancied to be the North American shopping list, trying to come up with the item that Oliver would buy.

In the hard times, the genteel Uruguayans of Montevideo, down on their luck, would find themselves forced to sell off family things. *Remates,* they called them—auctions. Garage sale was more like it. Oliver had gone to one, only one such public sale at a fine brick house on the Rambla in the suburb of Carrasco. Across the road muddy, brown waves of the Rio de la Plata had hissed over the broad beach, a chill wind gusting from the sea. The family, decent people, huddled to one side, trying not to cringe as strangers fingered their possessions.

Puig got a small score with his last item, succeeding at making Oliver thoughtful. "The Soviets are interested in people like me, you know. People from these little, unimportant Latin countries," Puig said, less friendly, but not ugly either. He was too amiable for that, even with all that brandy and Scotch inside him.

"What about the Soviets, Pooch?"

Sly triumph came into Puig's eyes. "Yes. It's as they

say. Mention the Soviets and the North Americans take notice. You see why we Latins feel we are only pawns in your eyes."

"Oh, come off it, Pooch."

"Nevertheless," Pooch was getting up, holding onto the table as he rose. "Nevertheless, I have enjoyed the lunch, Ted. Here is my card." Puig concentrated on writing a telephone number on the card and handed it to Oliver, who was standing now himself. "Think of what I've said. I don't care for the Russians, you know. It would be a great pity if, after all that Uruguay has passed through . . ."

Leaving that unfinished, Puig turned to walk carefully ahead of Oliver to the door. They said good-bye outside the restaurant. Oliver watched Puig make his way across the street, savoring his immense relief that the conversation was over without Puig once having mentioned her name.

Chapter 4

Although there was work awaiting him on his desk, Oliver went back into Delmonico's and asked a waiter for a phone. The waiter gave a half bow, flicked his napkin, and led Oliver to the phone. Oliver thanked him and dialed a number.

"Bueno?" a voice answered.

"Good, Ivor. What about a nice cup of tea? Nothing urgent, but if you're available."

"Oh, God. Anything to be free of this dreadful trade report."

Then Oliver called his office to tell Mrs. Pott that he would be back in half an hour or so.

"Mr. Drew told me to remind you that you have to go to the airport."

"What for?"

"The new person, you know." His secretary was careful.

"The hell. He's going to meet him, isn't he? Lemme talk to him."

"He's gone for the day. I'm alone here."

Oliver cursed and thought, isn't there some way? "What about you, Mrs. Pott?"

"Oh. I have choir practice. Anyway, that wouldn't be suitable, would it? He wouldn't want me meeting him. And I don't know him. Mr. Drew said you would understand."

"Would you call home for me, in that case, and tell

Marge that we've got a guest for dinner?" He would have to do that much—damn! After a pause, Oliver asked if the plane was on time. Mrs. Pott said that she had called and they had said it would be, but he knew how the Mexicans always said that, no matter what. Oliver hung up as she was talking.

Ivor Buchanan was sitting at a small round table tiled with the same blue and white tile as the floor. Across the coffee shop of the small hotel which catered to Mexican families from the country, two, small children were struggling on the tiled floor, grunting over a stuffed panda. They paused to regard Oliver, a careful glint in their brown eyes, as he came up the steps from the street. Ivor Buchanan's table was at the end of the room farthest from the children. There was a beer on the table before him and he held a newspaper in front of his face. He pulled the paper down as Oliver came up to the table, and stared wordlessly at Oliver as he sat down.

"Thanks, Ivor. I don't know," Oliver said to the waitress. "Coffee."

"Had one of those nice American days, have you?"

"Made complete by lunch with Don Julio Antonio Puig—Camps, I think the matronymic is."

"Mm."

"I knew him in Uruguay. He looked me up. That's how I ended up having lunch with him."

"Ah, yes?"

"I know he's been around to see you people."

"You Yanks have the money."

"But you Brits had Uruguay, in your own way. If Puig were not Uruguayan, he'd be English or Welsh, whatever. If he couldn't be Argentine, that is."

"Not Welsh, I hope."

"Scotch, then."

"Scots."

"Well, maybe Pooch doesn't know you ran out of money. He doesn't seem to know that we have, too. So?"

"To form a new political party? Etcetera. Etcetera."

"Yeah. What's he after, Ivor?"

"This is another of those occasions that leave me deeply grateful that Her Majesty's Government have left these sordid games to others, the happy consequence of which is that I need no longer peer into the black heart of the avaricious Latin."

"Puig isn't like that."

"No? As you know, I do draft the skillful piece—once a fortnight, I should say—explaining to HMG on behalf of His Excellency, for the fiftieth time, it may be—because he will not understand it—why the Mexicans will not buy British." Buchanan drained half of his beer. "By the by, I am grateful for the interview with your Economic Section head. He kept disgorging bulletins and studies, great sheaves of paper that will prove most useful when I can bring myself to crib from them."

Buchanan wore his wavy-brown hair long, so long that it flowed back along the side of his long head, past his ears, giving him the look of an Afghan hound, an intelligent one. His eyes were large, blue, the nose long, narrow, Afghan. A lank lock dangled from Buchanan's temple toward his dandruff-flecked, pinstriped shoulder. Buchanan, tracing Oliver's glance, put his beer down and tucked the hair back into place.

"I don't think that Puig has a black heart. But, anyway, what's he up to, Ivor?"

Buchanan made a grimace with his mouth and shrugged. Oliver was curious to hear whether Puig had mentioned to Buchanan the Soviet interest in Uruguay. Better keep that to himself. There might be something to work on if Puig were being courted by the Soviets. Oliver said: "You said 'etcetera.' "

"Did I?"

"Twice." Oliver sipped his coffee and waited.

"That's a presentiment," Buchanan said. "I have it on fairly good authority that he is not infrequently to be seen with our Russian colleagues."

"Don't you find that useful, I mean, potentially?"

"No. I am quite serious when I speak of my dislike of these smarmy types, groveling after money. How can you possibly feel content with one of them between you and the Soviet johnny? They only keep the bidding going. I can't be bothered. And I refuse to bother HMG.'' Ivor finished his beer. "How is Marge? I'm thinking of going over to Ixtapa and scuba about on the long weekend. Shall we make up a party?"

"Gosh, Ivor, I don't think we can. But thanks. Give us a rain check."

"Inform Marge, if it would make a difference, that my companion that day you saw us in Zihuatenejo, the one you referred to, in your coarse way, as a bimbo, will not be accompanying me in the future. If you would say the right word on my behalf to that red-hot mama that works for your ambassador—what a cozy pair we'd make!"

"She's a real cold fish, Ivor."

"I would warm her. You may tell her that."

"You're inviting a rumble between my ambassador and His Excellency. To say nothing of the problems between the Department of State and an agency that shall remain nameless."

"But my intentions, old chap, are of the most honorable."

"What about Mrs. Pott, then?"

"You recklessly endanger what little goodwill remains between our two countries."

"So, no interest in Puig. I'm a little surprised, Ivor."

"Surprised? Whatever for? You surprise me, actually, even thinking of using him in any way whatsoever. Down at heel, going about hat in hand, like a beggar."

"Come on, Ivor, you're pretty hard on him!"

"Not at all. A bad record in the Tupamaro time, I hear. Worked with the police against them. Bloody Ulster Constabulary stuff."

"And the Tupamaros the bloody Marxist IRA, I might point out."

"Yes, yes. Where's the right in these affairs?"

"I'll tell you something, Ivor, there's not the slightest

goddamn doubt in my mind about the Tupamaros being wrong. I was there, you know."

"And perhaps just a bit too close to it?"

"Oh, crap, Ivor. Forget it! What about Puig: What have you got specific on him?"

Buchanan shrugged. "Indeed, what more could you possibly want?"

"I'm not aware that your service works exclusively through Anglican curates. I mean, one works with what one has to work with."

Buchanan gave Oliver a scornful look. "Deep statement, that. I must give it thought. In any event, as you asked, I advise you to stay well away from Señor Puig."

Chapter 5

The evening traffic on the Reforma was no worse than Oliver expected, but he was more annoyed than usual at the thought of being late to meet the plane of Whitney Oates's brother-in-law. Oliver thought he would never get past the light at Avenida Hidalgo, the lanes slow, the cars taking forever to move up into position to turn toward the airport.

"Bastard!" said Oliver, as one of the green minibuses cut him off. "Bastard!" he said again, thinking of Oates's brother-in-law. Wouldn't you know? Oliver asked himself, knowing the thought to be quite unfair, that he'd come in during the worst of rush hour.

The virtue of promptness is the more noticeable when missing. Among the lessons taught an intelligence officer in his early days of service is the importance of being on time. If childhood training or military service had not already accomplished this, he is brought up short in training sessions until he shows some respect for the exigency of the minute hand. More than one CIA career has been blighted for being late—no matter what the explanation—for a date with a senior officer. Fair or not, an odor of sloppiness, a whiff of stupidity, seeps from a personnel file for the blunder of standing up a superior. Being late for Whitney Oates's brother-in-law's plane would not be serious—rather an attractive thought, actually—but the pouting brother-in-law would be quick to let Oates know of it, adding another petty mark against Oliver in Oates's black backbiting book.

Oliver pressed the accelerator and managed the petty victory of cutting off the offending green minibus as they both whirled right on Eje 1 Norte. Traffic was looser there until Boulevard Puerto Aereo itself. Cutting into an obviously illegal parking spot, trusting to the diplomatic plates to protect him—a trick deserving censure when others did it—Oliver slammed the door and skipped briskly across the darkening parking area to Arrivals. His relief at learning the flight was late, just then touching down, was enhanced by a brief gloat over the tardiness of Nicholas Van Schaik.

Pacing and turning on his heel, Oliver stopped occasionally at the edge of the crowd gathering outside the customs area. Hotel touts were pushing forward as the first passengers came in sight. Oliver moved away from the others to scan faces as passengers came into the light, eliminating the obvious categories, waiting for the appearance that would fit the pattern in Oliver's head. Then a round-faced and pudgy North American in his thirties, one of those persons who looks middle-aged in youth, conventional in his wrinkled gray suit, the discreet dark gray topcoat over one arm, the expensive carry-on luggage in one hand, stepped to one side of the stream of people coming toward the waiting crowd. He sent lost glances about the hall. Oliver gave himself a quick nod to salute his acumen and started toward the fellow. Might as well get it over with. But before he went any farther Oliver turned when a voice in his ear said: "Are you looking for me, sir?"

A tall, young man was looking down at him. He had untidy, dark red hair above a face at once elegant and rough-hewn, an outdoor sort of face, teeth shining in a wide grin, an amused look in his chestnut eyes. At first Oliver took him to be someone from the airline, a pilot, maybe, although the wrinkled, tweed jacket looked out of place.

"Nick Van Schaik," announced the other to a speechless Oliver.

By the time he had tipped the porter—Van Schaik had no pesos—and put the bags in the car, Oliver was able to speak evenly to Van Schaik. "Thought you might like to have dinner with us tonight. Nothing fancy."

"Yes, sir. That's great. I'd like to drop my things off at the hotel first. Freshen up a bit."

That was not how Oliver had planned it but, never mind, he could hardly object. In passing he saw that he might have turned that suggestion briskly aside had it been made by the pudgy person at the airport, the obvious brother-in-law, instead of this unexpected passenger. "Of course," was what Oliver said.

As Oliver pulled into the thick traffic of Fray Servando, Van Schaik looked out the window and said: "So. Never thought I'd be in Mexico City. Not much like Tijuana, is it? That's the closest I ever got before."

"That seems to be the usual story," Oliver commented, as irritated by his own sententious comment as by Van Schaik's tiresome announcement. He could feel Van Schaik turn to look at him.

"Guess I ought to say," said Van Schaik, "that I didn't know anything about this assignment until I got back to Washington. Did they tell you? I had a run-in with Slasher O'Rourke and he gave me the boot and next thing I knew I was assigned here."

Oliver grunted, pretending to be more intent on his driving than demanded even by the anarchy of cars forcing their way through the intersection of Eje 2 Norte.

"I know about Drew and all that," said Van Schaik. "I can see how you might resent my being forced on you this way. On the other hand, I was grateful to Whit at the time. I thought my goose was cooked. Now, I've got another chance, and really, sir, I appreciate it. Can't help wondering, now, of course, what with Slasher—"

"Yuh," Oliver grunted. Van Schaik's frankness was

presumptuous. Oliver had planned to bring the grievance up himself.

When Oliver did not elaborate on the grunt, Van Schaik said, turning to look at Oliver, "Well, anyway, I wanted to let you know. I really appreciate—"

"Sure," said Oliver. He could not continue grunting without appearing sullen, although that was how he felt. "I understand. The only thing—what Drew's been doing, the mena—the work with his Latins, you know. I'm afraid we'll lose it."

"Yes, sir. Well." Van Schaik was watching the traffic. "I spent some time with the desk, what I could. Not much support there for Drew's operation. As a matter of fact—"

"Yeah. People make fun of it, don't they?"

"Yes, sir. They say it's not an operation, actually. That's the main criticism. That it's not our work, more State Department stuff. Now that—"

"But State won't do it. And it's not true anyway. Some of Drew's people will be assets later to other stations."

"What they say—I'm just repeating what they said on the desk—it's too airy-fairy. 'Assets,' right. But not agents. Not solid, controlled agents. With the new—"

"Oh, that textbook stuff. 'Control.' The guys talking 'control,' those tough staff types in headquarters. Parlor toughs."

"Yes, sir," said Van Schaik. "The big thing now is the Soviets, and in particular—"

"Nothing new about that."

"Well, sir. What they're asking for is for every station to forward a Soviet program. There's a dispatch coming down to you. The Comprehensive Soviet Program Planning Document—"

"Yeah, we got it. Only thing now we gotta decide is whether to work on the Soviets or fill out their damn program-planning document." Van Schaik laughed politely as Oliver continued. "Everyone has to discover the Sovs at some time in his life—this is Insurgentes, one of the main drags—and now the director has to carve out his own bold new approach. Embassy's up to the right this way. We put you at the Maria Isabel, right across the street. We'll fight our way there now." Oliver slumped in his seat when the traffic stopped moving. "So," he said. "Welcome to Mexico. It's a great place to work if we ever get our act together." The line of traffic moved grudgingly. "They say anything about personnel?"

"Yes, sir. They said they're going to write you about the personnel situation."

"They've been going to write for some months now. Did they say what they're going to say when they get around to writing?"

"That it's tight but—"

"Tight! The condition we're in? Can't be *that* tight."

"It's the Soviets."

"The Soviets! Whatta they got to do with it? They handling Personnel now?"

"No, sir. They're moving now," said Van Schaik. Oliver looked at him uncomprehendingly. Van Schaik was staring ahead. "The cars, I mean."

"Oh." Oliver sped ahead to stop any more cars from cutting in front of him, then pulled to the right to turn into the lateral that led to the front of Van Schaik's hotel.

As they walked back to the car from the Maria Isabel, Oliver said, "You're married, aren't you?"

"Yeah. She'll be coming down later on."

They entered again the thick traffic on the broad Avenida de la Reforma. "What you said. Something about the Soviets and the personnel situation."

"There was some big reorganization of the station. Something happened, I take it."

"Yeah." Oliver was wary. "A complete turnover here. All new. Haven't been here long myself, guess you know. Did anyone—" Oliver stopped. Surely Whitney Oates would not have told even his own brother-in-law what had happened in Mexico—why a "reorganization" had been necessary. "So—it's just Drew and me. Now you. And Mrs. Pott, of course. But what are they saying about personnel and the Soviets?"

"It's a counterintelligence study of the situation here. Very closely held. I didn't get to see it. Whitney told me about the recommendations. The gist of it is that the counter-intelligence people have this hypothesis of you as a honey pot."

"God!" exclaimed Oliver, slamming on the brakes then and under his breath cursing the car that had cut in front of him. "Sorry," he said. "Can't let the driving here get under your skin. 'Honey pot,' eh?"

"The idea is, as long as you're here, the Soviets will be swarming all over station operations."

"Flies after a honey pot! Such a delicate figure of speech."

"The CI study said the situation might lend itself to sophisticated exploitation—they didn't say exactly how—"

"You bet they didn't."

"—but that, in the meantime, the station should go through a prophylactic period, they call it, an innovative holding operation, in order to throw the Soviets off the scent before we build up again here."

"But Whitney doesn't have to buy that. He's in charge. This is Mexico. I mean—it's his responsibility to see we get what we need to do the job here, not a bunch of slit-eyed CI types. We can't lie here belly up like a possum, praying the Soviets will go away. An innovative holding operation. Jesus! What kind of thinking is that?"

"Well, now, of course with Slasher—"

"Look," said Oliver. They had crossed the Periférico at the Petréleos monument and Oliver shifted down, pressing the throttle to move faster now, up the long slope of the Reforma. "You might as well know now that Whitney and I are not exactly what you'd term real close buddies. He resents the hell out of my being here in Mexico. He's your brother-in-law and I won't go around saying what a horse's ass he is all the time, but you might as well know how it is with us." Oliver pointed at a restaurant on their right as they went up the hill. "Big Nazi hangout in the forties."

Van Schaik nodded: "Hm!"

Van Schaik was too young for Nazis. "All right, that's it, then." Oliver was able to smile, wondering just how Oates had described Oliver to Van Schaik. It would be undignified to ask, but Oliver could not help saying, "I would like to have heard Whit's description of me." He laughed.

"Whit can be a stuffed shirt, sometimes, I know. But look, the thing is—I mean—what I was trying to say, sir, Whitney's out. Slasher O'Rourke is in."

"Slasher O'Rourke? What do you mean, 'in'? In what?"

"South America. The division, I mean. Whitney's going up to be Chief of Long-Range Planning, whatever that is. Guess they want a real hard charger in South America now. Well," Van Schaik gave a short laugh, "they got one, all right. He'll shake everyone up."

"Didn't you say you and O'Rourke had a falling out?"

"Yes, sir. My wife had never been in the Far East before and she had a bad case of culture shock. She got pretty unhappy, and O'Rourke decided I had to come home."

"Just like that? Sounds pretty arbitrary."

"Yes, sir. O'Rourke has a hair trigger. He's sort of a Jesuit. I guess you know him."

"Well, yeah. I know who he is. Never worked with him. Sounds like a charming fellow." Oliver was thoughtful: this changed everything.

"So," added Van Schaik, "maybe I won't be around here too long. I tell you one thing, sir. I don't know about Slasher and any prophylactic period. Especially with the Soviets. A real hard charger."

"So you said. I hope he'll charge real hard at the personnel problem. 'An innovative holding operation.' What's that supposed to mean? We could dangle Mrs. Pott at the Soviets. Exciting, new, operational thinking in

Mexico: an opening gambit. Plump, middle-aged alto lures KGB officer into bass part in Easter chorale."

"That'd be okay. Slasher likes activity. Any kind of activity."

The gate was open and Oliver pulled up to the front door.

At the other end of the table from Oliver, seated at her right, his head turned toward her, Van Schaik was making Marge laugh at something he said.

"What was that?" muttered Oliver, but they went on talking, and he went back to thinking about the change in the South American Division, wondering what it might mean to him. The other two laughed together again. Oliver spoke louder, "when did you say your wife's coming?" They looked toward Oliver now.

"Well," Van Schaik played with the handle of his knife. "She had a bit of culture shock—" He turned back to Marge. "—I was telling Mr. Oliver—"

"Ted," said Oliver.

Van Schaik bobbed his head and grinned. "First time she had been out of the country. Add to that," Van Schaik nodded to Oliver, "the trouble with Slasher. You know."

"How long have you been married?" Marge asked Van Schaik.

"Just a few months. This time."

"Oh," said Marge.

"I had a divorce. I just got married again."

Oliver spoke to Marge. "You've heard of Slasher O'Rourke."

"It's not a name you forget. Why 'Slasher'? Seems to me I've asked that before."

"The way he treats people, I guess," Oliver said.

"Comes into a new place and tears everything up. Brings his own team with him. Discovers everything's wrong. Have to get rid of everyone there. Then the word goes out that everything's under control, Slasher's doing great things. About that time he and his team jump over to the next stepping-stone."

"I don't know why your agency tolerates that sort of thing," said Marge, looking at Oliver.

"Well, 'tolerate.' I don't know—Slasher's one of those hard chargers you figure belongs more to the corporate world. Fighting his way up the ladder in Detroit, Wall Street, someplace. You wonder how that type wanders in with us. Milking the corporation for what they can get out of it, then moving on." Oliver sat up in his chair and smiled at this wife. "Anyway, Slasher O'Rourke has replaced Whitney," he told her.

"Oh, dear. But it doesn't sound like much of an improvement," said Marge. She glanced quickly at Van Schaik. "What I meant—"

"You got the idea," said Van Schaik.

"I still don't understand how someone—" Marge started.

"Well," Oliver said, "skip the cultural anthropology—point is he's there. He impresses the management. They don't know what it's like to work for him."

"People say you're not safe above him, anymore."

"How do you think you'll get along with him? Do you know him?" Marge asked Oliver.

"By reputation," said Oliver. "Only. Wish we'd kept it that way."

Van Schaik and Marge were talking again. Oliver allowed himself to brood, against his judgment, about O'Rourke. It was not that he was made nervous by the unfamiliar, Oliver told himself, or that he feared the unknown, but he had settled so comfortably into a constant restless irritation with Whitney Oates that it had not occurred to him that a change from Whitney might be for the worse.

Van Schaik was saying something and repeated it: "Mrs. Oliver was saying—"

"Marge."

Van Schaik ducked his head again. "Marge. Anyway, she was saying how much she likes Mexico. How's it strike you?"

"When people ask me that, I say that any place where

you can see black-crowned, night herons flying out of the center of the city at dusk, the way they do at sunset as you drive along the Reforma past Chapultepec—that's a good place to be."

"Aha," said Van Schaik.

"Ted, I've told you that normal people don't know what to make of that kind of remark."

" 'Course, you have to look up to see them." Oliver grinned at his wife. "Look, Mexico is just another place to work, but it's a good one. We're in it, but not of it, not a part of it. It's like any other country, in the sense that we have to know what we can do and what we can't do, and when to do it and when not to, and how far to go and when to stop. That means we have to know Mexico—Mexican politics—cold, even though Mexico is not the target. Mexico is the water we swim in, the valley we walk through, the woods we track in, but it's really incidental to us."

"No political work."

"No politics. Actually—"

"What about Diego?" asked Marge. "What could be more political?"

"Who's Diego?" Van Schaik looked from Marge to Oliver.

"Well, okay, I'll get to that," said Oliver, getting up to refill the glasses with wine. "The thing is, the Soviets are too cagey, most of the time, to try any fast stuff with the Mexicans. When the Sovs get feeling too clever—well, then they get burned. You wonder if they'll ever learn to leave well enough alone, just get a free ride from the anti-U.S. sentiments of the Mexicans, especially of the intellectuals. The Mexicans waltz around the ballroom with the Sovs to show how independent they are, make us chew on our handkerchiefs with jealousy. But for the KGB and the GRU, Mexico's just a dandy platform to work against the States. An unsinkable aircraft carrier, as it were."

"So, that's the game."

"I'm not one of those who thinks it's a game."

"Ted!"

"All right." He grinned at his wife. "She means I'm being pompous. Okay. The Great Game. *Kim* and all that. Sure. That's all right. Makes us feel sort of dashing. But it's not a game—you know—that dumb newspaper talk. Maybe when we all retire we can sit around and look back—'The Great Game.' Well, all I'm saying is that the Sovs aren't part of Mexico and neither are we. You live here and you may even enjoy it, the way Marge and I do, but that's not central. You and I will always have to be thinking about something else. Like the KGB."

Marge protested, "that makes you sound like some kind of a zombie."

Oliver pushed his chair back. "Nick's the zombie. You must be pretty well done in, all that flying. I'll run you down to the hotel."

"What about this Diego fellow?" Van Schaik insisted.

At the same time, Marge said: "You have time for coffee."

They walked over to where the fire dully glowed through gray ashes, their wineglasses in hand. "Diego is Secretary of Government. He's in that job partly because of something we pulled off that made him look good—"

"That Ted pulled off," inserted Marge.

Oliver looked at her and shrugged. "Anyway, we screwed up some KGB dirty work, serious, heavy dirty work, aimed at Mexico. It's fair to say that he's in that job because of us and I'm in my job because of him."

"You've got it made here, then."

"By no means. Wish I did. Look! The Mexicans know what the KGB is doing here day in, day out: running operations against the States. But they can't do much about that, even if they wanted to, and they don't."

"They could throw the Soviet Embassy out."

"Well, that's not in their interest. They did cut them back, but the Sovs simply slip their people back in with the cooperation of the Mexican External Relations people. Who keeps count?" Oliver took a cup of coffee from

Marge: "Decaf? Look, the Mexicans are realists, Diego too. If the Soviets work against the States from Mexico and the Mexicans turn a blind eye to that, then we get a chance to work against the Soviets in Mexico and the Mexicans turn the same blind eye to that. But if either one of us steps over the line: watch out!"

"Where's the line for us?"

"That's where a chief of station earns his pay: knowing where the line is and working right up to it."

"But Diego is a real charmer," said Marge. "I don't claim to know him at all well, but he's suave and not as—well—as calculating as Ted makes him sound."

"He's charming and calculating at the same time. We don't get a free ride. I stay away from him unless I have something to say. Even then, sitting across from him, you can see his mind ticking away—what about all those awful things he hears about the CIA? What are they really up to? Okay, I went bail for him once, but what am I after now? Diego's your Latin mixture of sophistication and credulity."

"And charming and calculating," said Van Schaik.

It was Oliver, not Van Schaik, who sagged tired in his chair. The lunchtime alcohol was pressing on Oliver, and he thought briefly and resentfully of Puig. He looked over to where Van Schaik and Marge were sitting. She was laughing at some story he was telling about Thailand. At last Van Schaik stood up, offering to take a cab, realizing then that he had forgotten again to buy any pesos. Some insincerity showing, Oliver said: "No trouble at all."

On the drive back down the Reforma to the Maria Isabel, Van Schaik was as quiet as Oliver, the exuberance he had shown with Marge replaced by a tired silence. That becoming noticeable, Oliver said: "So. Any other bombshells from the home front?"

Van Schaik stirred and yawned noisily. "No, sir. There wasn't time—oh, one thing. A case the bureau's got, someone who comes to Mexico to meet his Soviet handler. I was supposed to get a briefing but there wasn't time. They assume it's First Chief Directorate." The CI people are going to write. They say it's very delicate."

"Isn't everything, with them?"

Van Schaik yawned again.

When Oliver reached home, he tiptoed about the bedroom, thinking Marge to be asleep. But she turned to say: "I like the new person. Don't you?"

"Yeah, I guess he's all right. You can't visit Whitney's sins on his brother-in-law, I guess."

"This terrible O'Rourke—but I suppose you're grateful to be rid of Whitney Oates."

"I don't know. I never thought—I guess I was getting used to him."

"It's good I'm leaving," said Drew the next morning. He had come by the office for his mail. "I've done the O'Rourke bit. Once per lifetime is enough."

"C'mon, Harley. He can't really be that bad." Oliver put his feet onto the scarred top of the coffee table.

"On the contrary: worse. Van Schaik seems to have put it to you well enough. Oh, O'Rourke has his coterie, his admirers. Those who seek certainty, who like being told exactly what to do. Little Nazis. Our superiors are impressed by his aggressive executive style. Not the decent ones, but that race may be dying out. Just you and me left. Then only you." Drew sighed loudly, more of a groan. "Oh, I'm so glad. Dear France! Peace in France. I'm too old. It's a young man's game, isn't it? Peace."

"Thanks a lot for dropping by to jack up morale around here."

"Oh," Drew was wiping his brow with a blue, silk bandana. "You'll get along all right."

"Yeah, thanks again, Harley. I do seek certainty, being told exactly what to do."

"I didn't mean that and you know it. It's true, Ted— I'm tired, I told you. With you, it's different. You know."

"I never thought I would find myself looking back

fondly at the time of the great horse's ass, Oates. It's beginning to seem like an era of real warmth and love. Go on. Tell me more about O'Rourke."

"Really, there's nothing more to be said. You must not fall into the error of thinking him stupid because of his use of cliché, his dictating torrents of turgid officialese. Interesting, that. He always dictates: never writes. Executive camouflage? Does it remove him a pace from responsibility for the result? Or, it may be only that he cannot write.

"Underneath a more than animal cleverness is a truly feral nature. He smiles at a world he assumes to be hostile and thus disarms it. He asks for your trust—'Trust me'—and plunges a knife into your vitals as he asks."

"Okay. That'll do for today."

Drew laughed. "You asked me." He was silent and then he grunted. "You don't like my retiring, Ted."

"Sure. You leave and it's lost, everything, everything you know. What sense is that? And who will I have to talk to?"

"I've never said this, Ted." Drew used a knuckle to give his nostrils a nervous rub. "But, frankly, my motivation—I think my motivation's gone." He stirred in his chair. "Thirty, forty years ago it wasn't like this. We thought we were defending something, out here"—Drew gestured with one hand—"so that they back there—well, you know."

"Yeah?"

"The enemy is still out here—the threat changed, yes, but still to be reckoned with." Drew looked at Oliver.

"That's right."

"But back there. That's what's changed."

Oliver nodded. "I know but—"

"I'm not asking you to agree with me or to defend it. I'm just telling you I find it offensive and I need to get to the south of France."

Oliver moved slightly in his chair, started to say something about how the south of France would not be a damned bit better, really, just different, but to hell with it. They sat quiet for a moment. Then Drew unclasped the pale white hands he had folded about his belly, waving them as though fanning himself, before clasping them together again with another grunt.

"Yes?" asked Oliver, recognizing the oracular portent.

"I wasn't going to say this. However, I owe it to you. I predict Slasher will find you threatening and will find a pretext for moving you out of the way, out of Mexico."

Chapter 6

One mid-morning a few days after Van Schaik had arrived in Mexico, he and Oliver were driving through the suburb of San Angel. "There," Oliver said as he slowed down, "up that street is the house where they killed Trotsky. With an ice axe." He made a face. "Imagine! An ice axe! Supposedly it was just handy. You've got to wonder if Stalin wanted something especially brutal done to Trotsky's brain."

When Van Schaik had peered up the street, Oliver drove on. "Mexico has a bloody past. The Aztecs, cutting peoples' hearts out—"

"Sounds like O'Rourke."

"—the Noche Triste, and then right on up through the revolution. I don't know why it adds to a city's charm so. Take Paris, where they've marked the spots where someone died during liberation. You go to the Alhóndiga de Granitas in Guanajuato and you stand right there at the wall where the Spanish lined up the revolutionaries and shot them. How'd you like it, standing there, waiting your turn? Goya in Spain. Same epoch, same thing, only with the French. *Al paredón!* Maybe it's not charm, exactly," added Oliver.

"I'm sure my French will help me," said Van Schaik. They had been talking about his lack of Spanish.

"Help or obstacle—two dialects of modern Latin. Friend of mine claims that North Americans have only one other language at a time. Anyway, all right. We're in Coyoacán now. Name has something to do with coyotes. Here's your real charm, cobbled streets and the old houses. Look at that faded tomato-soup color on that stucco, there, on the corner. The persimmon color over there on that wall. Hard to reproduce. As you might expect, this is where the arty crowd hangs out, including, of course, our man Harley.

"Speaking of artists, did you know that Siqueiros, the painter, was tied up with the KGB, I mean, when it was NKVD? Yeah. He led a gang that attacked Trotsky a few months before they finally got him with the ice axe. Attacked the same house, up that same street. Pablo Neruda—there's another tied up with them. He got Siqueiros a Chilean passport so he could get out of Mexico."

Oliver slowed down to turn a corner. "How do you explain it? Siqueiros, the great painter, Neruda, the great poet. The darlings of the smart set, doing Stalin's dirty work."

"What's Harley Drew like?"

"Like? Well, you'll see in a minute. And you'll get to know him pretty well, sitting at his knee, as it were."

"I mean, to work with."

"Well, he's not a Zen master. He's not going to slap your face every time you make a mistake. Harley's an old-fashioned gent. When he leaves, a great hunk of experience goes with him. It's like a piece of glacier calving off, this huge block of ice the size of Rhode Island—" Oliver took his hands off the wheel to gesture—"splashing into the sea. They shouldn't let him retire. You've got to wonder what value they put on him, whether they know what they've got. He's like someone's library, full of books on politics, on Latin America, Eastern Europe. He served in Moscow once. Harley's like an old house full of books and fine furniture, a formal garden, that's about to get bulldozed to make way for a shopping mall."

"Jesus! I mean—" Van Schaik laughed. "You make me feel—"

"No, no. I'm carried away. But it's an opportunity. Keep your ears open and ask all the questions now you'll wish you asked him later." Oliver brought the car to a stop by a beige stucco wall. "Here we are. A good deal like the place Harley has in France. He's convinced stucco is elegant."

The black-painted wooden door set in the stucco wall came open and a dark face, green-eyed, large-nosed, appeared solemn in the opening. Addressing the white-coated butler as Paco, Oliver introduced Van Schaik as Señor Nicolás and the three passed through the graveled dooryard, Paco crunching ahead to push open one of the two high wooden doors that opened onto the red-tiled atrium.

As they stood with Drew on the Chinese rug in the living room, drinking coffee, the room bright with light from the French doors giving onto the garden, Oliver was saying, "Nick will take over Pooch in English while he works on getting his Spanish into shape. In the meantime, you've got to give him a crash course in *hispanidad*."

"I thought you rejected Puig's offer."

"I did. In reply to my cable reporting the interview with Pooch we have such eloquence that, well—" Oliver pointed to Van Schaik, "see if I can get this right." Oliver sank into a gray overstuffed chair, putting his head back to look at the ceiling.

"Let's see: 'Hereinafter in future indispensable not summarily reject such forthcoming opportunities prior fullest consultation this headquarters.' "

"Yes, sir. That's it. The Slasher is in charge."

"Ohhh," Drew groaned.

" 'In such instances complete exploration potential . . .' how does it go there?"

" '. . . potential essential—' " began Van Schaik.

"Wait!" Oliver held up one hand. "I got it: 'In such instances complete exploration potential essential primary first step requisite preliminary source evaluation.' Olé!"

"You left out the 'narrow' bit, sir, you know."

"Did I? So I did. That may be the best part. 'Disturbed lack appreciation widening parameters Third World mission demonstrated this case. Experience has shown narrow perceptions not conducive fullest exploitation . . .' Then how does it go?"

" ' . . . producing oftimes less than optimum desired results,' " Van Schaik finished.

" 'Hereinafter in future' is my favorite," said Oliver.

" 'Potential essential' is pretty good," Drew commented.

The three sat in silence for a few moments.

"More coffee?" asked Drew.

"Yeah. Please. Okay, shoot. *Hispanidad* 101."

"Ted pretends I'm an authority. I don't," said Drew, leaning forward in his large leather armchair to put the Spode cup on a Japanese red lacquer table. "Jiggle that bell for Paco, would you? And he'll bring the pot. Generalize about Latins all you like, but remember throughout that in the end you're dealing with an individual. Someone said that socialists declare they have founded utopia and then they try to work back from the theory to where they really are. There's something of that in the Latins, an insistence that their world is not as you see it but as they want you to see it, as they want it to be, as they wish it might be."

"And Uncle Sam expected to make it all come true."

"Oh, you make too much of that, Ted. Don't mislead our young friend. He no doubt arrives laden with prejudices as it is. Do you not?"

"Mister—Ted told me coming over that if we try to help in Latin America they cry 'intervention,' and if we don't, they accuse us of neglect."

"I wish he wouldn't say such things."

"But, in the case of Puig," asked Van Schaik, "how does he fit into that?"

They both turned to Oliver, who was looking up at Paco, who was pouring coffee. "*Gracias*, Paco." When the butler had left, Oliver continued. "A paragraph on

Pooch? His family had money once but lost it. That says a great deal about him, right there."

"Does it?" asked Drew. "And how so?"

"His grandfather, I think it was, went through the inheritance. Pooch's father scraped a living as an *escribano*. We don't have anything quite like that, do we, Harley? A cross between a notary public and the family solicitor. Dusty files bound in red tape on the shelves of a Dickensian law office. Shabby genteel. From Pooch you got the idea that his family was displaced gentility, as though he'd been robbed of a ducal inheritance. He went into his father's office after studying in the law faculty in Montevideo. He wasn't particularly happy, but reportedly fun to be with in those days, despite that— popular with the young fast set. He managed to marry into a landed family. Really a nice-looking, lively girl. Handsome. Surprising. I didn't know them till later. But you wonder how it is an elegant woman marries a guy like Pooch."

"What was she like, his wife—" began Van Schaik.

"You know him quite well, then. I had a different impression," said Drew.

Oliver did not reply to either of them. "The trouble was," he continued, "the wife's family were serious farmers. No airs about being landed gentry. The father and the brothers, that is."

"And Puig?" asked Drew.

Oliver grinned at Van Schaik. "Kindly note the subtle difference in the pronunciation. Harley doesn't approve of nicknames."

"Pshaw," said Drew. "I don't address Paco as Francisco. It's not that at all, but rather your setting Nicholas, here—Nick—a bad example. From that manner, it's only a short step to talking of spicks, dagos, gooks, ragheads—the lot." Drew flicked a fat hand at Oliver.

"Oh, come on, Harley," Oliver protested.

"I was merely asking you to be polite," Drew resumed, "and saying that I had thought your acquaintance with Puig to have been more casual."

"Yeah, well." Oliver shifted about in his chair and was silent for a moment. "I thought I'd go into it a bit for Nick, here. I mean, first you find that none of these countries is quite like another. And then, as Harley said, you come up against the individual once you get through your generalizing. Uruguay is like Argentina—'European.' That's what everyone says about Buenos Aires— it's a 'European' city. What'd they expect? Des Moines? Uruguay is a lot like Argentina, a small Argentina. The same mixture of Spaniards and Italians, the lingering British tradition, Montevideo the swollen capital, the countryside full of cattle and ostriches, more animals than people. Main difference from Argentina is size and that the Uruguayans don't overthrow their government every year or two.

"Pooch went up to his wife's place one weekend, to the family *estancia*, near the Brazil border. It's all rolling green pasture, a lot of deep blue sky, treeless except for scrubby stuff on outcroppings of rock and along the streams in the gullies. Around the farmhouses there'll be a large ombú tree or two.

"Anyway, Pooch came out the first morning in his tweed hacking jacket and jodhpurs, a hat on his head, gloves, the country gentleman, you see, and the father and the two brothers are working the animals, sloshing around in the manure, whatever farmers do in the morning. Pooch was going to ride and he had made some remark the night before about creole horses, a superior remark, that is, how they're awkward cobs. The younger brother, a good-looking blond boy, Federico, Freddie— a first-class rugby star later in Montevideo—said something along the line of: 'Oh, we've got the horse for you to ride.'

"Maria Elena, the sister—Pooch's wife, that is—tried to stop it, but the father and the older brother told the boy to go ahead. Pooch must have suspected something by this time. The boy came out in a minute, leading a huge bay stallion that was skittering around sideways and throwing its head up in the air."

"Jesus," said Van Schaik. "I don't want to hear the rest."

"Yes," said Drew. "That's quite enough. Nasty beasts, horses."

Oliver grinned. "Pooch didn't like the looks of it and said something like: 'There ought to be a martingale'—you know, one of those straps below the neck that keeps a horse from throwing its head up. Pooch tried the cinch to be sure the saddle was tight, not to be caught by that trick. And he stuck his knee up into that place just behind the left foreleg, and the horse jumped straight up in the air and began snorting and waltzing around the yard. A couple of gauchos came clumping over in their boots to help hold the animal—"

"You were there," said Van Schaik.

"No. I heard about it later."

"From Pooch? I mean, did Puig tell you?"

"No. Someone else." Oliver shook his head impatiently. "But Freddie held the horse by the head until Pooch got up and had the reins and then he let go. Pooch is short-legged and not much to look at on the ground, but on a horse, with his long torso, you don't see that. He's got a good seat, erect, his feet straight in the stirrups, and he looks good up there. I guess he's a pretty good horseman, or was, anyway. The horse began to rear and stamp but Pooch did a good job of handling him and made him stop whirling around and put him into a trot, all right, but then the horse broke and reared and came down hard, Pooch sprawled on his neck, and ran like hell down a dirt lane between two fences. Pooch couldn't get his seat in the saddle to lean back and hold him. At a turn the horse swerved—one of the little tricks he had—and Pooch lost a stirrup and off he went."

"What a nasty thing to do! Was he hurt?" asked Drew.

"Nothing serious, although he had trouble walking when he first got up. He was a couple of hundred yards away and he could hear the men—all the gauchos had come out to watch—whooping and laughing and rolling around. The horse was long gone and Pooch picked up his hat and had to limp back up the lane, mud all over, to where they waited for him.''

"How dreadful! What rubes!" exclaimed Drew. "I hope that was the last time our friend graced them with his company."

"No." Oliver was thoughtful. "No. He went back. Of course, things were never the same between him and the men of the family, especially the younger boy. As a matter of fact, Puig said something once about her—about his wife's—family, something about their being very 'rústico.' Rubes, I guess," Oliver added for Van Schaik.

"Yes," agreed Drew, "but far too polite. It's nightmarish; the yokels, the yahoos, taking it out on the sissy, the city slicker."

"Funny thing, Harley, your speaking of socialism. The father was kind of a parlor socialist, real dogmatic. Your up-country Uruguayan, especially the landowner, is usually hidebound conservative. Freddie was named for Friedrich Engels. The father was down on the U.S. Didn't know anything about us but carried on at a great rate about imperialism. Things he read. He wasn't dumb, by any means, but in politics self-taught, indiscriminate in his reading. I guess he was a good farmer—he'd graduated in agriculture in Montevideo—but narrow. There you are: 'Narrow perceptions lead to less than optimum desired results.' "

"A bucolic autodidact," said Drew.

"I suppose. The father took aboard all the crap he read, as long as it was anti-U.S. At the same time, he was never unpleasant about it, I mean, personally—just boring. He didn't credit anything I said. He gave me no points for having lived in X number of countries, and him stuck up there in his cow pasture. I confess I got a little tired of having to listen politely to his endless crap."

"Why did you have to be so polite to him?" asked Van Schaik.

"Oh, I don't know. Now the elder son, the other brother," Oliver continued, "he *was* unpleasant, dour, dark-browed, not that he said much. Come to think of it, he was one of the few Uruguayans I ever met that seemed really unpleasant. They're nice people. I was told not to take it personally."

"He try to get you on that horse?" asked Drew, wheezing with laughter.

"But didn't you say you weren't there?" said Van Schaik.

"I wasn't there with Pooch, not there for the business with the horse. There was another time."

"So Puig is to be for you something of an exercise, like learning to ride a bicycle," said Drew to Van Schaik.

"Not like that horse, I hope."

"More than an exercise," said Oliver. "Tell him," he said to Van Schaik.

"Well, sir, you heard the quotations from Slasher. They want us to use Pooch, Puig, the way he volunteered to Mister—to Ted. We send him back to Uruguay as a source on politics there."

"More than that: they like the idea of his joining or starting or taking over a party," Oliver added. "Nonsense!"

"Why nonsense?" asked Drew. "Is this our purist intelligence officer speaking? Our classic antipathy to political work?"

"Not at all. Uruguay is not Central America. They're quite capable of carrying on democratic government without our sticking our noses into it. Until the Tupamaros came along, Uruguay was democratic—to a fault, if anything. Could give us a few pointers on honest elections. Parties sort of screwed up but, hell, look at ours! The Tupamaros with their twisted ideas, fascist, Peronist, Marxist—all at once. Whatever the differences are, the Tupamaros drowned them in blood. The idea was to bring on repression which would lead then to a popular revolution. Cruel nonsense. They got the repression, all right. They fired the petard and damn well were hoisted by it."

"You feel strongly," said Drew.

"I was there. What's more, I had to pack my bag and haul ass out of there one day. They had me targeted."

"You never mentioned that," said Drew. "Who?"

"The Tupamaros." Oliver waved his hands impatiently. "It's a long story."

"Red Brigade types, weren't they?" asked Van Schaik.

"Yeah. Baader-Meinhof gang. Kidnappings, assassinations. But getting back to Pooch. You can walk up to a politician on the street in Uruguay and ask any damnfool question you want, within reason, if you're polite about it, and get an answer. You don't need to mount an operation. Sponsoring Pooch's return to Uruguay is an example of running an operation for operations' sake. Or politics for politics' sake."

"The Slasher is very action-oriented, and any—"

"That would be one of his phrases," said Drew.

"—any kind of activity is better than none."

"And one of our real weaknesses," said Oliver. "But look at it this way, Harley. The way they've been down on your work, if the Slasher's so wild about fritzing around in Uruguay where it's completely unnecessary, maybe he would see the need to keep your stuff going in Central America or someplace like Bolivia, where it's all so damned fragile. What do you think, Nick?"

"Hmm. Well, sir, frankly, the way Slasher looks at things, it depends on what he would enjoy more, making his predecessor look dumb or shaking you up."

Drew nodded. "An eminently sound analysis. A bright young man you brought with you today. One emendation to that otherwise impeccable statement: Slasher would prefer to accomplish both, if possible."

"Wait a minute, you two. You mean. . . ?"

"Yes. He'll ask for a briefing on Mexico, and when they start pissing all over—excuse me—criticizing Mr. Drew's—"

"Harley. And, I fear, 'pissing,' would describe it."

"—Harley's work, Slasher'll decide right then whether to cut them off at the knees. Maybe it turns out to be a key element of the widening parameters of our Third

World mission. Or fix your wagon, in a manner of speaking, by ordering you to terminate the mena—operation in about five minutes' time. Excuse me, Mister—Harley."

"My poor peregrines."

"And that's how you think it'll be, Harley?"

Drew nodded. "Exactly, allowing for a certain infelicity of expression on Nick's part. That, and your being older than Slasher; he doesn't like having older men under him. Interesting. Makes him uneasy, an occasion for perspiring. He sweats a good deal. Some trace of guilt, you might say, as unlikely as that may seem."

On the way back to the office, Oliver remembered another point in the correspondence from headquarters on the matter of Puig: "He really reamed me out for having talked to Buchanan about Pooch, didn't he?"

"Yeah. That's something else. Slasher doesn't like the Brits. You know, you can't assume Slasher wrote that himself. He brings his claque along with him, and they know how he thinks, any one of them could write that with his eyes closed. As a matter of practice, they know that Slasher would want to start by terrorizing all the station chiefs. You can be sure every place in South America is getting some kind of a rocket."

"Charming. Hell, I *knew* Pooch would go to Buchanan first. It's the sort of thing you just know, by feel. Pooch is an incurable, congenital anglophiliac—his idea of a gentleman is British." Oliver put on a superior tone: " 'Hopefully ill-advised revelations to Buchanan did not compromise this useful opportunity.' Balls!"

As Oliver turned onto the Periférico he said: "And they showed no interest in the Soviet angle. How come? If we have to fool around with Pooch, let's push him a bit in that direction. Start right in on that tomorrow. I don't agree with Buchanan that you can only use Eagle Scouts against the Sovs. Since when did we wait around for perfection in this business? Or in any other, for that matter? Nuts to Buchanan and his ilk!"

Chapter 7

"Don't worry. Pooch likes to talk, preferably about himself, but, anyway, talk. Just keep on asking questions and listen to the answers and he'll never guess you knew squat about Uruguay to begin with," Oliver said the next morning as he led the way through the corner of the Monte de Piedad. He and Van Schaik had taken the subway to the Zócalo stop, walking across the vast Plaza de la Constitución, Mexico's great cathedral looming on their right.

"This place's not as fancy as Delmonico's, by the way," Oliver called over his shoulder as they dodged other pedestrians at the crossing. Oliver wondered if the contrast would seem excessive. He led the way into the narrow avenue of the Cinco de Mayo that went west from the plaza. He stopped some yards farther on before a glass door. The legend, CAFÉ CINCO DE MAYO, in raised gold letters, formed a crescent on the glass door. Oliver stopped to look back to the towers of the cathedral, framed by the buildings at the open end of the street.

The dominant green color within gave an underwater effect to the long room. On the right stools were set against a counter. Oliver led the way to a small table for four at the far end of the room.

"You're right. It sure isn't Delmonico's. You trying to tell Pooch something?"

"It's not that bad, Nick. It's a coffee shop. Out of the way—out of our way, that is. The habitués are Mexicans, office workers from around here. No foreigners. No one knows us. So, maybe it's a few cuts below Delmonico's—"

"A few cuts!" Van Schaik laughed.

"You think I went too far? A little asceticism won't hurt Pooch. He musn't get the idea that working with us is one great, giddy round of parties."

They sat down and Oliver looked about them. "All right, spare, maybe. You can make meeting arrangements that suit you when you get to know the town." The waiter came and they each ordered an espresso. "But he shouldn't think every meeting is the occasion for an expense-account banquet."

"He's six minutes late. Typical, I suppose," Van Schaik said a few minutes later, as they sipped the rich, hot coffee.

"Anglo-Saxon late but not Latin late. Actually, it isn't typical of Pooch. Anyway, once we get through the preliminaries, I won't hang around. You just start moving in and take over."

Ten minutes later, when the waiter had been by again, Oliver said: "Something's happened. No doubt about the time or the place."

"Would he stand you up?"

"No. I don't think so. Oh, no!" said Oliver in the same breath. "Aghh—" he gargled. "I might have known."

Van Schaik stared at him and then followed Oliver's eyes to the door of the café. A blond woman, short, slender, pretty, was coming quickly toward them, her skirt swaying as she avoided the tables, her heels clicking on the hard floor. She wore a dark blue suit over a white blouse. She was looking directly at Oliver, a half smile on her face. Her long-lashed blue eyes went to Van Schaik in quick appraisal as she reached the table. She said something in Spanish to Oliver that Van Schaik could not understand. Her eyes were intent on Oliver as she took her leather bag from her arm and laid it on the bare tabletop. She had easily drawn the eyes of everyone in the room, male and female.

Oliver put his hands on the table and struggled to get up but sank back in his chair without doing so, staring at her, saying nothing. She looked at Oliver a moment longer before pulling out a chair and sitting down across from him, folding her small hands on the tabletop. She glanced at Van Schaik again and narrowed her eyes at Oliver, smiled with her even white teeth, not with her eyes. Oliver stayed slumped in his chair.

"Say something," she said in Spanish. "Present me."

"The Señora de Puig Camps," said Oliver in English, straightening slightly and waving a limp hand. "Mr. Van Schaik."

She nodded at Van Schaik but went back to looking at Oliver as the waiter came up to the table. She shook her head when the waiter spoke to her, still keeping her eyes on Oliver. She was not smiling now, but they continued to stare at each other. The waiter stayed nearby, looking at her.

"I should have known," said Oliver, in Spanish. "He doesn't speak Spanish," he added. "What happened to Pooch?"

"He's coming. I had to see you first." She used the familiar form in Spanish. "We have to talk, you and I. It is supremely important. Important to you, understand?"

"Another espresso," said Oliver, to get rid of the waiter, and turned back to the woman. "How long have you been here?"

"Not long." She shook her head impatiently to protest Oliver's continuing to use formal language with her. Her short blond hair swirled about her head.

"You and Pooch—you're together again?" Oliver decided to use the familiar.

"In a manner, only in a manner. And you married." She took a sip of water. "What is she like? Is she one of the tall, big-voiced Americans in a tweed skirt or is she one of those shy, sweet things that wear fuzzy pink sweaters?"

"Neither the one nor the other. Taller than you. Darker than you. Very pretty. Look, Maria Elena, this is rude."

"Maria Elena, is it, now?"

"Absolutely."

She turned to Van Schaik. "Would you like Spanish lessons?" she asked in her accented English.

Van Schaik looked at Oliver. "Well, sure—"

"He doesn't want an Uruguayan accent."

"I teach any style you like." She smiled at Van Schaik.

"Look, Maria Elena," said Oliver. "What—"

She spoke in Spanish again. "I tell you. It is urgent. Every day except Monday, from ten to eight, I am at the Botica Karina—that's in Londres—waiting on your American tourists." She wrinkled her nose. " 'Oh, miss! Do you speak English?' "

She rose abruptly. "Come by there at fourteen hours, my lunchtime." She raised her eyebrows at Oliver. She smiled at Van Schaik, who had leapt to his feet. "Think about the lessons," she said to him in English. Oliver had drawn himself up more slowly.

"Wow!" said Van Schaik, watching her thread her way through the tables to the door. "You didn't say anything about her."

"How could I have known? They separated years ago." Oliver sat back down and stared at his hands on the table. "I did, actually," he added, looking at Van Schaik. "Remember the business with the horse?"

"Yeah, but what a knockout!"

"Little old for you, Nick. It's that damned Rule of Three."

"What's that?"

"Oh, you know. You set something up and you think it's between you and the other guy and then he goes and blabs to everybody. Whew! I didn't expect that."

"Here's Pooch."

Puig came toward the table smiling. This time Oliver got up to greet him, as did Van Schaik, whom Oliver introduced to Puig. Before Oliver could say more, Puig said: "Sorry about that. I hope you didn't mind. Maria Elena wanted to say hello. You know. Women." He spread his arms and smiled with his head on one side.

"I must say, Pooch, considering, uh . . . I wish you hadn't told her," said Oliver, still rattled.

"Oh, she always liked you. She didn't like all the Americans, you know. You were always someone very special."

Very special—Pooch had to pick up every idiotic phrase! "But what—" Oliver began. He had started to ask how Puig had described to Maria Elena his current connection to him. What Oliver really wanted to know was what Puig knew of his past connection to Maria Elena. Oliver's voice sputtered to a stop as the two ideas collided in his head. Anyway, it seemed that Puig might not have heard him; Puig was beaming at Van Schaik, his new friend. Puig's eyes were darting about the place with wonder. No, it's not the old Jockey Club, Pooch. Puig stared now at their coffee cups.

"Let's sit down. I'm going to have to run along," said Oliver. But, before he left, he said, Van Schaik was interested in exploring Puig's ideas about Uruguay. Puig was listening, leaning forward, creasing his brows to demonstrate seriousness, glancing at Van Schaik to show himself ready, nodding to illustrate comprehension. By not even a sly look did he remind Oliver of Oliver's categorical refusal of Puig's propositions of the other day.

Oliver was not pleased to hear Van Schaik tell Puig that he had been sent to Mexico specifically to work with Puig. That was all right in one way but it would puff Puig up too much. Oliver would have to warn Van Schaik about that: if Puig got the idea that he was invaluable to the Americans in Uruguay, he might be unhappy at finding himself being used against the Soviets in Mexico.

When Oliver got up to leave them at the table in the Café Cinco de Mayo, Puig did not object, coming to his feet to give Oliver an athletic handshake, patting Oliver's shoulder with his left hand. On his way out Oliver turned to look back at the two of them. Puig was waving a finger at the waiter. He would get the menu, make the best of the bare surroundings. Van Schaik was a good-looking fellow, Oliver noted. His appearance would have influenced Puig in his favor. There was something raffish about the pair of them. They gave the coffee shop a certain style.

When Van Schaik came back to the office, Oliver was at his desk, staring out the window, still wondering whether casually to mention Maria Elena to Marge—just in case—or to let it go as it was. How casual could he make it all seem? Better let it go. He could see himself getting tied up in explanations and looking guilty when it was all entirely innocent, none of his doing, nothing to do with the present. Why bother Marge with it? They'd never meet.

"I'm signing up for language lessons. With her, I mean."

"You know, we gotta think about that. I'm not real sure that's a real good idea."

"Yes, sir. Thing is, Pooch likes the idea. Actually, he said it would be good cover for our getting together."

"What kind of cover—?"

"They've got an apartment in Polanco. I think maybe they're a bit strapped for dough."

"Not surprising. So, they live together?"

"Sure, why?"

"They were separated for quite a time. I didn't know they were back together. I mean, I haven't thought about it one way or the other. It's nothing to me. What're they doing in Mexico, anyway?" Oliver got up to put the blinds aside and gaze out the window. The smog was bad and the buildings farther down Rio Danubio were fading into the yellow murk.

"He's been moving around, in Argentina and Chile for a while. She's been in Uruguay all along and just came up here recently. Puig hasn't been back. For a long time, I mean. Here." Van Schaik opened his spiral notebook.

"*'Junta de vigilancia.'* Some kind of counter-Tupamaro outfit he was in. I guess they did some pretty tricky stuff. Rough stuff, I mean."

"Yeah. It was rough, all right." Oliver stared, without really seeing, down the street.

"That's why he talked about taking soundings in Uruguay. But he says it's okay now. No problem. What do you think?"

Oliver turned to Van Schaik. "One thing for sure. That's his lookout. We're not stepping forward as some kinda official sponsors. He has to get his own ass back there."

For a moment Oliver couldn't think what it was that was bothering him. Then he remembered and went back to thinking about Marge and Maria Elena.

Chapter 8

A few days after Van Schaik met Puig the sun was sending amber shafts of hazy morning light onto Drew's white Chinese rug. Oliver was sitting low in a soft gray chair, jacket off, tie loosened, listening to the music flowing from the hidden speakers, finding himself again considering how to deal with Maria Elena's inconvenient presence in Mexico. Until he became aware of movement at his left, his eyes had been gazing without seeing into the garden. A short, thickset figure in faded blue coveralls backed into view, posed immobile for a moment, and then moved back out of sight.

Oliver went to the French windows. The gardener was using both hands, elbows raised, on a pair of long shears, to clip the green, shiny-leaved hedge that grew waist-high along the wall on the left side of Drew's garden. The man worked with rhythm, an active phase of clipping, a pause to move his head in short arcs to spot escapees, clipping again, stopping now to squint along the side of the hedge, clipping. At regular intervals he would back up to gain perspective—that was how Oliver had first seen him—putting his head on one side and then another to view his work.

On the far side of the hedge long-legged pale red geraniums climbed the garden wall, house finches fluttering from them to the eaves of the house above Oliver's head. Oliver backed to his chair, lowering himself carefully to be sure that the acts of the gardener remained in view.

The morning ritual was soothing. Partly it was the pleasure of watching another work. On a deeper level Oliver saw hedge clipping as Aztec ceremony.

A moment later, when Paco shuffled quietly across the rug with coffee and a croissant, Oliver's eyes were nearly closed. Paco put the silver tray on the coffee table, jerking his head at Oliver in a less deferential version of the respectful bow with which he had been taught to address Drew. Oliver winked at him. Paco raised his eyebrows and turned to drift back out.

"Who's that?" Oliver pointed.

"My cousin from Amecameca."

"What's his name?"

"Same as mine, señor. Francisco. We call him El Gordito."

Little Fatty. "I bet that Señor Drew doesn't call him El Gordito."

Oliver and Paco watched the gardener at his restrained horticultural ballet. He was not fat, despite the nickname. Because he had no neck, possibly. The large head sat right on the shoulders, his stocky, squarish figure carved from a block of *noguera*, a squat column of dark walnut. El Gordito's face was chocolate, angled, a strong, straight nose, a heavy chin, the eyes slits. Really authentic: he could have been an Aztec eagle warrior of the Templo Mayor.

Paco shuffled back out.

The music came to its end and the speakers popped as the machine was turned off. A moment later Drew himself appeared, swaddled in a large blue bathrobe.

Seeing Drew's eyes on them, Oliver leaned to pick flaky crumbs of croissant from the rug. "Manage to plow through the old silent meditation one more time? What was that?"

"Chopin's Second. Rubinstein at Carnegie Hall, 1958."

"You sure got Paco cowed. When the music's on, he slithers around like a duck-billed platypus. I knew him when he would have been whooping and shaking."

Drew, breathing heavily as he sat down in the red leather chair, did not reply.

"Not to Chopin, of course. More like 'Guantanamera.'" Oliver looked over at Drew. "What's the matter? You off your feed?"

Drew exhaled noisily. "Possibly so." He ran his fingers across the thinning hair on the top of his head. He, too, looked into the garden.

Oliver was studying Drew's face. "How does young Van Schaik strike you?"

"Ah, yes." Drew put both hands to his face and rubbed his eyes. Putting a hand on either arm of the chair he fluttered his fingers on the leather. "The reason for the new wife's not coming?"

Oliver got up to walk to the window, putting his head on one side, then the other, imitating the gardener. "Van Schaik's? Culture shock, he told us. Hey, Harley. Getta load of this guy clipping your hedge."

Drew ignored him. "She's his third. How old is he? What seems to have happened is that he went out to Bangkok ahead of her and, in the brief interval before she arrived, he managed to seduce Slasher O'Rourke's secretary. When the wife came, he treated the secretary with such sudden formality that she went to pieces. Older woman. Not quietly either. The new wife was no more pleased than the secretary. That's why Slasher sent him packing."

Oliver sank into the gray chair. "You sure or is this just more talk?"

"It's just talk all over the Agency. I wouldn't hang about International Arrivals waiting for the wife if I were you."

"He referred to Slasher as puritanical."

"Hardly. Slasher would consider a junior officer's copulating with his secretary without permission to be a form of lese majesty."

"So Van Schaik's skirt-crazy."

"Apparently. But fitfully uxorious along with it."

"Damn."

Drew shrugged.

"He's got himself a language teacher," said Oliver slowly.

"Did he examine her teaching credentials or were there other, overriding factors?"

Oliver did not reply. He sipped at his coffee, holding the flowered cup in both hands. He motioned at the red lacquer table with his head. "I brought your mail."

"Thank you."

"Just passing by. I've got a meeting."

"Something to interest you has come up with Enrique," said Drew.

"Let's see—he's the Nicaraguan."

"No," said Drew, frowning. "He's the Salvadoran. Gualtero is the Nicaraguan."

"Oh, yeah. What about Gualtero?"

"No, Ted, it's Enrique I want to talk to you about. A Soviet is ingratiating himself."

"Oh? Who?"

Drew looked at his hands. "Well, we didn't get to that. He was in a hurry. I'll see what I can find out." Oliver sat across from Drew, staring at him. Drew coughed and looked up at Oliver. "I tell you, I'll find out. You know how I feel—"

"I know how you feel and you know how I feel. I protect the menagerie the best I can, but you lend me the occasional hand with the Sovs. Otherwise, you'll have one of Slasher's storm troopers sitting here, looking at you with his little pig eyes."

"Not with my retirement papers being processed. I'll be in France by then." Drew rubbed his face again with one hand.

"Yeah. And look at you. Beginning to regret it already."

"Ted, it's not that." Drew sighed again. "There's something we have to talk about." He squirmed about in his chair to loosen his robe. "This letter." He drew himself up, fishing about and gasping until he could find the pocket in his robe. He wiggled from the pocket two folded pages of notepaper covered with writing in a blue ink and handed them over to Oliver.

"It's in Russian," said Oliver.

"Yes."

"I don't read it."

"I know. It's from—it's signed—'Galina.' This appeared in the mailbox on the door yesterday morning. Paco found it there." After another struggle, Drew found an envelope which he passed to Oliver.

Oliver turned the envelope over to look at both sides and put it on the table, picking up his coffee cup. "Postmarked Leningrad. I can read that much."

"Nevertheless, a small but careless gap in their operational data: postmarked, but it was not mailed. Paco found it in the box about nine yesterday morning. As I regularly get local mail, bills, the odd invitation, Paco checks the box daily. The thing is, we don't have a delivery until noon or one, at the earliest."

"By hand, then. See anyone?"

Drew shook his head.

"Galina?"

"When I was in the Soviet Union."

"Is she the one, uh. . . ?"

"Yes. They wouldn't let her out. And of course Security was dead against it. I said I would resign were she able to come."

"Mm." There had always been talk of a sadly romantic incident in Drew's past, on the basis of which Drew had a unique standing with all wives everywhere.

"Now. This letter." Drew frowned at it and rubbed one hand over his face. "You see, it's been so long. Word came out that she had died in a camp. I put it all aside, did my best to be done with it." Drew began to lean forward and then heaved himself forward in the chair, lifting himself to walk to the window to stare out at El Gordito. "Of course, I see now, there was always—I had not succeeded at killing off that one last germ of hope."

"How about the writing?"

Drew shrugged. "They would be bound to take pains

in the interest of verisimilitude. It says that she wants to see me."

"And naturally you would like to see her."

"Do I? I wonder." Drew sat back down. "It's been so long. I'd come to terms with it. And is it really she?"

"A really dirty trick, if not."

"Do you think them incapable of that?"

"Where is she supposed to be?"

"There's the rub. Claims she had applied to emigrate but has been refused. She—the letter—suggests I proceed to Helsinki and wait to hear from her there. There are instructions."

"Very neat," commented Oliver.

"But plausible if she's in Leningrad."

"This has to go to headquarters."

"Certainly, Ted. But not yet. Give me a day or two to think about it. It can hardly be sent to headquarters without bearing my reaction with it. Pour yourself coffee."

They sat quietly for a moment and then Drew spoke: "Friends of mine have a place in southern Maryland. I spent a weekend with them before coming here. It was late fall and I was up early, walking—"

"You? Up early? Walking?"

Drew did not respond except by rubbing his eyes again with one hand. "It was one of those bright fall mornings, misty, the grass sparkling with frost, and a patina of frost over the fields, soft earth colors, from lavender to magenta. You think of fallow fields as brown, but put your head to one side—" Drew leaned to put his head nearly down to the chair arm, closing one eye and peering into the garden "—the way painters do, and you see the true colors. I don't think he's cutting that close enough," he added.

"I was following a dirt road that slopes down toward the water, a deep ravine with large beeches and tulip trees on the left, the fields falling away easily toward the water on the right. You cannot imagine a more peaceful scene.

"But then . . ." Drew closed his eyes and let out an

explosive breath. He opened his eyes. "I am nearly as sickened now by what I saw as I was at the time."

"What was it?"

"A red fox held by a foreleg in a trap, the poor creature swinging about, tugging at the trap, the leg torn and bloodied. The animal would stop hurling itself about to give me a quick, penetrating look and then yank away at the leg, trying again to escape. In the course of this it had worn a bare circle of earth about the stake that held the trap in the ground."

"God!"

"Yes, you do well to speak of Him. I may have said that myself. I turned away, sick—not physically sick, but my whole being filled with the despair of being powerless in the face of evil. Do you understand?"

"Yeah, Harley."

"I went back up the road without thinking of anything but getting that scene behind me. A pickup truck coming down the hill toward me had stopped to avoid hitting me. The farmer, the man who ran the place, was in it, and he said 'Good morning' to me. By the way he looked at me, I could see that my distress was evident. 'There's a fox in a trap, there.' He looked ahead and said, 'Good. They get all the quail. There hasn't been a rabbit hereabouts for a month or two.'

"Now even in the state I was in I knew better. This is one of those farms mowed clean, no hedgerows, no cover save in the ravines where they can't go with their machines. No habitat, you know, for quail, or rabbit, or songbirds—hardly enough for foxes—only what refuge the beasts can find in the land that's not tilled. But I was in no condition to give this fellow an environmental lecture.

"The farmer was no doubt a good man—my friends thought highly of him—but he indulged himself in a small cruelty with me. He gave a little smile and said that the trapper would be coming for the fox. Did I need a lift back up to the house? I told him that I would walk back—all I wanted to do was to get away from there, from him, from the look of baleful pleasure on his face. But he would not let me go that easily. He kept me there to administer the countryman's vengeance, his way of asserting himself over the soft city cousin—the streak of meanness they showed your friend Puig on the *estancia*.

" 'Don't worry about the fox,' he said. The trapper would be along. 'What they do'—he insisted on my knowing—'is they club the fox with a heavy stick they carry. When it's unconscious, they put a foot on the chest and force the air from it and it suffocates. That way it dies with no mark on it. Fetches a good price, a red fox like that.' "He was pleased with himself. I could not speak and turned to go back up the road without a word. The farmer could not have known the magnitude of his cruel triumph, that beyond the immediate horror through which that poor animal was passing, the fox was for me a metaphor of Galina."

Oliver could think of nothing to say.

"Well," said Drew, "enough of that. But give me a day or two to think about it."

"Of course, Harley," said Oliver.

"Look there!" Drew wiggled a finger. "Would you mind speaking to the gardener? I don't like the way he's doing that."

"He doesn't know me, Harley. You'd better talk to him."

"Drat it! Stubborn! Will do things his way." Drew moved about in his chair, breathing heavily, the steps preparatory to rising.

Oliver stood. "I gotta go." He looked at Drew. "You're looking at this the right way. Just don't do anything rash." Oliver picked up his jacket and tightened the knot of his tie. "I gotta go."

Chapter 9

Later that same morning Dr. Michael said to Oliver, grinning as he said it, "In a word, I would say 'elitist,' rather like you in that." Oliver was irritated again by Michael's mocking manner, as restless as Michael had made him from the moment he picked him up.

Michael had climbed in on the passenger side of the front seat of the Toyota, looked over at Oliver and said, "Right on time. A precision most commendable. I dislike having to wait."

Michael was slight in build, a good fifteen years younger than Oliver, which—Oliver admitted later—may have made his manner more annoying. His hair was dark, curly, thick down the back of his neck, arranged to flow over his collar, carefully tended, as was his beard. "Oh, yes," he went on, as Oliver turned the car out into traffic, "I seem to remember that I am to make some absurd remark so that I would be sure who you are or that you would be sure who I am. Now I can't remember what it was. How, then, am I to be sure you are the person you pretend to be? Let's see, 'Ted' is it?" Michael grinned at Oliver.

Oliver was at that time having to lean to look into his side mirror as he tried to force his way back into the traffic on Avenida Juarez, where Michael had been waiting on the wide sidewalk that runs along Alameda Park. "Yes. Ted. To answer your question, to begin with, I'm in a gray Toyota. I flicked my lights twice just before I picked you up a minute ago at exactly ten-forty. I have on a gray tweed jacket. Damn," he added mildly as another car refused to let him enter. "There." Oliver waved at the car behind him. "You were supposed to ask me if I would like to read your magazine. I would have said I'd already read it."

"Although you would not have. I hope you're not shocked at my waving a dangerous leftist publication at you."

"You were supposed to have it in your right hand. You had it in your left."

"Oh, sorry! I'm afraid I've never been very good about following orders. But, a natural mistake given my views, don't you think?"

Oliver shook his head. "At that distance it's hard to know what paper someone has in his hand or even what hand it's in. I wouldn't pass you up because you had it in the wrong hand."

"Confirming that there is no sense at all to the whole silly spying rigamarole."

"Don't the Soviets have a silly rigamarole with you?"

"Oh, yes, even more involved and just as senseless. So, you don't object to my leftist reading matter. Perhaps you're not familiar with it."

"Isn't it as much fashionable as leftist? What someone said once about the disadvantage of our political and literary capitals being separate."

"Oh? And what are we to infer from that?"

"That New Yorkers are confident about passing judgments on the political world without direct experience of it."

"And you?" asked Michael. "Passing judgments from the world of spies? Please!"

"But you are working in my world now. And it's not spying so much as politics. All of it, espionage, covert action, the whole lot—a subdivision of politics."

"Oh, that's quite good. Thus you insist on the dignity of what you do. No doubt you refer to it as a profession. Espionage as a subdivision of politics—may I use that?"

Michael gestured with the rolled-up magazine in his hand.

"Sure, use it. It would pass as an original idea with your readers. I've read some of your stuff," Oliver added. Michael did not say anything, but Oliver could feel his eyes on him.

After a moment Michael asked, "Where are we going, may I ask?"

"Sure, you may ask. Up Constituyentes onto the Toluca road, over the pass at Las Cruces, and then down to La Marquesa. We can pull over down there somewhere and stretch our legs. I've read some of your stuff," repeated Oliver, looking toward the folded magazine. "You write well."

"Better and better," said Michael, grinning at Oliver. "I'm grateful for even the awkward compliment. But I fear you have not read all that I have written. Or that you did not read between the lines."

"I read your piece on the Montoneros, and on Chile too."

"And?"

"I guess that's what's meant by revisionist history."

"Oh, I don't think that applies at all. Not deliberately revisionist. I wonder what you do mean. Perhaps you meant 'reductionist'?"

"No." Oliver considered. "It's not that what you write is wrong."

"Thank you very much."

"You're above the fray, detached, an observer. It's all happening to someone else, you're an anthropologist—"

"Really!"

"Oh, I'm not saying the writing's not good. But you're above the fray—not only you, but your type of writer."

"Absolute rot! What do you mean by 'type'?"

This could get tiresome. Oliver asked, "Why don't you write on Mexico?"

Michael shook his head. "Every Tom, Dick, and Harry writes on Mexico! One is so put off—that sort of person!"

"Meaning?"

"Oh, raving about Cancún. Cozumel! Vallarta!"

"That's hardly Mexico—"

"Try again: why 'revisionist'?"

"Well, I don't think you can excuse terrorists because they use a Marxist vocabulary," said Oliver. "I happened to be in Uruguay when the Tupamaros were getting started. Using a word like 'liberation' doesn't justify them."

"Oh, were you! We must chat one day. But because of their sins we were justified in destroying them."

"The Tupamaros destroyed themselves."

"Are you asking me to believe that we were not behind the scenes, pulling the strings, directing the repression?"

"We?"

"You, the CIA. I happen to know some people—not the sort of people you would know."

Oliver grinned. "You're only proving my point about New Yorkers."

"And you confirm my opinion of the CIA," Michael spat back. "I didn't like the idea of meeting you here."

"They told me it was your suggestion that we meet—"

"They misinformed you," snapped Michael. "Curiosity overcame my compunctions. It so often has in my life. You see, I've never known anyone in the CIA."

"What a thrill for you."

Michael was grinning at him again. "Oh, delightful. I must tell you that I don't especially look forward to having to go over everything twice."

"We have different interests from the Bureau," said Oliver. "The thing is, my interest is strictly—"

"Oh, good. Otherwise it would suggest that one of your organizations is redundant, isn't that so?"

Oliver said something monosyllabic under his breath as he moved to peer around a lopsided, overloaded truck that was grinding slowly uphill in the middle of the road. Oliver suddenly accelerated through a cloud of black diesel fumes. Michael put both hands on the dashboard as the Toyota roared past the truck and slowed again.

Michael laughed. "Did I touch a tender nerve?"

"What I started to say was that my interest is in who you met, what you can tell me about him."

"Won't they want to know that, too?"

Oliver was polite. "Look. Why don't you just let me ask you some questions and rely on me not to waste any more of your valuable time than necessary?"

"I stand rebuked." Michael showed white teeth in a grin. They were winding through the pass and were starting to run the series of curves that would take them downhill through the forest to the valley on the other side.

"This pass, along here, that we're going through, is called Las Cruces because, in the days of Spanish rule there were bandits, highwaymen, that preyed on travelers here."

"How romantic! You can see them hiding behind the rocks, in among the trees, waiting to pounce."

"When the sheriff's men caught them, which I guess they occasionally did, they would crucify them, spread-eagle them on X-shaped crosses, setting an—"

"Echh!" Michael shuddered. "I appreciate the no doubt well-meant travelogue, but try another subject."

"Okay," said Oliver. "Let's assume the man you met is an officer of the First Department of the First Chief Directorate. That makes him especially—"

"What does that mean?"

Oliver looked over at Michael. "I thought they might have—what that means is that the Soviet who deals with you is assigned in the KGB to working against the United States."

"So I have always assumed."

"All right. The point is that I'm interested in the man himself, what you can tell me about him." Oliver turned off the highway, opposite the marshy pond at the bottom of the valley, onto the road that winds through the Valle de los Conejos toward Tenango de Arista. Oliver parked the car at the roadside before reaching the turnoff to Chalma, getting out on the driver's side to take a deep breath.

"Where are we?" Dr. Michael asked across the roof of the car.

"A place with a lot of sky, as you see. A quiet place to talk. A picnicking place. No one much here on a weekday." There was no one to be seen in the open country save three men on horseback disappearing into pines on the slope a good two miles away down the wide grassy valley. Descendants of the bandits in the pass, I daresay," said Oliver, indicating them with his head.

"No, but where are we? I want to know."

Oliver slammed the car door, the sound of it swallowed by the space around them, and took another breath. "The Valley of Toluca. This part, right here, is called the Valley of Rabbits."

"How absurd! I wonder why."

Oliver shrugged. "The air's good here, isn't it? That's enough reason for coming." He and Michael walked slowly through the short grass toward a blasted tree, orange fungus on its aging trunk, sparsely leaved on its few scraggly branches. It stood alone on the crest of an undulation in the green pastureland.

Michael proved to have been minimally observant when Oliver succeeded in getting him around to describing the meeting with his Soviet handler. Oliver was able to get some idea of the man, even though it meant having to sort the useful facts from Michael's constant sardonic attempts at wit. The Russian was older than Michael, closer to Oliver in age; well, but somewhat younger. Height? Hard to tell, sitting in a car together. Not short. Not stocky, but more powerfully built than Oliver, very good English, well-informed. "Nice manners," Michael did not resist adding, looking sidewise at Oliver.

Where had they gone? Out the Puebla road, stopping at a high pass where the toll road and the other road meet. They had turned there to return to the city.

"Rio Frío," said Oliver.

"I believe it was. I'm vastly entertained that you are so much alike."

"In what way?"

"Oh, in many ways. I'll have to think about that. But, to tick off one item, both of you picking me up in a car, driving madly to a wildly scenic spot. The next time, he said—well, he asked if I would like to see the pass through which Cortés came to Mexico from Vera Cruz."

"Between the two volcanoes. That's a fair way out of town, between Popocatépetl and Ixtaccíhuatl. The Paso de Cortés at Tlamacas. The Americans came that way, too, in the Mexican War. Didn't he throw in anything about that example of perfidious imperialism?"

"He may not know. He told me he's just getting around to reading a history of the conquest. So he may not know yet about that particular attack on our helpless neighbors. But it may surprise you—he doesn't seem interested in swaying me with a lot of vulgar rhetoric. Not like the other. A first impression, of course."

"What do you mean: 'first impression'?"

"Didn't I say? He's new. To me, I mean. He said something—what was it now?—that led me to believe he is new to Mexico. Oh, that his family hadn't joined him yet."

Oliver nodded. "They've had a big turnover."

It was there that Michael had made the remark about the Russian's being "elitist," like Oliver.

"What's that supposed to mean?"

Michael was grinning again. "Are you pretending or don't you really know?"

Oliver kept his tongue in check. "Let's go over what else he said, what you noticed, what else might give us an idea of what makes him tick."

Rather than complying, Michael said: "Why do *you* do this? What makes *you* tick."

"It's my work. My field."

"Delightful! So matter of fact! Why do you do it? For kicks? Or are you a patriot? Ridding the world of the communist menace."

Oliver was impatient. "And you?"

"It's not the same, is it? I can assure you that it is not. How do you think I got into this? What makes me tick?"

Oliver gazed at Dr. Michael for a moment. Then he said, "it probably wasn't money."

"Thank you," said Michael, bowing his head in a pretense of gravity.

"Sex?"

"Tch-tch. For shame! Guess again."

"That leaves vanity."

Michael burst into high-pitched laughter. "Wonderful! It amuses me to leave you guessing." He leaned to pick up a dried brown pine cone and threw it at the tree. He spread his arms wide. "This is charming—so vast! The sweep!" He let his arms fall against his thighs. "Continue the interrogation."

"Did you tell him you would like to go to the volcanoes?"

"Absolutely not! I can't stand those dreadful places: they speak to me of cold and of death. Oh, I nearly forgot. He had an ice axe in the back of the car."

"An ice axe? Describe it, would you?" Oliver was turning to lead the way back to the car and he stopped now to look at Michael.

"Oh, you must know. An ice axe. A haft of about two feet, maybe more"—here Michael put his hands apart and then used them as he went on—"it comes to a point on one side of the head and there's this sort of broad, flat, thingummy thing at the other."

Oliver stared at Michael. "Huh," he said. Michael began to repeat the description when Oliver nodded. "I know." Michael had an amused look in his eyes, his eyebrows raised. Oliver gave a short laugh. "It's the coincidence, that's all. Just the other day we were talking about Trotsky. You know—"

"What a delightful surprise that you know of that!" Michael laughed. "He was not amused when I brought that up to him."

"What's surprising are the gaps, things we assume they would know and they don't."

"Oh, you mustn't think they're stupid!"

"I didn't say—"

"Oh, but he's not stupid! He knew, he knew."

By the time Oliver pulled to the curb, a block from the Hotel Camino Real, he thought he had wheedled from Michael all that he could, and Oliver was sure he had spent all the time with him he could stand. The constant sparring was tiring. As Michael put his hand on the door handle and turned toward him, Oliver remembered a basic question: "One more thing: Did he call himself Peter, as the meeting plan called for?"

"Oh, that was cute. Yes, indeed I was told, as part of the meeting arrangements, that he would identify himself as Peter. And he did."

"I see. Just Peter."

Michael looked pleased with himself, and Oliver wondered what would come out of him next. "As we parted, very much like this, I said to him—to tease this confidence, this equanimity, this tough-guy pose, the way he, and you, too, take us for granted—I said, 'Your name really isn't Peter. Tell me, what is it?' He stared at me for a moment with those marvelous green Russian eyes and then said quite charmingly, 'As you wish'—did I say he has something of a British accent? Quite stylish, really. 'As you wish,' he said. 'My name is Gennadi. You may call be Genya.' "

"Hm. Good. Well, good-bye, Dr. Michael." Should be nice to the sonofabitch, thought Oliver, offering his hand. "And, thanks. And my name really is Ted."

"Oh, yes, I assume so. Good-bye."

Oliver stood in front of the smoldering fire, holding in one hand a Scotch whiskey poured over ice, still smarting over having been so effectively patronized by young Dr. Michael. He turned to put the drink on the mantle and knelt to poke at the fire. When he picked up the drink again, the Scotch whiskey made him think of Puig and his thoughts went directly from him to Maria Elena. He took a gulp of whiskey.

"What are you brooding about?"

Oliver started at his wife's question. He was certainly

not ready to mention Maria Elena, if ever he would be. "The usual administrative crap. That's why I was late." True enough. He had been going over the finance books kept by Mrs. Pott. "Here I am, practically alone for all purposes, and it seems sometimes there's as much financial business along with all the other stupid reporting— as if we had a full complement. We'll drown in the stuff."

"Well, they'll send you more people."

"I dunno. Got to eventually." He was staring at the fire then, as it began to blaze.

"But, even so, isn't it better with Whitney gone? Even with this Slasher person? Aren't you pleased?"

"I don't know yet."

"But you detested Whitney!"

Oliver was uncomfortable at appearing childishly hard to satisfy. "Look. Something strange has come up with Harley. There was this great romantic interlude, way back. Now—"

"You mean the Russian girl?"

Oliver stared at Marge. "You know?"

"Yes, he talked about her."

"Well, he never said a damned thing to me until today."

"Well." She turned on the couch to tuck one leg under her. "He wouldn't, would he?"

Oliver frowned. "All I'm trying to tell you is, if he says anything, I mean, he might—"

"He did. He's coming by tomorrow."

That sent a shiver through Oliver. He could not put off seeing Maria Elena. Next thing you knew *she'd* be telephoning and dropping by to see Marge.

Chapter 10

Oliver went to his office the next day to take his raincoat from the coatrack and to tell Mrs. Pott that he should be back by three-thirty. "I have to see someone," he added, not saying where he could be found, as he usually did. The rain had stopped by the time he reached the sidewalk. He stood well back from the street as cars swished past him over the wet pavement, sending sheets of water over the curbs, splashing through the puddles standing in the street. When he crossed the Reforma he found water flowing from the eaves of the buildings, from the edges of awnings. The other passersby, coming out of doors into the street now, were, like Oliver, zigzagging along the sidewalk to avoid the last streams and drippings of rainwater. When Oliver reached the corner of Calle Londres he stopped to find the Botica Karina on the other side of the narrow street. Then he turned to walk up the opposite side. He was a good ten minutes early.

Oliver supposed that he must have heard the Trout Quintet, "La Trucha," before that night in Montevideo. But he never heard it again without the cheerful music bringing that night back to him. He had arrived late at his friends' house on the Rambla, and the white-tied musicians, professionals from the Sodre, had already begun playing.

They sat in an alcove off the living room, facing the larger part of the audience. The overflow, of which Oli-

ver was a part, had been seated in the sun porch—in a transept, as it were, the quintet playing in the apse—so that Oliver sat looking at the main body of guests in enfilade. He found himself studying, halfway along the uneven front row of chairs, the clean profile of a young blond woman whom he thought he remembered having seen before, from a distance, perhaps at the tennis club. She sat listening with chin high, showing a smoothly curved neck. He could not tell, the way she was sitting, who was with her, a matter that gradually became of interest to him. Oliver found he was paying more attention to her than to the music, too much attention, perhaps, for her head slowly turned and suddenly she was looking Oliver square in the eyes. Disconcerted, he let his eyes go to the musicians.

Their eyes drifted toward each other several times more before the music was over. After the applause the crowd rose, some to speak to the musicians, others to push toward a dessert buffet on a candlelit table in the dining room. Oliver found his host and, taking him by the elbow, asked him about the woman.

Amused, smiling, his host had led Oliver through the crowd into the press around the buffet table. She was aware of their approach. Oliver could see one corner of a blue eye. As they came closer, she turned from the man with her to give the host a dazzling smile, letting the smile include Oliver. She was shorter, smaller than he had thought, well-proportioned. She gave Oliver a calm, thorough look on being introduced, holding his eyes as he held her hand. Her escort, a darkly handsome fellow, showed himself barely polite as she and Oliver stood looking at one another. He announced abruptly in a loud voice that they had to leave. As the others left, Oliver hung about to learn more about her from his host. The hostess came to stand with them, putting her arm about Oliver's waist. She was pleased that Oliver was taken by the girl, excited that they had met under her roof. She would get them together. Oliver was immensely pleased himself when she said the escort was not the girl's hus-

band—oh, no, she was separated from him. That escort of hers was a playboy, a cretin, really, a well-known bore, the hostess added, wrinkling her nose.

And at that moment, finding himself in Mexico, Oliver realized that he was longing to talk to Maria Elena again, and at the same moment he saw that it was nearly two o'clock. He turned back up Calle Londres, and started to cross the street to the Botica Karina. As he looked across the street, the door to the shop came open and Maria Elena came out, turning over her shoulder to speak to the man behind her. Oliver stopped, backed up, thinking it might be Puig. The man was Ivor Buchanan. They were talking and did not look toward Oliver. They walked down Londres to the corner and there they disappeared from sight.

"That was a quick lunch," said Mrs. Pott, looking at the clock.

"Umm," said Oliver. He had not eaten lunch.

"Mr. Van Schaik is here."

Van Schaik was sitting at the coffee table in Oliver's office. "Sir, you're looking at the greatest living expert on Uruguay."

"Tell me," said Oliver, sitting down in the chair behind his desk, "all about it."

"I have a pretty good idea of who Pooch thinks he can team up with in Montevideo once he gets back. But I'd like to try it out on you. Pooch has an awfully plausible way with him."

"That he does. But don't try it on me. I'm too dated. Headquarters."

"Okay," said Van Schaik slowly, looking down at the papers on the coffee table in front of him. "I'll pull this together. The Soviet—I'm not sure what's to be done—Pooch, Puig, is not terribly eager about cuddling up to them. However, he's been seeing—been under cultivation, I think it's safe to say, by one in particular—one Alexeyev. Gennadi Alexeyev. 'New to Mexico, like me,' Puig said. No Spanish, an English—"

Oliver's mind had gone back to considering the surprising sight of Buchanan with Maria Elena and he did not at first hear what Van Schaik was saying. He held up one hand. "Hey! Hold it right there. Maybe we got something. That Bureau case. I saw him yesterday."

"Oh, yeah. What about him?"

"Well, mostly he's a wise-ass, but aside from that he's being handled by a Genya—a Gennadi—who's new here. Cut back the way the Soviets are, there can't be a whole mob of Gennadis milling around Tacubaya. English speaker. No Spanish."

"Good English, says Pooch. He asked Pooch to give him Spanish lessons. Pooch wasn't having any."

"Hmm. Well, what about Mrs. Pooch, then?"

Van Schaik frowned and turned to look out the window. "Well, sir, I don't think—I thought of that. I told Pooch that wouldn't be too good an idea. You know."

"Maybe not. But I'd like for us to get to know this Gennadi guy. Have you started your lessons yet?"

"Yes, sir. I mean, no, not really. I start tomorrow."

"Yeah. I can't help thinking—Spanish teachers are a dime a dozen in this town. You could go to the institute. Seems a waste of Mrs. Pooch when we could use her against—"

"Thing is, we've got a definite date for tomorrow," said Van Schaik, shuffling the papers on the table. "She'd be disap— I mean, she seems to be looking forward to it."

Oliver looked at Van Schaik through lidded eyes.

"I ought to be going." Van Schaik stood up.

Oliver had decided—not quite sure why—not to tell Van Schaik about seeing Maria Elena with Ivor, but something in Van Schaik's manner led him to change his mind. "I happened to be walking through the Zona Rosa at lunchtime and there, across the street, was Ivor Buchanan walking along with Ma—with Mrs. Pooch. You know—"

Van Schaik was open-mouthed, dropping his papers on the rug. He knelt. "Ivor Buchanan?"

"Yeah. You met him at the British—"

"Yes, sir, I know him, all right. We have a tennis date—what's he up to?" Van Schaik was scowling up at Oliver, shuffling his papers.

"Good question. Don't say a damned thing to him about this. They didn't see me. It's something we gotta look into." Van Schaik didn't seem to be listening.

Chapter 11

Oliver jaywalked through misty rain, dodging the cars slicking through the dusk, the street shining like a river with the light from the headlights and the open shops. He hopped safely to the curb at the corner of 18 de Julio as the rain blew harder, stopping to roll pants cuffs above his ankles, striding faster down the long slope leading to Plaza Independencia at the bottom. The gleaming sidewalks were crowded despite the rain that swirled to the avenue between the high buildings. The wind tugged at his raincoat and he put his head down, pulling his collar up against Montevideo's midwinter storm. At the bottom he reached shelter in the arcade at the side of the plaza where the fronds of the palms were tossing wildly in the gusts. Standing at the edge of the arcade, he squinted into the rain that sparkled like wires where the light caught it. Pulling his collar higher, he ran blindly toward the Teatro Solís at the side of the plaza.

The concert—tonight a group from Leipzig was playing Bach—would begin at six o'clock. Oliver had started much too early, unable to hang about the office one impatient moment longer. Challenges that a week ago he would have welcomed—the question of how to handle a threat of blackmail, information from an untried agent that did not fit what was known about the personnel of the Soviet Embassy, indications that a seemingly friendly inspector of the Montevideo police was taking money from an agent of the Cubans, a quarrel with headquarters over a plan to make a compromising offer to a KGB officer—were that day's problems, and they were to Oliver mere petty distractions.

All that afternoon he had been glancing at his watch, jumping up from his desk, leaving work half done in the typewriter, peering through grimily translucent windows at the gray rain. He was ready to abandon the pleasures of command, the absorbing rush of the taut hours. His pride at gaining a working mastery of that part of Uruguay that belonged to him—the Soviets and the other East European intelligence services, the grim conspiracies of the dogmatic left, the perilous aberrations of the bitter right, the work with the police, his business, his life—all seemed a small thing.

Oliver hurried up the dark steps at the entrance to the Restaurant de 'l Aguila that sat on the left side of the Teatro Solís. She was not there. It did not occur to him that he might look silly, darting from one column of El Aguila, with their Corinthian capitals, to another on the higher porch of the theater itself, half trotting in and out of the dark under the columns, like a dog quick on the scent. He found her—she was early too—and she had been watching him hunt her down. She was laughing as he hurried toward her without speaking, reaching for her, pulling her to him. They stood close at the side of a dark column, both wet and both cold and quite unaware of it.

"It's closed," Maria Elena said when he finally led her to peer through the glass door of the Aguila. The tables from lunch, a session that would have gone on much of the afternoon, were made up with white linen for the next meal. Clean glass and bright silver flickered in the dark room. Oliver pushed at the doors, and a waiter in shirt-sleeves came to peer at them through the glass, surprised. Shaking his head, he opened the doors an inch or two. Oliver asked if they might get a drink. The waiter looked past him to the rain rushing by on the wind. Seeing Maria Elena, he smiled and opened the door to let them in. He latched the door and turned to walk flatfooted toward the kitchen.

They watched him go through the darkened restaurant,

his footsteps echoing in the empty high-ceilinged room, and they could hear him calling out in the back, in the kitchen. Maria Elena and Oliver were standing close, smiling at each other, when a bartender in a blue apron and shirt-sleeves came to switch on a light behind the mahogany bar against the wall at the right. Oliver helped Maria Elena with her wet coat as they walked to stand at the bar.

The bartender, drowsy from his nap, hair untidy on his head, thought a martini to be a straight vermouth. He watched with neutral expression as Oliver mixed a splash of vermouth with gin over ice in a tumbler. Maria Elena watched, too, taking the bartender's part by commenting that no Uruguayan would drink such a mixture. Did they ever run out of Scotch, they would drink grappa before that medicine. The bartender laughed and agreed with her. "I know you," he said to her, glancing then at Oliver.

"Sure," she said. "I used to come here for lunch. With my husband. Julio Puig Camps. You know him. We're separated now."

"Oh," said the bartender, looking again at Oliver. Maria Elena made a face when she tried Oliver's mixture and smiled gratefully when the bartender poured her a glass of red wine. They stood at the bar and ate chunks of bread and yellow cheese the waiter had brought them.

The bartender was talking of the Argentine bank robbers that had come to Montevideo the week before. There had been a gunfight in an apartment house and all three of them were killed.

"Yes," said Oliver. "I went over there afterward. Place stunk of tear gas."

Maria Elena exclaimed, "You didn't tell me!"

"It's near the embassy."

"They killed an inspector, did you know?" asked the barman.

"So I heard," said Oliver.

"He lived over on Avenida Italia, not far from me." That's what the bartender had wanted to tell them.

"You'd see him walking his grandchildren on a Sunday." The bartender took the wine bottle from behind him and poured wine into Maria Elena's glass. "We don't like those hampónes coming over here. Uruguayans don't go in for that Argentine mob stuff. But we know how to handle those boys, if we have to."

"We're nice people. Not like those porteños." Maria Elena laughed and nudged Oliver in the ribs. But the bartender was quite serious.

He was a fan of Nacional, like Maria Elena. They talked about fútbol and Oliver listened. When the bartender directed an occasional sporting comment to Oliver, Maria Elena would do the answering. "He knows nothing," she finally said, and the three of them broke out laughing.

The red, gold, and white of the small theater, the black-clad musicians, the warm wood colors of their instruments, the music itself, were a blurred background to a portrait of Maria Elena in clean profile, light from the stage bright on her face, a picture that stayed sharp with Oliver when he could no longer remember the music they heard that night.

At intermission Oliver called a taxi and took Maria Elena to his apartment. He woke up toward morning to quiet. The rain had stopped and the wind dropped off. Maria Elena was asleep. Oliver got up to go to the doors to the balcony, pulling the curtains apart, sliding the door open.

He stood there looking at the lighter gray of the sky in the direction of Carrasco. He was standing in a puddle of rainwater and started to turn when Maria Elena came to stand beside him, as naked as he was. He leaned to kiss her and to whisper: "Maria Elena!"

"No." She put a finger to his lips. "I told you. When we are together like this, and from now on, you call me Marucha." She took him by the wrists and led him back to bed.

And from that night Oliver went with renewed spirit to his work. In the months that followed, Maria Elena was *to grow jealous of it, of having to wait for Oliver, irritated by knowing that while he seemed happy at being with her, he was often thinking of his work. She was annoyed at having to compete with this unfamiliar rival.*

The diffused light of elapsed time threw on those days a false kindness, a soft light with no shadows. The light in the Mexican courtyard where they sat now might be uncharitably bright, but the sun felt good on his hands. Oliver closed his eyes and bent his head back to feel it warm on his face. He let his head fall back down and opened his eyes at Maria Elena. Her eyes turned from his and she looked around the courtyard, at the persimmon-colored walls, at the balcony above them, at the azaleas blooming in terra-cotta pots, the young Norfolk pine in its larger pot, the fountain in the center.

Oliver would have been glad, in the ordinary way, to see just about any face from Montevideo, any old friend, found it comfortable talking of those times, feeling warm about it, pleased at the end of it. Maria Elena Ortiz de Puig Camps was not that kind of old friend. He would not give offense, could he help it, but he was wary of her making claims on him. He was as cautious with his new life as a miser with his gold, nervous about what Maria Elena would ask of him.

She sat to his left, halfway around the round table with the green cotton cloth. She had taken off her white sweater, pulled it around her shoulders. She slowly stirred the lemonade in the glass in front of her with a thick plastic straw. Oliver raised the barrel-shaped goblet of Carta Blanca to her and took a sip from it.

"I don't care for their Mexican beer," she said, watching him.

"Really? It's better then we have at home, Anyway, you're a wine drinker, aren't you?"

She blinked and turned her eyes away from him again.

He picked up the menu. "What would you like?"

She shook her head and picked up the menu at her elbow. Now Oliver watched her. To counter a warmth he could not help feel at being near her again, he was compiling an inventory of her imperfections, examining her, noting that she looked older, as she should, and if less pretty, inescapably handsome. When they had walked from the shop in the Zona Rosa to find a taxi, she had drawn long looks on the street not only from men but from women. When they had come past the reception desk a moment ago, walking on into the courtyard of the Hotel de Cortés, it had been the same. People at the other tables were stealing looks at her now. When people came in from the busy street to the lavender stone of the courtyard, their eyes went right to her.

The wrinkles around her eyes, the new lines at either side of her mouth, he had listed as demerits; they could as well be listed on the other side of the ledger, hardly subtracting from her smart appearance. Maturity had given her a new poise, a different order of charm from that of her early twenties.

He found himself wondering if he got up from his chair, right then, whether she would go with him as easily as she had that night at the Teatro Solís. He was annoyed with himself for drifting so easily into temptation, and at the same time, feeling stuffy for refusing the test.

As though she sensed something of that, she was looking at him, half amused, half annoyed—her eyes were narrowing—more annoyed than amused now. She had looked like that in the taxi a few minutes ago when she had said: "The sanctity of the marriage vow was of no consequence in Montevideo, I remember."

Her eyes had narrowed almost shut when he had replied, "It's completely different. You and Pooch were separated."

Her mind had gone back to those remarks, too, for she said, waving the menu at him, "You never used to talk like a lawyer. Bringing up technicalities." She tossed her hair and put up a hand to smooth it in back. "You would find yourself an escape clause now were it in your interest to do so."

She spoke louder than Oliver thought necessary, and

he could not help a quick look around the nearer tables to see if their neighbors had heard. The several faces looking their way turned at his glance. They had been admiring Maria Elena rather than listening to her.

"I told you, I—we—have something very good. And the two children too."

"So domestic!"

"Frankly, Maria Elena, I do not intend to endanger what I have."

" 'Maria Elena!' again." She mocked him. "You always did think of yourself first. In everything."

That stung. It was so unfair, so female. Oliver found himself taking a hasty inventory of low points in their year-long, long-ago relationship. Had it been that way? He quickly decided that it had not. "And," he decided to point out, "of course, you're back with Pooch."

She turned her head away from him. "I'd forgotten how tiresome you can be! I told you: only in a manner." She twisted her head back quickly, laying both hands flat on her blouse. "It is convenient to me at this moment. Understand?" She let her lip curl. "He has someone, as usual. One of your little North Americans, a teacher, very serious, so earnest, studying at the university for a degree in anthropology. A doctorate, is it? One can understand the preoccupation of the Mexicans with their own past. What I fail to understand is why you Americans insist on being mixed up in it."

Phooey, thought Oliver. "You know her?"

"Know her? Hardly. They sneak off together. One afternoon I went up to them where they were walking on Campos Eliseos, in Polanco, near our apartment—she lives nearby." She laughed. "Poor thing. Went all red, then white. She was terrified."

"Um," said Oliver, imagining the extent of his own discomfort had Puig confronted him with Maria Elena in Montevideo. "Pretty?"

"You might think so. Mousy. A blonde. Dyed blond. A thin little thing with small bones. Rather like me, in some ways."

"Mousy."

Maria Elena laughed.

"Let's order," said Oliver.

"The salad, the avocado," she said, tossing the menu to the table.

Oliver had been holding the menu without looking at it. He was on the edge of asking Maria Elena what Puig knew of their affair in Montevideo. It would be stupid. The question was absurd. Of course Puig had known. What could Oliver ask? How did Puig like their having an affair?

Oliver signaled to a waiter in a mulberry jacket with black lapels. When the waiter left, Oliver leaned forward. "You said there was something important—"

"I thought you might be interested," she said, letting her dark lashes close softly several times over her blue eyes. "They are going to kill you because of Freddie."

Chapter 12

Oliver had been sitting back in his chair, his hands clasped, his elbows on the arms of his chair. He did not change his expression or his position. He did swallow. " 'They'? Would you repeat that?"

"You had better listen carefully. And you should think carefully, too, of what you say. Don't make one of your jokes. I tell you: they are going to make you answer for Freddie."

"Now, wait a minute, Maria Elena." Oliver put his left elbow on the table, leaning toward her on his arm, pointing a finger at her. "I wrote you." He spoke with a deliberate patience. "I was very sorry to hear about Freddie." He had been sorry, too, for her sake. "I wrote. You never answered."

"So? It was so late that you wrote. What was there to say? It was all over."

"I wrote as soon as I heard."

"There! Let's be frank. Why pretend? You would have known. Why even bother to write?"

Oliver gave an exasperated laugh. "Maria Elena. For one thing, I was out of the country. Out of the States, I mean. For another, Uruguay was behind—I mean, I wasn't working on it anymore. No one thought to tell me."

"One thing is true that you say. When you are done with us we are behind you and you think you can forget us."

"It's not that way, not the way you put it."

"No? What is different now," she said, "is that I am no longer innocent."

Oliver laughed. "I don't remember your innocence."

"You see? That isn't funny. I was innocent politically."

"And now?"

"Now? Now I know what you were doing in Montevideo."

"I thought maybe you knew then. You never asked questions."

"What you did then was of no matter to me." This brought a short laugh from her lips. "I didn't know of such things. What question would I have asked? Now I know all about those things."

Oliver doubted it. He leaned to be closer to her. "Who do you mean, 'they'?"

She shook her head without taking her eyes from his. "I'm taking a great risk telling you. If you know who betrayed Freddie—that indeed it was not you—you had better tell me now."

She was looking at him intently, leaning toward him with eyebrows raised. At one time Oliver thought he would never be closer to another human than he was to her, that no two people could have been more intimate than they were. They had done a lot of looking into each others' eyes. Her stare now made him uneasy. He would keep his head. "In the first place—" he began. The waiter came with their lunch. She agreed to another lemonade.

"In the first place: Was Freddie betrayed?"

Maria Elena's eyes narrowed. "Stop the pretense. You know he was."

Oliver threw himself back in his chair, shaking his head, half smiling. "Maria Elena! You're going about this the wrong way. Honestly, I don't know what you're talking about."

She looked less certain. "You always deny everything." Here, Oliver supposed, she was referring not to him but to the CIA. "You cannot avoid responsibility for what took place in Uruguay."

"Oh, yes, I can. And do. That was your own little show, your own doing. Not yours, personally. But not ours, not at all. Look, I'm going to eat. Eat your salad."

"That's not what people say. They say you were there to train our police in methods of torture."

"Maria Elena! Do you think the Montevideo police—any police in South America, in Latin America—need training from us in torture? Do you think—really, now—that was what I was doing in Montevideo?"

Her eyes shifted away. "I'm telling you what people say."

"Who are these people?"

She shrugged. "Everyone."

He shook his head at her, broke a roll and buttered it. She watched his hands, waiting for him to speak. Oliver knew he was not clever at this, hotly impatient, rather, with the slippery generalizations. But this was something more than an argument about politics, this statement that he had been found guilty and condemned to death for a crime unknown to him. "Maria Elena. Look. Never mind what 'people say.' Let's talk about what we know, what you know and what I know."

She drew herself erect and raised her chin and stared at him. "I've been talking to people who know as much as you do. You always thought, you always think, you know more than the others—you had better take this seriously, for your own sake."

"I take being killed very seriously."

"There. Another of your jokes. Mind you, Ted, I have other people I can talk to, my own sources."

"Other intelligence officers?" Oops! He had warned Van Schaik against telling Buchanan that Oliver had seen him with Maria Elena.

"That's my affair. There are others who know as much as you do—maybe more."

Pah! "Eat your salad," he said. "Let's start—"

"Stop telling me to eat my salad!" She seemed strangely annoyed. People were looking at them.

"Don't eat it, then!"

They ate in silence. The food was good, and Oliver had been hungry. According to Maria Elena, the meal could be his last. He looked over at her, smiling, but she was eating, head down. One didn't know sometimes if a woman threw the drama and mystery in for the hell of it or whether she was really mixed up.

He kept on eating. He'd let her talk. The parrot in the cage near the fountain suddenly gave a series of frightening squawks, startling everyone in the courtyard, and the people at the tables laughed. Maria Elena smiled too.

They refused coffee and he paid the check, helping her into her coat as they went out to the street. They walked past the fortresslike building of the Secretaría de Hacienda, stopping at the zebra crossing for the cars to pass. Oliver guided her across to Alameda Park. Rock doves were thick on the sidewalk at their feet, fluttering noisily off for no apparent reason. "Let's start at the beginning," said Oliver, offering her his arm. Maria Elena took it—a good sign, that, a sign of trust.

She went back to the beginning too.

Oliver would remember, she said, how the family had fussed over Freddie for neglecting his studies in the faculty of agriculture, how his family, his friends, his teammates, worried when Freddie began missing rugby practice. He was going instead to the noisy meetings, painting wall slogans, chanting in the streets, building a record with the Montevideo police for hooliganism of the political sort. It was Freddie who helped haul the tires to the intersections for burning, who stretched the banners across the fronts of university buildings, who planned the lightning demonstrations, the group coming suddenly together on Avenida 18 de Julio to smash the windows of the Pan American Airways office, that convenient symbol of imperialism. Freddie was easy to spot, the racing, hoarsely shouting, blond fellow—*muy exaltado*—gaining a new notoriety in police files.

"You remember all that," she said to Oliver.

"Yes. And how you worried about him. How he changed. How he came to disapprove of us," added Oliver.

"That was toward the end. He was never unpleasant about it."

"No, never unpleasant," Oliver agreed. But if not unpleasant, damn close to it. Freddie from the first had struck Oliver as a handsome, cheerful, uncomplicated fellow, blond and blue-eyed like Maria Elena, four years younger than she. The two were close, the mother having died when Freddie was born; the elder brother—even as a youth, apparently—was as darkly grim and charmless as Oliver knew him later.

No great brain, Freddie, but amiable, tolerant of Oliver, not jealous, although he must have realized how it was between Oliver and his sister. Or so Freddie had been when Oliver first had come to know the family. Later, in the months before Oliver left Uruguay, Freddie began to challenge Oliver, dispute him, spout dreary stuff about the United States. He was never surly like the elder brother. Oliver annoyed Freddie by not accepting Freddie's premises, refusing to rise to the bait, talking calmly, rather, of the United States that Oliver knew.

Keeping those thoughts to himself, Oliver said, "I was truly sorry to hear, Maria Elena—I liked Freddie—what happened?"

They were walking toward the empty bandstand that sat like an elaborate basket in the center of the park. There were few people in the park that time of day, aside from the usual clutches of working-class couples, clasped together on the benches, or standing on the grass, silently embracing. Oliver spotted an empty green-painted iron bench along the walk where a ground dove was scuttling about, head down, tail up, urgently searching the grass behind the bench.

As they sat down, Maria Elena said Freddie was restless, moving from one political group to the next, tending always toward the more radical and violent. Because of the name he had earned at rugby, he was sought after, although his political development, according to the father and the elder brother, was rudimentary. The father, during one of these times, had been particularly worried about Freddie's being active in the youth wing of the Partido Comunista del Uruguay. Oliver would remember that the PCU was probably the most obedient of the Moscow-line parties in all the Americas. The father, a good socialist, disapproved of the Soviet Union and of communists. The father had worried in the same way about the elder brother in his time at university, when he, too, had his fling with the communists, even holding office in one of their main front groups. But the elder brother had returned to country life to give himself over to the work of the *estancia*, never seeming to look back or to regret abandoning the party and politics for farming.

Freddie left the party, too, Maria Elena said, to begin an even more intense involvement with a faction that openly called for violence, a group that despised the standpat communists as fiercely as the communists themselves despised the bourgeois government of Uruguay. When Freddie was arrested marching with the sugar workers, smashing store windows in the center of Montevideo one First of May in the late sixties, the family saw what a dangerous political choice he had made. "It must be what parents feel when a child goes beyond their reach, joins a religious cult. Or takes to drugs. Freddie had left us. And it was dangerous. Be honest, Ted," she went on to say, looking at him intently. "You knew all this."

"Sure, the politics of it. I knew that Sendic and the sugar workers were the nucleus of the Tupamaros. But that's not the same as knowing—at that time—that Freddie had gone over to them."

"Hmm," she said, looking from one of his eyes to the other. Even here, Oliver saw, strollers through the park slowed to look at her. "When the Tupamaros were doing the kidnappings—it may have been the Brazilian, Dias

Gomide, or the American, Fly—the police began looking for Freddie himself in earnest. That was early on, when the Tupamaros were sympathetic, exposing political corruption—people still called them Robin Hoods, before the worst of it.''

She paused to look at Oliver. He only nodded, not looking at her. Robin Hoods! Before the worst of it! In that Robin Hood time they were already killing. The cold-blooded killing of the American official, Dan Mitrione, the Tupamaro leader Sendic would later casually and cynically shrug away as a mistake. Oliver did not like passing judgment on Freddie, dead, but he would not excuse him either. Better dead all of them with their politics of death. He made his hands into fists and jabbed them into his raincoat pockets, frowning at the hedge across the gravel walk from them.

The elder brother strongly disapproved of Freddie's being with the Tupamaros, Maria Elena was saying, but did nothing except to write Freddie off as hopeless, an idiot, lost. Maria Elena tried to reach Freddie but he was hard to find. Then, when he did turn up he was brusque, thin, hard-faced, with a grimness for all who were not with him—for her too—not the tender younger brother anymore at all.

Maria Elena went to the *estancia* to consult with the elder brother about Freddie. But the elder brother was coldly angry at having been interviewed by the police, being confronted with his own record from their files. "Stupid!" he had said through clenched teeth. "Can't they leave me in peace? Can't they distinguish between those infantile left-wing adventurers and the party?" The brother was no comfort: Freddie was politically naive, a fool for lending his good looks, his name as an athlete, his popularity, to the Tupamaros. "They'll achieve nothing, those gentry"—the brother was savage—"except to make the rightists respectable and, in the end, the repressive forces popular."

Maria Elena looked up at Oliver. "How right he was. God knows he was right about that!"

After another bold Tupamaro incident, one of the kidnappings, the police had come to search the house and the outbuildings at the *estancia*. Maria Elena had been there. The police did not bother to be polite this time. The elder brother had been furious, understandably so, but unreasonable, she thought, in directing his fury at the reckless, absent Freddie more than at the police. "Very cold," Maria Elena added. "He resented being in any way involved. It was left to me to deal with it, and I could not abandon Freddie."

She was silent for a moment and then went on. "At the end, Freddie was alone at a farmhouse, not far from Montevideo. A policeman had been killed and the police were bumping about stupidly like angry bees at a windowpane. I got word at the *estancia*, from one of his comrades, where Freddie was. My brother offered nothing. He turned his back on me and thus on poor Freddie as well. I went straight to Montevideo. I thought Freddie might send word somehow to the apartment in Montevideo, try to come there to hide."

"I didn't know about all this," said Oliver. "Pooch said nothing of it."

"Puig! He would not," said Maria Elena scornfully. "Oh, he called to warn me that the police were after Freddie. As though I didn't know! He told me to keep out of it."

"Well, he was looking after your welfare."

"Oh, was he? Puig hated Freddie for the humiliation— I told you—the incident with the horse. My welfare! And that's something else. Tell me the truth: Puig was working for you in Montevideo, wasn't he?" She pulled away from him to put distance between them on the bench, folding her arms.

"Certainly not!"

"Tell me the truth! It's nothing to you. To me it's terribly important."

"Maria Elena, I promise—"

"If not then, later, at the time I'm speaking of."

"Why Puig? Where did you get the idea that—"

"Puig had the motive— Oh, never mind!" She looked around at the green of the tended park as though surprised to find herself there. She got up. "I must get back. Can we get a taxi? We stay open during siesta—the tourists. Anyway," she resumed, standing there, again not seeing the park in Mexico, "the police went straight to the farmhouse where Freddie was. They surrounded it and told him to come out. There was some shooting and they fired tear gas through the windows. They broke down the door and when Freddie came out they shot him down."

Oliver took her arm in his. "Maria Elena, I'm sorry." And he was, again, sorry for her. She did not look at Oliver but shook her head, and they started to walk on the path back to Avenida Hidalgo. "How do you know all this?"

"Oh, I know it well enough. There was someone there who did not like what was done. He sent me a note to tell me what happened that day. I don't know who he was. I had no way of finding him. It was on his conscience. It had bothered him and so he wrote me. I have no reason to doubt what he said."

It had taken everyone some time to understand, more time to be willing to admit what was happening before their eyes. No one, not even intelligence officers—especially not intelligence officers, thought Oliver, grimly—saw at first that the Robin Hoods were not laughable but deadly. Violence and killing were too remote, romantic, things that happened in stories, in the movies, in distant lands—nothing to do with peaceful Uruguay, with Montevideo, not in these days, not to us, not now.

They were at the curb and Oliver held up a hand for a taxi.

Maria Elena was looking at him. "That is not all he wrote in that letter. He said that the police did not just stumble onto the farmhouse but that they had intelligence that Freddie was there. That's where you come into it."

"I? I was long gone from there."

"Yes, you were not there because you had left. Left in

a hurry because the Tupamaros had you on their list." Tears came to her eyes. "Why couldn't you have told me that at the time?"

"Maria Elena—look. It was secret, the way we found out. If I had stayed on, you would have been dragged into danger too. Where did you—"

She stamped one foot. The tears were angry. "Never mind about that! Don't pretend you left to protect me."

"That's not what I—" He began to feel foolish, arguing with her while waving one hand in the air. He took the hand down.

"Listen! Don't act superior. It was Freddie that told the Tupamaros about you."

"How did you learn that?"

Instead of answering that, she gave him a triumphant look. "So, you did know that, then!"

"Maria Elena, you should drop this. You can't bring Freddie back." Sententious but true. "You'll end by making yourself bitter. What's more, it's dangerous, your going about investi—"

"Dangerous! Yes! The danger is for you!"

"Nonsense!"

"You know Freddie told them about you, don't you?"

"That was suggested, later on, as a possibility." He flapped his hand at an orange Volkswagen taxi.

"Let me tell you something else that has been 'suggested as a possibility,' " she said, speaking to be heard over the roar of the Volkswagen engine. Oliver opened the door of the taxi. The front passenger seat had been removed, and she bent to climb into the backseat. "It has been 'suggested' that your CIA told the police where Freddie was to be found."

"Maria—" Oliver glanced at the taxi driver, who didn't seem to have picked up the English, giving him the address in Calle Londres. The driver nodded, set the meter going, leaning to pull the door shut with the chain drooping from the door handle. "Maria Elena," Oliver began again, "be reasonable—"

"I *am* reasonable—more reasonable than you!"

When he answered with half a laugh, she flipped her head away from him to look out the window on her side.

"Maria Elena. All I mean is that if you can tell me this much, you should be able to tell me more. You know: who? when? wha—"

She turned to look at him. "I have warned you. What more can I do? If indeed it is as you claim, and your people were not involved, then you'd better find out quickly who was. They are going to avenge Freddie."

By the time a frowning Oliver was ready to try once more to pin her down, the taxi had pulled to the curb. Oliver got out first, deciding to pay the taxi off. He could walk to his office faster than the taxi could take him. Maria Elena was bent over, coming through the door of the taxi, and Oliver caught her arm as she straightened. "Wait!" he commanded, passing money to the driver. Maria Elena twisted herself free, and when he turned, the door of the boutique was swinging closed behind her.

Oliver picked his slow way along the walk through strings of early afternoon shoppers, clots of late lunchers, hardly seeing them. He felt he should be able to take the threat of death more personally, but so far, with the evidence in hand, he was unable to feel fear. If a doctor had told him he was shortly to die of an incurable condition, giving the reasons for the diagnosis, he might object to the opinion but he would take it seriously. The allegations of Maria Elena carried with them no such confidence. To begin with, Oliver told himself—for he was viewing the case as an intelligence officer must— there was no sourcing. She might have overheard idle boasting and misunderstood it. One of Freddie's comrades might have tried to impress her with an assurance of vengeance. Oliver easily admitted that he wanted to dismiss the threat, not fear that it might be true, but from fear of the reaction in Washington.

He would be obliged to report it. Maria Elena's no doubt well-meant warning might have the result only of his being ordered home on the pretext of saving him from assassination. Death is always just around the corner, thought Oliver. The animals don't know that: we do, but we live as though we don't. He knew he had been far closer to death in the past, continued his argument. Think, too, of the times death brushes past without our knowing it: Let's put this amorphous rumor in a real context. Why should anyone take it seriously?

Oliver reached his office, having pretty well drafted in his head a rational, pooh-poohing cable to Washington. He was ready to type it up. But Mrs. Pott, of course, had to jump up from her desk in her own excited and mistaken sense of priority.

"The pouch is here," she said. "I've put it in order. I'll bring it right in."

"No rush," said Oliver, holding up his hand as he passed her desk. "I've got to think—"

"You really ought to look at it." Mrs. Pott giggled— not the amused giggle, the embarrassed one.

"Oh?"

"Mrs. Pott was absolutely right. The first item reported the indignation of the Bureau, CIA headquarters relaying it in scandalized tones that suggested Oliver had singlehandedly brought on an irreparable rupture of the relations between the Bureau and the Agency. On his return, Dr. Michael had complained that Oliver had treated him "with arrogance," that Oliver had implied ". . . the Bureau was asking [Michael] the wrong questions. . . ."

Oliver read on with horror. Oliver had accused ". . . New Yorkers and Michael himself of being narrow and provincial. He had attacked New York writers for lack of involvement in what they wrote about, as though a writer had to be a CIA agent to write of those subjects, sneering at Michael, derogating intellectuals, castigating Michael because he was not a García Marquez, a Vargas Llosa, a Carlos Fuentes." Michael must have written it all out. Maybe the Bureau people had recorded it. They could hardly have gotten all this ranting down verbatim. "Oliver typified the Philistine callousness that disregards the role of the intellectual, strips him of stature and influence, leaving him—so unlike the place of the intellectual in Latin culture—quite without respect or power."

Finally, Michael had said—Oliver could see the miserable little wart spitting it out—". . . [Oliver] suggested Michael was cooperating with the KGB for money, for sex, but mostly out of vanity." The Bureau was "deeply upset," said headquarters. On the basis of Oliver's treatment of him, Michael was reconsidering his relationship with the Bureau and was threatening to stop seeing the Soviets. Only by ". . . appealing to his patriotism"—Oliver snorted—had the Bureau ". . . kept this most prominent writer motivated to continue this most unique and valuable activity."

Oliver kicked his chair away from the desk, marching out to where Mrs. Pott sat. He pointed his finger at her. "Where's that report of the interview with that, that—"

"I have it here. I thought—"

"Just read me the comment I put on it, would you?"

Mrs. Pott turned a page. "You mean here, at the end? Out loud?"

Oliver nodded, hauling a chair to the side of her desk, sitting in it, staring at the floor as she read.

" 'While I am of course grateful for the chance to interview subject,' " read Mrs. Pott, " 'and for what appears to be a good identification partly as a result of it, I was uneasy the whole time with Michael. He seems to be playing at some sort of game. While I can't put my finger on it, beyond his cute way of fencing with one, he seems to regard all this as a joke, himself a superior being, me his unimaginative foil. I wonder what his manner is with the Gennadi Alexeyev (whom we are carrying as the KGB officer handling him) and, for that matter, with the Bureau people in New York. In passing this report and these comments to the Bureau, please ask them to describe his relationship with them, especially if I am to see him again here. What are they getting from this? What do they think his motives to be? What do the Soviets get from it? Such information from the Bureau, before I saw him this time, obviously would have been useful.' "

Oliver blurted out a word. "Excuse me, Mrs. Pott," he added hastily.

She pretended not to have noticed, continuing to read. " 'One other point which, even if explained, should be pursued: in earlier correspondence it was stated that Dr. Michael said he would like to see the CIA station chief in Mexico so as to pass on his immediate impressions. Yet, as you see, above, Michael said that seeing me was not his initiative but that of someone else. What's going on here?' "

"They won't have seen your report yet, you know. Your comments on Dr. Michael. There hasn't been time."

"That's so. That's good." What was not good was the Bureau people taking down Michael's words as though they were scripture. What was not good was headquarters assuming the worst without asking Oliver for his side of the story.

That afternoon a message came ordering Oliver to Washington for consultation.

Chapter 13

"Still clipping away, I see," said Oliver, standing the next morning at the French doors to watch El Gordito at his ballet steps in Drew's garden.

"Not still," said Drew. "Again. He has commissions in other private gardens in Coyoacán, in the Pedregal. He gives me what time he can. You see, he works a week in the park at the volcanoes, and then, during his week off from that, he does his gardening."

"Hey, that's interesting," said Oliver, going from the windows to sit in the gray chair.

"Indeed, you are easily interested." He dismissed El Gordito with an impatient wave of the hand. "Speaking of interesting—I met the Uruguayan wife last night. Now, she *is* interesting."

"Damn!" said Oliver. "One big happy family!" Oliver bounced out of his chair to pace up and down the Chinese rug.

"Well, really!" said Drew, watching this. "No need to blow up. A reception at the Chilean Embassy. She was there, with her husband Puig, whom I had met, as you will remember, on a previous occasion. All quite natural. You make too much of it."

"And does she know of our connection? You know she's giving language lessons to Van Schaik, don't you? If she can just cozy up to Mrs. Pott, now, she'll have the whole damn station in her pocket. Probably has—I'll check to see if Mrs. Pott is giving Maria Elena a lift to choir practice."

"Really! You do make too much of it. It was all quite natural. We can't live in an autoclave. I found it entirely suitable to ask her to tea—this afternoon."

"Tea!" Oliver threw himself into the gray chair. "God Almighty!"

"What is it? What have you against her? Charming. I would—"

"Oh, come on, Harley. We can't have people getting that close to us. All right, I wasn't going to—but maybe I'd better. You see, I just sent something off to headquarters about all this."

" 'All this'? What 'all this'?"

Oliver looked at his watch. "Van Schaik's coming at ten, isn't he?" He leaned forward to rest his arms on his knees. "I don't really want to go over this with him. Lemme think."

Where to start? Oliver stared bleakly into the garden. He found the house finches irritating, chirping and whistling where the tall geraniums grew above the French doors. He would expurgate, for Drew, the account of Montevideo so as to say the least about Maria Elena and himself. Difficult: they were inseparable so much of that time, every night—except when Oliver was working, and even then she might be waiting for him at his apartment. Keeping her out of the narrative would be tricky. Oliver gave a mental shrug: surely he could trust Drew with his confidence at least as much as he could trust the people at headquarters. Unfortunate: What had been tucked away, nearly forgotten, in the files, would now be dug up by the new arrivals, unfeeling archaeologists, Slasher and his crowd.

"Well, to begin, we were working with the police in Montevideo. As to be expected, there were the types in the police who thought the way to deal with the radical left was to haul them in and bounce them off the walls."

"Isn't sadism pervasive in those circles? Of course, I never dealt with the police."

"Don't be lofty, Harley. And stereotypes don't become you. Some of them used the rough stuff because it was the only way they knew to get information. Seemed convenient. No doubt some of them enjoyed it, but I'm not sure sadism is a sufficient explanation. Uruguay has a very middle-class orientation, just as we do, but it goes without saying that there are differences. The police, including the officers, by and large, came from the less-well-off middle class, and the enlisted ranks from farm boys and the urban working class. So, you have resentment of the intellectuals with their snooty, superior ways, the spoiled university brats jumping up and down, taunting you. What I mean is, you don't have to be a certified sadist to enjoy knocking people like that around a bit if you find yourself alone with them in the *jefatura*.

"Our job was to convince the police to use intelligence operations instead of applying an electric charge to the subversive testicle, find out what these groups were up to—you know—analysis, define the threat, deal with the problem intelligently, lawfully. You don't strut about snapping your galluses and preaching to the police about this—they are somehow strangely unimpressed by loud-mouthed North American righteousness.

"So we argued on pragmatic, technical grounds. Some of the younger officers, some of the army officers in the top command structure of the police, the smarter politicians, saw the need for reform of police interrogation customs as well as we did, maybe better than we did. So they used us to accomplish what they could not do directly themselves, let us run with the ball, and quietly came around to pick us up when we ran into trouble. What we did with the police was training, simple training, no less—how to go about it—clipping, cross reference, filing systems, penetration operations—talking always in our technical, practical, pragmatic, down-to-earth way, and they were dropping the rough stuff, torture. I don't have to tell you, Harley, but this was good political work, a real contribution. And it was going well until Congress passed that damn fool law prohibiting work with foreign police forces, one of the dumber things Congress has done."

"Yes, I have no doubt—but what does that have to do with my having Mrs. Puig to tea?"

Oliver stared into the garden and thought about the question.

When the report came from the Montevideo police that the Tupamaros intended to seize a North American official, it was Oliver who got the embassy to alert all North Americans, family members as well. Oliver had no grounds for doubting the specific words of the report, as much as he would have liked to have known more about the source, and to judge its reliability for himself.

The police were careful, jealous of the source, didn't want the Americans elbowing in. Fair enough: previous reports from the same source had been borne out by events. The warning had to be kept general, because of the sensitivity of the police source. Once families got on the phones talking about the threat against an American official, the word would spill all over, alerting the Tupamaros to the leak in their ranks.

The trouble with generalized warnings is that they draw jaded responses—the small North American community, put on alert so many times by then against one reported threat or another, had grown blasé. This time Oliver took the ambassador aside and suggested he warn the deputy chief of mission and the heads of embassy sections, in particular, to be careful.

A long weekend was coming up and Oliver was going to Costa Azul with Maria Elena. They liked the anonymity of the modest resort. Maria Elena would not be known at the small brick hotel, the Gran Lido Azul. They had their own room giving onto a wide, sheltered balcony above the beach, the surf hissing on the sand part of the night. Later the waves would boom along the coast, making the stones of the shingle rattle, the waves marching up the beach on the inflowing tide.

Maria Elena would tell friends that she was thinking

of going to Punta del Este. There were so many parties in Punta during the season that her absence from any one could easily be explained, were someone later to ask.

At the last minute on Friday the ambassador told Oliver that he would be needed at the Saturday reception for the visiting congressional delegation. Annoying, but not unusual. Oliver had worked it out. He and Maria Elena sat in the sun, swam, walked on the beach all Saturday afternoon, knowing no one, speaking to no one outside the hotel. After the long, late lunch they had stayed, red from the sun, in the room. When the sun was low, Oliver took a shower, put on a white shirt, and his good, dark blue suit, telling Maria Elena he would be back before midnight.

The moment the minister of the interior came through the wide doors from the hall of the embassy residence, he caught Oliver's eye with a quick gesture of his head before bowing over the hand of the ambassador's wife and greeting the ambassador.

He came directly through the crowd to Oliver, pausing only to snatch a Scotch from a waiter's tray as it passed, inviting Oliver to step to the patio outside. Handing his congressman and an Uruguayan politician over to an economic officer to interpret for them, Oliver joined the minister.

"I am afraid, Señor Oliver, that I have ominous news for you," said the minister solemnly. Solemnity was unusual in the amiable political hack whose interests were cheerfully admitted by him to be young women and the raising of prize bulls, the order, he was wont to announce, reversing as he grew older. He left the details of politics to his deputy and security matters to the chief of police. But he had been good about the CIA role. "Myself, now, I'd like to hear their communist balls cracking in a vise"—all of the left was "communist" to him—"but I suppose you chaps have it right. Let me know when you have problems with the police."

Oliver was amused, wondering what categories of information the minister would regard as ominous. At the *same time there was the not-unaccustomed tingle of pleasure at the implication of excitement that comes with bad news. The minister's somber manner suggested a new crisis, a pleasing emergency, a different problem to attack and solve. Oliver later would look back ruefully at his selfish reaction. He would see soon enough that he was not immune, not at all untouchable but, rather, as naked as the next man.*

The police source, said the minister, had called for an emergency meeting to pass on the identity of the target of the Tupamaros. The minister rested his glass on the balustrade to take a piece of paper from his pocket and hand it to Oliver—with the melodramatic sweep of an actor, Oliver was pleased to note, grinning to himself.

That was the end of the grinning, the end of any feelings of superiority for a while. Oliver's feet went cold in the mild evening.

Theodoro [sic] Oliver, norteamericano, secretario 2ndo de embajada del EU, domicilio Bulevar Artigas, 179, Dpto. 17E. Coche, Chevrolet Nova, camioneta, azul oscuro, llantas blancas, placa diplomática 213 . . .

The note went on to describe Oliver, his weekday patterns of movement, where he might be seen at lunch, his address. While Oliver never showed himself aware of surveillance—the report noted—never taking any obvious steps to lose his followers, nevertheless at times he would disappear and those watching him could not describe just how it happened. This suggested that Oliver was, as the report phrased it, involved in "special activities."

There was the address, too, of Maria Elena's own apartment in Pocitos. At the end the note said that Oliver would be spending that very weekend at Punta del Este, showing a new value to Maria Elena's cover story. That inaccuracy did not diminish the reliability of the report, rather—if anything—adding to it.

Almost physically sick—for the consequences were im-

mediately apparent—Oliver closed his eyes for a second before asking the minister: "May I keep this?"

The minister said: "That's for you. I'm sorry, Oliver. Truly and personally sorry. We are at your orders. Let me know what you decide." The minister must have known as well as Oliver there could be only one solution. "Will you have the goodness to inform your ambassador?"

Oliver thanked the minister, tucked the note in his pocket, took the ambassador aside, made his excuses to the ambassador's wife, and drove off to send a cable to Washington. Later he drove in the moonlight along the Rambla to Carrasco, the moon glinting on the sea to his right, past the airport, through the small towns, pretending for a time that the note had not said what it did. It was like pretending that someone dear had not died, that things would be as they always were, that nothing had happened. By the time he reached Costa Azul, he'd given up playing with evasions.

At the darkened hotel he found the gate locked. He stood in the moonlight tossing pebbles and shells over the wall onto the balcony outside their room. Finally, pitching his jacket over the wall, he scaled it, dropping into the soft sand on the far side. He shinnied up a tree from which he put one tentative leg precariously across to the railing of the balcony. His good suit, too, he thought, hurling himself to sprawl onto the floor of the balcony.

When he awoke Maria Elena by slipping into bed with her, he paid no heed to the complaints about her sunburn, saying good-bye to her without her knowing it. When she went back to sleep, he stayed awake, first wondering how he could bring himself to leave—he could resign, stay on in Uruguay—another evasion. Then he lay in bed planning how he had to go about it, what his duty required of him.

Maybe he would send for her later.

Of all this Oliver gave Drew a bare but complete outline and then brought him up to date.

"I see. I had no idea." Drew had been listening intently, breathing with his mouth open, obviously fascinated by the story. "And did you leave? I mean, right away, just like that?"

Oliver nodded slowly. "The way we handled it was to have me go to Buenos Aires on a business trip, apparently on temporary duty. Appeared normal to everyone. And if the Tupamaros smelled a rat, it was too late to do anything about it. I just never went back to Montevideo. Clever enough. And cruel too. I had to pretend to Marucha. I couldn't say good-bye. I called her from Washington, wrote her, of course—"

"Marucha?"

Oliver shook his head. "Maria Elena, I mean."

"Oh." Drew had a slight frown on his face. "Well, the way it is now, it wasn't the end after all, was it? Here she is in Mexico."

Oliver regarded Drew without replying. Drew clearly had been drawn by the pathos of the story. Now, Oliver saw, Drew was jealously comparing it for sadness with his Galina story, beginning to resent Oliver's competing with him in the lost romance department.

Oliver grinned at Drew, and Drew's frown grew heavier, confirming Oliver's thoughts. Drew was close to being cross. "Well, Ted. Indeed. I see. But why are they after you now?"

"I reason like this, Harley," said Oliver, throwing one leg over the arm of the gray chair. "Freddie was the one who fingered me, and whoever 'they' are, they know that. Then, with the usual twisted, half-assed, conspiratorial mind, knowing Freddie set me up, they jump to the wrong conclusion, e.g., Freddie fingers me, I finger Freddie. Or the Agency did, to get even, to eliminate the glamorous young Tupamaro leader. I oughta make that clear, Harley. Freddie was a popular figure then—even if practically forgotten now—and the police really hurt the Tups when they got him. You can see why—whoever it was who tipped off the police—why the Tupamaros, the holdouts, the bitter-enders, would be gnashing their teeth to this day, wanting to get the guy that did it."

Oliver clasped his hands in front of him, his eyes following the rigid design in the Chinese rug. "Having said all that, I still wonder why. The survivors of the Tupamaros, the bloody remnants, are back in circulation. A bitter bunch of bastards, but I agree with you—what do they get out of going after me now?"

"Cui bono? A political statement? Vengeance? A symbolic victim? A way of rallying their forces?"

"Yeah," said Oliver. "All that, I suppose. As it was, I got into hot water on account of this, when the story came out. Got chastised because of Maria Elena. Bad judgment: some of the CI types—there was a move to stick my head on a pike at the entrance of the main building. All that happened, in the end, was a stern note in my file, you know, pompous, 'ahem, erh, uh.' It looks terrible when you put it baldly, you know; 'CIA station chief's girlfriend revealed as sister of leading Tupamaro cadre.' Criminally negligent. I see this terrorist running down the street with a knife in his teeth and stop him to ask if he has a sister."

"I can't complain." Oliver stood and stretched. "The security people—they have to live in the real world—were pretty understanding, actually. Anyone'd have thought Freddie was just going through the normal, asinine phase for that age. You know—the gonads. What's the outlet? Religious hysteria out of style in Montevideo in that epoch. And no war: no platoon leaders, no way to scare your ass off. Half the students in Montevideo were trendy, little, revolutionary punks, getting it out of their systems before elbowing into the ranks of the bourgeoisie. Most of them get over it. Freddie didn't. Exaltado—rabid. How do you account for Freddie?"

"The question is: What are you going to do?"

"Tell you, Harley. I'd like to find out who 'they' are. I can't cut and run on the basis of Maria Elena's remarks. And if I did disappear, wouldn't they grope around and find another candidate? Do me a favor and canvass the menagerie."

"Oh, there are some Tupamaros. We need to focus on them. I'll get on that. What about the Mexicans?"

"And anyone who blows into town from Uruguay, or Cuba too. Yeah, the Mexicans. I hate to use up our credit, but, yeah. If only we had better data, I might hold off—"

They could hear Paco at the door. When Van Schaik came in, Oliver was by the windows, starting to tell Drew of the scathing message that erupted from his meeting with Dr. Michael, complaining about summarily being ordered to Washington instead of being asked for his side of the story.

"The Slasher strikes," was Van Schaik's comment.

"But what's the penalty?" asked Drew. "The Slasher has no weak-minded compassion for him who stumbles. Do I hear a distant drumroll?"

"All right, you guys. Forget the politics. The business of Michael and the Bureau: Does it strike you funny?" asked Oliver.

"Yes, but cui bono? say I," said Drew.

"Well, who?" asked Van Schaik.

"Cui? The Soviets, for one party, I say," said Drew.

"Yeah," said Oliver. "Well, headquarters must see that, the Soviets getting a charge out of setting the Bureau and us against each other."

"Aren't journalists out of bounds?" Van Schaik commented.

"That's what I thought. Maybe not for the Bureau. Boy, if ever there's a guy I wouldn't touch—one of the new breed. Well, to hell with it. We got a free identification. 'Gennadi Alexeyev, first secretary of the embassy, says Pooch. And now he's after your Gualtero, Harley,' or is it your Enrique? Yes, Enrique. Excuse me. Why is Genya, whom we carry as first department, courting a Salvadoran?" Oliver went to stand at the window, watching El Gordito.

"As it happens, Gualtero knows him too."

"Is that so? You can see why headquarters thinks the Soviets are all over us. Everyone—"

"Please, Ted. Enrique is an important cog in Mexico of the propaganda machine of the Salvadoran guerrillas. He is in touch with all sorts of people in the States. He's quite sure that's what Alexeyev is after."

"Yeah? The Soviets must have the Salvadoran guerrillas penetrated up the kazoo. Add their penetrations of the Salvadoran apparat in Mexico, whatever sense they can squeeze out of the Sandinistas, what they get from the Cubans, and what can little Enrique do for them?"

"I shall see that he does nothing."

"Okay, Harley. Has it occurred to you that the Soviets know he's in touch with us and intend to run him against—"

"One moment you make scathing remarks about 'CI types' and in the next you're seeing Soviets under the bed. Really, Ted, let me draw Enrique gently away from Alexeyev." Drew turned to speak to Van Schaik. "You understand, Nick, I know. Enrique's negotiating his return to Salvador to reenter party politics there. With the training he's had from me, he can make a real con—"

"If they don't kill him first," Oliver commented.

Except for a frown, Drew ignored that. "It may sound immodest, but, you see, Nick, with a few strategically placed Enriques in the Americas, we raise the odds for decent, strong, democratic government. I have chosen these trainees—I call them that, 'trainees,' a known category the dullest of the common denominators in headquarters can apprehend, will take aboard—I have chosen—"

"Boy, talk about cynical!" Oliver said.

"Not at all—a bow to the practical," he said, not looking at Oliver. "I have selected them for their honest ambition, their sincere desire to serve their people, for political sophistication—not to be confused with cynicism—" here Drew frowned at Oliver, who was winking at Nick "—pshaw, Ted. Stop it! This is no mere mechanical approach, fiddling with tactics or electoral strategy, that soulless, fascist, mechanical, Goebbels approach. Your hired guns. Realize, Nick, that these people have only the vaguest notion of what to do once in office should they get that far. The oratory comes easy and is essentially meaningless. The basic—''

''Too bad you're not working in the States,'' said Oliver.

''That's the truth,'' said Van Schaik.

''Please, Ted. Don't trivialize it. We can't abandon the contest to the others, to the gorillas. You must make headquarters understand that!'' Drew added, red-faced, slapping his chair arm. ''Bring it home to them!''

Oliver turned from the window to stare with raised eyebrows at Drew: ''To the Slasher?''

''Yes!'' said Drew. ''Especially the Slasher!'' swatting the chair arm again. ''The Slasher above all.''

Oliver grinned at him as he walked back to slump in the gray chair. ''Well, let's get back to what is in our own power to decide. This day's business, that is: Who can Nick pick up from the group? How about Enrique himself? He's got good English.''

''Yes. Enrique. He's going soon. Nick can learn from him. I will see him before he goes for the final polish.''

''Who else?'' asked Oliver. He knew that getting Drew to hand over his clients was like asking a doting mother to nominate sons to the draft board. ''Gualtero?''

''Too much of a handful. He veers wildly between anger at the Sandinistas and rage at us. A prima donna. A lightweight, I fear. He shows revolutionary fervor by affecting a dreadful Cuban accent. Not a good one for Nick, not to begin with.''

Oliver spent the better part of an hour fencing with Drew. Drew agreed to give up a Bolivian, a former minister of government, to Nick. Too readily noted Oliver, for future reference—something wrong there. The Brazilian technocrat, no: too difficult linguistically. Drew spoke Spanish to him, the Brazilian replied in Portuguese. Oliver extracted from Drew a heavily qualified agreement to give up the Chilean socialist to Van Schaik.

At this point Drew's disposition was so waspish—he was spitting out such terms as slave market, cynical exploitation, Anglo-Saxon cold-bloodedness, short-term advantage—that Oliver brought the discussion to a close. Anyway, it was enough. Van Schaik would have his plate full, struggling with Spanish, getting to know Drew's clients, and understanding the politics of their countries.

"I must insist that Nick not burn Enrique by playing him against Alexeyev."

"Well, we'll see," said Oliver. "It wouldn't blight his political future to tell us a bit about his new buddy, Genya. You know: Does Alexeyev play chess? Go to the movies? Drink margaritas? Read Shakespeare?"

"Such petty rubbish!" exclaimed Drew. Van Schaik suppressed a laugh. Drew sat frowning, his lower lip out.

"Alexeyev is an outdoorsman, by the looks of it, Enrique says," Drew said, less sulkily. "Binoculars. Surprised you, haven't I? Boots, a pack in the car." Drew took a notebook from the side table and tore out a page. "Here are the endless dreary details so dear to— Alexeyev drives a light brown, Ford station wagon, right, rear door and fender smashed in. Is that important? Diplomatic plates, of course."

"A KGB car with only one door smashed in? What color pack?"

"Really!" Drew spread his arms wide, looking heavenward. To Van Schaik he said, turning his head, "I ask you!"

"Well, what was it? Khaki? Blue? Red?"

"The pack is of magenta watered silk, trimmed with ermine, lined with the feathers of the quetzal bird." Drew waved both arms. "Thus do we stimulate the fabricator's powers of invention, assuaging our passion for endless and meaningless facts."

"What about a sleeping bag? A bedroll? How about an ice axe back there with the other stuff?"

Drew looked surprised. "Possibly—is that what Enrique was describing? *Pico*—pickaxe—he said."

"*Piolet*, it's called." Oliver had jumped up and clapped his hands together. "I gotta talk to Gordito."

Later, at the office, Van Schaik said to Oliver: "That's really something, the way he holds on to the menagerie."

"Well, you know. It's everything, life itself, to him. Anyway, you've got enough to do. I may have to pick up some of the menagerie types myself when I get back from Washington. Rather not—we have to set off in other directions."

"What I mean—he doesn't seem to be in any hurry to get to France."

"I know. I don't want to rush him. It's natural, when the time comes, he'd begin to fret about it. We're shorthanded and will be until I can get to Washington and knock some sense into their heads. Now, with Enrique, take him around it again, get a good description of Genya, what he wears, the license number of the car, a snapshot—you know—how he holds himself, how he walks, what he's *like*. We need all that."

Chapter 14

It was Friday and El Gordito was due back at work at the Albergue Vicente Guerrero, the lodge for climbers at Tlamacas on the southern side of the Paso de Cortés. Oliver had arranged to drive El Gordito to Tlamacas, looking forward to his first visit to the volcanoes in some ten years.

El Gordito was at the Cuauhtémoc metro stop at exactly the place and time agreed on for their morning rendezvous, carrying a handbag and a morning paper, his short hair neatly parted on his head. When he got in the warm car he peeled off a light jacket. They drove east onto Calzada Zaragoza, Oliver's attention tied up in the morning traffic. By the time they were passing the squatter settlement of Nezahualcoyótl, Oliver was able to lean back in his seat and talk.

El Gordito at close range was as dark-skinned in the face, a rich chocolate color, as Oliver had first noticed, the darkness no doubt deepened by his life outside in the sun. He was stocky, small in stature, but hefty, a blocky build, a piece of heroic, pocket-sized, Aztec sculpture. An upended box of a torso, muscular, forceful, hatchet-faced, a strong nose and heavy chin, he could have been a model for Diego Rivera—a stylized warrior of the early Méxicas, standing later at the side of Emiliano Zapata, an idealized white-clad campesino, rifle held aloft.

El Gordito's job was less romantic. He drove the water truck up from Amecameca to the lodge. "It's dry up there. Every drop of water must be brought in. Drinking, washing, flushing, showers, the lot. I work the grounds too. Whatever is needed. The crowds on the weekend leave a lot of trash. And I spell the others at the desk in the administración."

"It's a national park, isn't it?"

"Correct. Under the Secretaría de Desarollo Urbana y Ecología. We're part of Recursos Naturales. The *albergue* is essentially for climbers. You rent a bunk. You can rent your gear, too, crampons, boots, an ice axe. You want to go to the right here for Chalco."

"I used to go out there a few years back. There wasn't much then. The old *albergue* was a mean little lodge, smelly and cold. I hear this is first class, *de lujo*."

"Right. Well, maybe not luxurious, but close to it. We take good care of it. Look. You can't walk on the floors in your climbing boots. Prohibited. Honest! It mars the wood."

"You have to be a climber to work there?"

"Oh, no. But some of the people—like me—we hire out as guides. And I work with the rescue brigade in emergencies. People get altitude sickness at four or five thousand meters and you have to get them down. Accidents too. Even the experienced ones. Or think they're experienced. Some of the rock is rotten, especially around the Abanico."

They were passing through brown, dusty country. El Gordito was a good companion, speaking only when he had something to say. As they ran on the blacktop two-lane road through eucalyptus trees, leaves rustling in a strong morning breeze, Oliver remarked on the dryness of the land.

"Rains will come soon. April. You know, I didn't eat breakfast. Just as you come in to Amecameca there's a good little *lonchería* on the right. I'll show you."

"Who comes there?"

"To the *lonchería*?"

"No, no. To climb Popocatépetl."

"All sorts. Americans. Europeans: and all sorts of

them—from the Netherlands, France. Young people, men mostly. Germany, where else? From all parts."

"You get repeaters?"

"Those who come back? Well. You see, there are the people who come on picnics. Ordinary people, with children, in buses. Then you have the walkers. Some of them with all sorts of fancy clothes and equipment, but that's for show. They just walk a way up toward the Ventorrillo or on the easier way toward Las Cruces. Not far, most of them. Then the boys come for parties. Dressed as though they were going to climb, but they sit up and talk all night, drinking rum or tequila. You can imagine how far they get in the morning! The Club Alpino boys, now—they're serious. There's some of them any weekend. The Club de Exploraciones too. The Red Cross and the rescue brigade. For a lot of people the volcanoes are an avocation. I know if my work weren't there, I would be coming out here on the weekends too."

El Gordito's eyes were set in slits, invisible in profile, hidden by the epicanthic folds at the corners. When he looked at Oliver, the smallest triangles of pure white gleamed in the corners of the eye, a spark in the brown iris that was as dark as the skin.

As they approached Amecameca—a metal sign on a post announced the population as HABITANTES 38,000, and shortly after a hand-lettered board on a tree claimed 53,000—El Gordito had one arm half raised, the forefinger crooked, as they drove down the avenue into town, one-story buildings lining the street on either side. "There," said El Gordito, suddenly pointing straight, "right behind that pickup."

Oliver pulled over and El Gordito got out to lead the way to the open front of the *lonchería*. Inside it was the size of a one-car garage. El Gordito was welcomed by the older woman in charge at an oilcloth-covered counter. A pair of young women giggled from behind a high counter in back, peering at Oliver and El Gordito through dusty glass jars of candy and crackers.

There was a bottle of ketchup on the table. The proprietress set down a white bowl of salsa Mexicana, a steel spoon in it. Almost immediately a plateful of eggs, refried beans with white cheese sprinkled on top, and a basket of warm tortillas appeared. El Gordito's small eyes opened with pleasure. Oliver had only coffee, twisting in his chair to look behind him to where El Gordito pointed. Across the street was the black front of a dingy car repair shop. Above that squalor hung the magnificent bulk of the volcano, Ixtaccíhautl, the Sleeping Lady, near enough to touch, you'd say. A flimsy cloud was drifting past the knife-ridged Arista de Luz, the sun sparkling on the flatness of her peak, her snowy breast, El Pecho, more than five thousand meters high.

Oliver turned back to shake his head to express his wonder, smiling at El Gordito, who was handing him a tortilla with a dab of beans in the center. "So, you climbed her," said El Gordito, nodding at Ixta.

"Yes, and Popo a few times, years ago. By El Ventorrillo and by Las Cruces, both." Oliver turned again, his back to El Gordito, to contemplate the volcano, the light moving on her, the clouds blowing past, a plume of snow blowing past her knees and over her feet. When he turned back, El Gordito was standing up, and Oliver paid the proprietress.

"This was all dust, this road," said Oliver, "when I was here last. Greenish-blue dust all over the car, on the rocks, covering the branches of the firs along the road. See how clean they are now." He slowed down to let a skinny black bull calf heave itself up the bank and dance off, its legs twisting, kicking its rump up in the air into the grove of trees.

The paved road twisted upward in sharp curves through open pine forests, the forest floors tawny with bunch grass, brown with dry needles. A burro loaded with firewood stood head down at the edge of the road and a farmer in sombrero stood by the burro, his mouth half open, to watch them go by. Robins fed on the ground in the open glades. At gaps where the road turned, the sky was filled by Popocatépetl, instead of Ixta. Oliver had forgotten the empty feeling, the dry-mouthed dread, that came over him when drawing near the great volcanoes. It rushed into his body without warning, and he let the car slow down, involuntarily, when it came over him. He had to change the gear down to recover.

"Steep here," El Gordito commented. "Imagine what it's like in that old water truck." He wrestled with an imaginary wheel, grabbing at a gear handle, made a roaring sound, laughing.

When they reached the pass the road forked, left to La Joya and Ixtaccíhuatl, right to Tlamacas and Popocatépetl. The country was open, the pines scattered, dwindling as they moved up toward timberline.

When they approached a stop sign, El Gordito told Oliver to go on, waving at the man who stood at the small white house waving back. Near the top of the road by the parking lot, a black-and-white-striped pole laid in its notch to block the way. El Gordito called out to a tall, brown-faced old man in a wool cap who grinned at them, showing gums and crooked yellow teeth below rheumy eyes. He motioned to Oliver to move the car to the far side of the road and raised the pole so they could pass.

At the left of the *albergue* itself, Oliver brought the car to a stop in black, volcanic sand beside a tall pine. As they got out, a voice called a greeting from an enclosed workspace at the end of the lodge: "*Gordito! Qué hubo?*" El Gordito took his handbag and his jacket, walking over to answer the unseen voice behind the fence.

Oliver yawned, taking in great gulps of the thin stuff the air had become at thirteen thousand feet. He walked slowly to the broad low steps of pink stone that led to the large plaza in front of the lodge. Across the plaza to his right was the square alpine-looking stone building of the Brigada de Rescate.

At the far end of the plaza Popo loomed, hung above him. The photos just don't do it, Oliver thought. They flatten it so. You have to stand here to believe it.

He yawned, either from a shortage of oxygen or from apprehension. At a sound he turned to see El Gordito coming up behind him. Ed Gordito put out his hand. "Thanks for the lift. I have to go to work now."

"I might go walking. Can I get a bite here?"

"Sure. In the café. To the left, there, of where you go in."

"Look. Join me for lunch, okay?"

Oliver turned to walk across the plaza, down the low steps to where the pink stone of the plaza ended. He stepped across the metal grating of a drain to walk up a steep sandy dune, a blasted pine and a pile of rocks at its top. The path went down from there and up again to the next dune top, just nearby, two large pines standing alone there, the last of the trees. Oliver sat carefully on the exposed, uncomfortable root of one of the large pines. He raised his binoculars to sweep them over the trails to the mountain. Bunch grass grew on either side of the wide paths. To the right the trail went up toward dark outcrops of rock on the way to the Ventorrillo. The trail to Las Cruces went off at a low, gradual swoop up to the left, climbing toward the crosses out of sight around the shoulder of the volcano.

Good tactical ground, this. From here you would be able to see climbers using the conventional routes, going up or coming down. Much of the time, anyway—there were dips in the trail, places where people on the trail would be out of sight. The harder beating of his heart at this altitude—Oliver was sitting some four thousand meters above sea level—and the rays of heat rising from the volcanic sand, made the view in the glasses jiggle uncertainly.

A Mexican junco fluttered across the path and landed to sway on a whitish-green stalk in a patch of arnica with dried-out, yellow flowers. The junco put one bright eye on Oliver before fluttering out of sight to the ground. The wind that had been blowing wispy, vaporous clouds across Popo's flanks was dropping off, and the air was quieter, hot. Oliver peeled his sweater off and put it around his neck. Somewhere nearby a Sierra Madre sparrow sang a few hesitant notes and repeated them, doubtfully, as though not sure it should be singing at midday.

The ashen slopes of Popocatépetl curved gracefully upward toward the peak. Just then the snow cover was heavy, looking as though it would be down as low as Las Cruces, maybe below there. On the right-hand side of the mountain as he faced it, the Abanico, a rugged fan of rock, jutted up from the side of the volcano, breaking the gentle curve; a tall triangle of jagged steps dusted with snow, old ice in its crevices, forcing itself awkwardly up from the slope.

The landscape was grand, forbidding, and when Oliver found himself yawning again, he knew it was nerves, the tension he felt near the volcano, an emotion tacking slowly back and forth between Cape Respect and Cape Fear.

In vast sweeps of tame, beckoning country, the green waves of forest, the sun on checkered fields, flatter and pretend, at least, to accept you. You want to answer that condescension, lighten your body, tear your feet from the heavy ground, leap without falling back to a mountain ridge, swoop over the treetops, catch a draft and soar over fields and forests like a hawk, embracing the air, a flick of a fanned tail from one ridge to the next, trading the observer's hobbled stance and reasoning mind for your niche in a painted landscape, leaving time behind.

Not here: cold, even with the sun glassy on the high ice of the glacier, shy from the air's uncertainty, wary of the careless provocation, the climber's margin is the space he keeps between a firm footfall and the last misstep. Rather than leap, he clings, and has no idea of rivaling the raven, his mind in each slow step.

Oliver moved slowly along the dusty trail, pausing at the last pine to gasp, the beginning of a throb sharp in one quadrant of brain, walking on toward the place, a good kilometer away, where the trail forks. The hill there was covered with bunches of brown grass, the last outpost of vegetation before the undulations of volcanic sand

and pumice. A raven croaked as it flew over, hoarse croaks, a pair, then another pair of harsh notes, until it went out of sight beyond the hill at Oliver's right.

To the left the long trek across Popo's slope, boots sinking in the black sand, to Las Cruces, where the one white cross and the black ones mark where climbers died. From there you pant up through sand or snow or ice, depending on the season, to the low lip of the crater. By the right fork, taking the steeper route, climbing past the rockfall, leaving it to the right, you reach the metal hut below the Abanico. Beyond lies the cwm from where you look across to cliffs formed by the broken edges of the crevasses. At sixteen thousand feet the col and another hut. From there the Ventorrillo route goes steep on ice past the crevasses to the stink of sulfur at the high lip of the crater. The ravens float, shaggy-necked, squawking lonely above the path that skirts the Abanico, a place of cold and nightmare, a high desert that repels and lures at the same time.

Oliver stood to look at the peak, Popocatépetl, lying like a resting animal, a throwback, a pagan incursion; obviously more than so many parts of black sand, pumice, rock, fire and ice, but not defined in modern man's language either. You can talk to the god you like here, maybe to God Himself. You'd do well to thank Him if you reach the crater.

Oliver turned. Miles away across the Paso de Cortés, the dun valley that runs between the two volcanoes, the ridge of Ixtaccíhuatl stretched as silent, remote and cold. The peaks were quiet, composed, self-possessed, assured, not needing man about. Dignified, even tolerant on their slopes, but impulsive, on the edge of menace.

Oliver looked with care at the white mountain above him. Here you'd better think as deliberately as you step. The thin air strips the seat of judgment, the cortex of the brains of its handy powers.

Oliver rested. Interesting: this key point where he stood. From there—despite the blind spots caused by dips in the trails, by the dunes covered with tawny bunch grass, by the turns around piles of red-black rock—you could see climbers coming back down from any part of the mountain. There were only three routes, ordinarily—Las Cruces, Ventorrillo, and the less-used way, between those two, past Texcalco steeply up to Glaciar Norte, just across the crevasses from the Ventorrillo route. The spot where Oliver stood—speaking tactically and figuratively—commanded them.

That steep but shorter Ventorrillo route! Straight up that sandy track until you come to the rocky path that bends to the right around the Abanico. There you'll find the Queretano hut. Four thousand six hundred meters. Beyond there, the next hut: Teopixcalco, that is. Forty-nine thirty—five hundred meters, say, below the peak. Only five hundred meters! A short scramble, it's been said. Try putting on your crampons before dawn at the Teopixcalco hut, roping up, and from there exploring one man's definition of a short scramble.

You'd be a fool to climb those slopes alone. Might be all right when the snow and ice have retreated to the crater. Oliver considered Gennadi Alexeyev as a man set apart, a loner in his embassy, detached. Oliver looked back over the words of the interview with Michael and found no tangible reason for that impression, no one word or phrase from Michael. It must have been the outdoor gear, the ice axe, in the back of the car.

The inference he grasped from that tool and its use, Oliver knew, rose from inside himself. Why not? One side of his head argued with the other. His mind ran easy in that thin air, giving in to hunches, no good data, nothing objective to depend on, unsystematic, satisfied with his impressions. A little oxygen, like a little alcohol, leaches good sense from the mind. You can feel it hissing, boiling off, good sense spilling from the cortex of the brain.

You telling me, O'Rourke, that so-called chief of station of yours down there is out looking for Soviets on a goddamned volcano?

Oliver might have been drinking rather than taking Popo's thin sharp air, his thoughts so light, his flighty mind too ready to follow a faint track after loose and irresponsible spirits, a cheerful set of intellectually bad companions.

He shivered. The keen air was acute enough to burn his lungs, the sun warming his front, and his behind cold. Oliver lumbered loose-legged but sensibly back down the path, wishing for a good jiggerful of one hundred proof air to sober him up, something thick and warm to wrap around the thinness of his blood, more than ready to turn his back on the mountain.

When he reached the dune with the two pines, he saw El Gordito standing in the black shadow of a pine trunk, his face as black in shadow, the sun overhead now. El Gordito's teeth were white. "I thought maybe you were going to do the *recorrido*—the whole blessed round trip."

"Hardly. What's the time for the whole run, by Las Cruces to the top and back?"

"Depends on your condition. And the conditions on the mountain. Mostly yours. Seven to ten or twelve hours."

"Let's eat lunch."

They sat at a trestle table in the café, and a smiling young waiter brought them menus printed on wooden trays and practiced English with Oliver. El Gordito asked for the usual, this turning out to be *carne asada* with *tostadas*, and a soft drink. Oliver had a cheese omelette and a beer. From the windows one looked miles east to the hazy valley of Cholula and Puebla.

"Come here at dawn," said El Gordito, pointing, "and you'll see the peak of Orizaba above the clouds, there, and over this way, Malinche."

There were few people in the café and most of those seemed to be colleagues of El Gordito, greeting him and nodding pleasantly at Oliver, looking him over after they sat down, politely curious.

"A middle-aged man, younger than I am, comes up

here." Oliver described Alexeyev as best he could. "A foreigner. Does that seem in any way familiar to you?"

"Most of the people are young who come to climb." El Gordito signaled the waiter for another soda. "The older ones, the older foreigners, stand out. Not an American?"

"No. But he would speak English. Would try his Spanish, I suppose." He'd probably have to—few of the staff spoke English.

"A German or a Hollander, I think, the one I know that sounds as you describe."

A North European, that is to say. "Possibly." Oliver could not keep down a surge of excitement. "Does he come alone or with a party?"

"I'm not sure. I think, alone. I say that because if he came with others surely someone could speak Spanish better than he does. Know what I mean?"

"What about him?"

"Okay. Just before I went off last week I was holding down the desk in administración. Domingo, over there, was eating lunch late. This fellow, like you describe, asked about the routes. Wanted to learn them. It was difficult for him to get it out, you understand me? Not unusual. Many of the foreigners who come here don't know how to talk. He wanted a guide, and I told him I could not help him then. I told him to come back. Well, he may have gone with someone else. I'll ask around."

"Did he have equipment?"

"His own? I think so. He didn't ask about renting it. Oh, I know he had an axe, a metal one, he showed it to me when he was asking what else he would need. I told him crampons. He nodded and then asked about rope. We were standing at that big photograph of Popo at the desk and I pointed things out on it. Las Cruces: sometimes rope, sometimes not, I said." El Gordito illustrated his description of the interview with gestures. "Ventorrillo—and I pointed to that—yes—" nodding violently "—yes, rope."

"An experienced climber?"

El Gordito thought. "Not on ice, I think. That is, if we understood each other. He was mixed up about when to use crampons and rope. Look. He began to point things out on the photo. 'Crampons here. Rope there.' 'No, no,' I said. 'Rope is not good on ice unless you have crampons and an ice axe.' You understand?"

"Sure. With rope alone you can't support each other on ice." Oliver went to the counter to pay the bill. The cooking was being done in plain view in the kitchen, half a story down on the other side of the counter. One of the women stood at the stove in a gray apron, stirring a pan of noodles. She reached in to pluck some noodles out of the pan and put them in her mouth. So much for the visible kitchen. Oliver was glad he had eaten before looking. He walked with El Gordito out of the café to the entrance.

"Listen, I'll be in touch. It would be worth something to me if you can guide him. But keep this between the two of us." El Gordito looked impassively at Oliver from small brown eyes. Oliver walked out to the plaza and peeled off a roll of pesos from his wallet. "This is for expenses. And here's my telephone number."

"There's no phone here. Just the radio. I'd have to go to Amecameca." El Gordito looked at the wallet in Oliver's hand.

"How do I get in touch with you?" Oliver handed more pesos across.

El Gordito smiled. "You can't."

It was dark when Oliver reached home. The air at eight thousand feet was thick enough for a decent breath. He took off dusty shoes and socks to find his ankles gray-black, the cuffs of his trousers bulging with gritty black sand.

In front of the fire he shivered again as he was telling Marge of his visit to the volcanoes. "Why did you go?" she asked. She did not like the volcanoes.

"Oh, on impulse." True enough. "I wanted to see them. It's been a long time. I was thinking it might be fun to climb again."

"Well, I hope you don't. You certainly can't go alone. Who would go with you?"

"There are guides you can get to go with you if there's no one else. Listen. Something important. Someone may call, a guide up there, and have a message for me. It might be something like—oh, I don't know—such as 'He's ready to go,' or 'We're going tomorrow. Or Sunday.' Something like that."

"I wish you wouldn't. Oh, what I must tell you: Harley Drew was here this afternoon. He wanted advice about Galina. Or, I should say, he asked for my advice. I don't know that he wanted it. There's a difference. He may have just wanted a shoulder to cry on."

"I hope he didn't."

She laughed. "You certainly don't have to worry about Harley."

"Has he anything new?"

"No. There's this Uruguayan woman he's been talking to—he says you know her. What's the matter?"

Oliver sank into a chair. "Little lightheaded from the altitude. Maybe I shouldn't drink." He took another gulp of whiskey. "I'm gonna kill that Harley. Sorry. Go on."

"And you talk about climbing again!"

"S'all right. I know who he means. What about her?"

"She thinks he should try to find Galina."

"Oh, does she? Who does she think she is? None of her business."

"I don't know why you get so upset. He asked her advice just as he asked for mine."

"Good thing he's got going there, going around tugging at female heartstrings."

"Really, Ted. Poor Harley, and you talk like that."

"Oh, hell, it's this whopping headache I've got."

"You see? Who would be foolish enough to climb with you, anyway?"

"Oh, someone might turn up."

Oliver's headache went away with an aspirin. But that night he dreamed in monochrome, mixed grays and blacks on a gleaming, cold, white canvas.

Chapter 15

'Federico Engels Ortiz Perez del Castillo. b. 1951, Montevideo, Republica Oriental del Uruguay,' the memorandum began. Oliver raised his eyes from the memorandum to look across the table at Ivor Buchanan. Buchanan turned his eyes from Oliver's to gaze out the open, wide doorway of the coffee shop that gave onto the street.

"That flower chap across the way. Great buckets of monstrous gladioli in front. Where do you suppose he finds the dreadful things?" Buchanan threw one arm over the back of his chair. Oliver regarded the spectacle of Buchanan striving for nonchalance.

Oliver went to the beginning of the memorandum and read it again. "Cuernavaca, I suppose," said Buchanan, answering his own question. "Or Chiapas. Chiapas, I wager. Ask a Mexican the origin of something or other and he'll invariably tell you 'Chiapas.' Which is to say, don't you know, he hasn't the foggiest. Very *folklórico*, don't you think?"

Oliver looked up at Buchanan and put the memorandum facedown on the table before them. "Can you give me a context, Ivor? I mean, all this happened some years ago."

"Context? Not sure what you mean in this case." Buchanan picked up his glass of beer and tilted it in Oliver's direction without looking at him. "Cheerio." He drank. "Ah! Context. You mean the chap, having been killed some fifteen or so years ago, why the sudden interest?" He put the glass down. "That what you mean?"

"When we send trace requests we have to explain them. Have to do the same with yours, say that you asked."

"Of course." Buchanan moved his chair about so that he half faced Oliver and half the street. "The usual way. The gladiolus is not your favorite flower, is it? No. I was sure not. In this case we're honoring a request. Thought of you chaps because you were closer to events in Uruguay at that time."

"Oh?"

"Tupamaros killed one of yours, didn't they? What was his name?"

"Mitrione. He wasn't one of ours, Ivor, but they killed him. 'Executed' him. Said later it was a mistake."

"Yes, kidnapped our ambassador, you know. Let him go eventually. Of course! You know all about that. Silly of me."

"So, this is a request made to you, and you are passing it to us to answer."

"That's a fair statement of the matter. Hope it's no bother. You must have these odd queries yourselves from time to time. The important bit, actually, is here toward the end." Buchanan reached to pick up the memorandum. He read from it. " 'It has been alleged that the incident leading to the death of Ortiz at the hands of the police was the result of information received. We should be grateful—' " Buchanan waved a hand. "And so on— 'What your files may show of the nature of the information, the source of it, and the motive of the source in passing the information to the authorities.' That proper language? I mean, is it quite clear?" Buchanan crossed his legs, jiggling the upper leg rapidly up and down.

"Oh, quite clear," said Oliver.

Chapter 16

Whitney Oates's golf trophies were gone.

Oliver got up from the red leather couch to walk to one corner of O'Rourke's office. He leaned to look at a greenish-white, ceramic head enclosed in a Plexiglas case that stood on a pedestal in the corner.

Slasher O'Rourke was sitting behind his desk talking to a lean young man who had brought a cable for him to sign. Mumble mumble. Oliver tried not to listen. The desk was not the large mahogany one over which Oates had once frowned at Oliver, but a metal red-topped table with an array of telephones on it. A pair of bookends with a dozen, new hardcover books between them sat at the front of O'Rourke's table, the spines facing outward rather than toward O'Rourke. Beside the books was a pair of large, stiff-feathered, silver-plated birds, the sort that people give each other as going-away presents in Argentina. Pheasants. Oliver looked at them again. No, not pheasants but a pair of fighting cocks in combat array.

A blue and white Guatemalan textile hung on the wall between the large windows behind O'Rourke's desk. On the wall across from Oliver was a red and blue textile from Oaxaca. Crossed on the wall above the couch was a pair of bandilleras, faded bloodstains on the orange and yellow streamers. There were striped, Mexican and sober, Peruvian rugs on top of the gray carpet.

Oliver went back to sit down.

The young man left and another young man, taller and leaner than the first—they looked drawn in the face, like marathoners—came through the door and stopped immediately inside. O'Rourke raised pale eyebrows at him and then looked toward Oliver. "That head looks like an original," said Oliver.

"It is," said O'Rourke, pushing his chair back to pull a laminated page from a drawer in the table. He leaned over the paper, running one stubby finger down a list, a shock of gray-blond hair falling over his forehead. "Olmec. Vera Cruz. Circa nine hundred A.D." He put the page back in the drawer.

"It's nice." Oliver was puzzled. So far as he knew, O'Rourke had never been in Mexico. "Where'd you find it?"

"I don't play golf," a grin that did not reach the eyes. "Like Whitney," he added, unnecessarily. "And I don't want a lot of tourist trash cluttering up my office. So I told my support officer to go out and get me something really outstanding. Rob a museum."

The tall young man inside the door guffawed and O'Rourke laughed too. "Asked him how he liked it around here. He said he liked it fine, so I said then get off your ass and go get me some really outstanding Latin American decor, none of your goddamned tourist crap. Right, Tom? Remember?"

The young man laughed again. "Sure do, Chief."

"So he got all this. You say it's good, and I guess it is. That bum had to go, though. A real loser. A disaster, remember?"

"I sure do." The young man shook his head slowly from side to side.

"You got something there to go?" O'Rourke asked him. To Oliver he said, "Those hunting prints over there belong to me. Got 'em in London. Have a lot more in the library at my house out in Potomac. Look better out there on knotty pine. Sorry I can't get you over. Something on every night this week." He was frowning. "How about lunch?"

"Don't worry about it." Oliver walked over to examine the hunting prints, pink-coated white-breeched men in black top hats sailing over stone fences on small-headed horses, both forelegs arched forward and both hindlegs stretching back. One set was framed with green mats and the other with red. O'Rourke had begun talking to the young man and it was not necessary for Oliver to comment.

"Sit down here, Ted. This goes on all day." O'Rourke had his hand splayed across a cable form on his desk and was looking up at the young man. "You got the sense of it. But you pitched it just a tad too strong. Pretend he's gonna come through." He looked up at the younger man, who had raised his eyebrows. "Pretend, I said. You and I know he won't. Give him rope, right? Then, next time—"

O'Rourke winked at Oliver, scratched something out, wrote something in, scribbled on the bottom of the cable, and tossed it lightly in the air to the young man, who caught it. "Yessir!" He left.

"Don't tell me what you're going to do," said O'Rourke. "Just do it. Know what I mean?"

About half the books on the desk concerned Latin America, and the other half seemed to be advice on management. They had a clean, bookstore look to them. O'Rourke was pulling a sheet of paper to him. "Personnel. Couldn't agree with you more, Ted. You're naked. Drew. I know Drew. A has-been. And Van Schaik. He's got a complex—know what I mean, Ted? You know. Who was it hadda screw every broad he met?"

"Don Giovanni?"

"Don Wan." O'Rourke shook his head. Then he balled his fist and thumped the desk. "Now I got the CI types telling me how to staff one of my stations. I'm not standing still for that, Ted."

"Good!"

"That analysis of the Soviets being all over you in

Mexico. A honey pot! Bullshit! You know it's bullshit. I know it's bullshit. The whole world knows it's bullshit. Even the idiots who wrote it know it's bullshit." O'Rourke leaned back in his chair with his elbows in his lap and spread his hands toward Oliver. "Trouble is, Ted, they got the old man with 'em."

"The old man?"

"The director, Ted." O'Rourke leaned forward. "Trouble is, they've sold the director. He thinks they've got second sight. Walk on water. They got him hypnotized." O'Rourke raised one hand. "This is one of those times diplomacy is called for. Lemme handle this."

"But—"

O'Rourke's blue eyes, wide with frankness, suddenly narrowed. "That flap with the Bureau didn't help any. The old man has the Bureau right up here"—gesturing—"next to the goddamned flag. When he got that call from the director of the FBI he blew his top. I mean, hot! Like he found a turd in his soup." O'Rourke put one hand on the gray phone on his desk. "I grabbed a copy of the magazine, showed the old man the kind of left-wing crap this guy, whatshisname—?"

"Michael."

" 'Sguy Michael writes. Got him calmed down. I handled it, but it didn't help, Ted," said O'Rourke, taking his hand from the phone. "Didn't help a goddamn bit." He smiled a pleased smile, showing fillings in back.

"Did you see what I wrote on—"

"I know. I know." O'Rourke put out a hand at Oliver, stopping traffic. "These things happen. Water over the dam."

Another young man came in. "Whatcha got?" O'Rourke took a cable. "No. I'm not gonna put up with that." The upper part of O'Rourke's large freckled face was frowning at Oliver over the smile. "One thing about O'Rourke. You can argue with him. Okay? But not this." He took a cable up and shook it at Oliver. "We got a real smart-ass down in Santiago. A case where he shoulda stuck this in the safe overnight and taken it out and torn it to hell up in the morning. Goes all over headquarters. Makes everyone look stupid, him especially. You never worked for me, Ted, so I'll tell you. Say what you like to O'Rourke but don't spread the dirty linen all over. A quiet letter through the pouch. This asshole in Santiago's the one ends up looking stupid, know what I mean? Not O'Rourke. I'll get the girl." O'Rourke pressed a buzzer at the edge of his desk.

In a moment a white-haired woman appeared, a spiral notebook held against her bosom. O'Rourke stared at her. "She's out," the woman said in a small voice.

O'Rourke stared at her another second. "Okay," he said. "Never mind. Look," he continued, turning to the young man. "Get this clown up here. For consultation. Got it?"

O'Rourke swung his chair toward Oliver. "What some 'a these guys don't know's where the action is. Some never learn. That clown. Santiago, for Christ's sake! Action's in Washington. Not London with the Brits either. Not Mexico, Ted. Right here." O'Rourke tapped a forefinger on the desktop. "In this building. The White House. The NSC. Congress. Here. You with me?"

"Well, in a sense—"

"Reminds me." O'Rourke pulled the paper on his desk toward him. "Those half-assed Daniel Ortega stand-ins of Drew's."

"That's on my list to dis—"

"It's on everyone's list. Hold off on it. Tell you why. There's this congressman on our committee's got a thing about leadership training in Latin America. Raises hell 'cause State's doing zilch, as usual. I tell the director about Drew's thing with you in Mexico. Director calls the congressman. We look good, State looks bad. Name o' the game. That's what it's all about. Keep up the good work. I mean, don't bust your ass. Just keep it going, Ted. Congressman goes off the committee next year."

"We can do that. Getting back to personnel," said Oliver. "Drew's leaving—"

"High time too. Lemme tell you something, Ted. This

director intends to see this agency is responsive. His words. This means we gotta get rid of the weak sisters. Build up morale. These days it's perform or out. Shape up or ship out." O'Rourke jerked a thumb past his nose as he looked down at the paper in front of him. "Soviet program. You've got zilch, Ted. That's what makes the old man hot. Soviet Division's talking in one ear, the CI types got him by the other. Write me up a Soviet program, Ted, get it up for them to snarl over. In my book, don't tell me what you're going to do, just tell me what you did when you've done it. Not the old man. Gonna hold your feet to the fire."

"Well, I sent for traces on Alexeyev, the one who looks like he's worth something. Working on the Soviets with only Drew and Van—"

"Ted, never make O'Rourke say things twice. I told you I'm taking care of that. But you gotta produce. I'm not talking about having some Soviet, that guy—who'd you say?"

"Gennadi Alexeyev."

"Yeah. You don't have to have him in a cage, know what I mean? I'm talking about a sound, well-thought-out Soviet program. I drag my ass up there once a month and report to the director what each one of my station's doings. 'What? Mexico's got no goddamn program?' " O'Rourke pointed a finger at Oliver. " 'Mexico! The main Soviet base in Latin America? O'Rourke! Our station in Mexico City sitting on its goddamn ass?' " O'Rourke sat back in his chair and picked up the paper again, saying, "Now you got the message. So you gotta give me something, Ted, like yesterday, know what I mean?"

"I bet the KGB picks up as many drops in Rockville and Fairfax City as it does in Mexico," said Oliver. "Add the GRU and I'd be sure of it."

O'Rourke put his chin in one hand and with the other hand pointed at the ceiling. He looked sadly at Oliver. "Say that here, okay. Say that upstairs—" O'Rourke whistled and shook his head from side to side. "Ted,

A BLACK LEGEND

what you know and what I know doesn't matter. It's the perception. Which reminds me . . ." O'Rourke put both hands behind his head, leaned back in his chair and looked out the window. "I read your security file."

"I see."

O'Rourke got up and walked to the window. "The director asked me, what he wanted to know—how is it with you and that woman now?"

"If you mean, is there anything—no."

"Yeah. What kinda relations?"

"That's all over, whatever there was."

"Well, what's she after? She thinks she's doing you some kinda favor saying how they're going to nail your ass for turning her brother in or—"

"I didn't turn the brother in."

"I know, I know." O'Rourke came back and sat down. "The old man reacted right away, we should yank your ass out of there. How does it look, someone kills his station chief, that sort of thing."

"I got yanked out the other time. I couldn't argue. A definite intent to kidnap, meaning, with the Tupamaros, interrogation, torture. This is different. I don't know what she bases this on. It's a very emotional thing with her, the brother. And I'm sure the director"—the old man?—"doesn't want us to be running from rumors. I'll get to the bottom of it."

"She lying?"

"Oh, no. She believes it, all right."

"Guess you'd know." O'Rourke winked at him. "Well, get to the bottom of it but better make it quick. Thing to do"—O'Rourke was looking at his aide-mémoire again—"send her husband—what the hell kind of name is that?—back to Uruguay. Get him on the road. We'll be sending something down on that. Don't wait for it. The old man doesn't like anything about it. You get yourself killed and Congress starts asking questions. 'What? You mean you were actually damn well warned?' " O'Rourke grinned. "Guess you and the director had a little run-in once." O'Rourke's grin stayed on his face as he looked at Oliver.

"Did he tell you about it?"

"No, I just gathered."

"Ask him to tell you. I can't," said Oliver, smiling back at O'Rourke.

"Yeah? What gets me—how come you're still around?"

"Well, talk about your bad pennies!" The woman took her hands from the keyboard, pushed her gray metal chair away from the computer terminal, and rose to hold out both arms.

"Hello, Diane." Oliver went into the gray-walled, two-person cubicle and took both of her hands, bending to kiss her on the cheek. "So. We still got a little continuity around here."

"God! I'm about the last of it. Sit down, Teddy." She pulled a chair from behind the second desk in the cubicle. "How's Marge?" She sat down, pushed the sleeves of her sweater up to her elbows, cocked her glasses up on her gray hair. "I got your query on Freddie Ortiz. Queries, rather. I pulled the stuff together. Checked with Montevideo. Nothing new there. Like to go over it now?" She took a cigarette from the pack on the desk and lighted it.

"Sure, if it's handy. I can mark what you could send down, go over what I should tell the Brit," Oliver said. "Won't need all of it."

Diane blew a cloud of smoke to one side. "Bother you?" She didn't wait for his answer. "When I saw the trace request I thought: Whatever happened to big sister?" She smiled quickly, her eyes darting from one of his eyes to the other. "Tell me to go to hell if you want."

Oliver smiled and shook his head. "She's in Mexico."

Diane fixed her mouth as though to whistle, eyebrows raised.

"That's over and done with." Oliver told her of Puig and Maria Elena. "But it's the reason for the traces. She claims to know Freddie was killed because someone informed on him. She accused me of being responsible. Or, if not, of knowing about it."

"On what basis?"

"Good question. If not personally responsible, then the station."

"Well, wait—that's nutty. You'd left Uruguay then."

"Exactly. Listen, Diane: Could the station—did the station—pass a lead to the police?"

"On Ortiz? Highly unlikely. The files don't show it. And they would, wouldn't they? Even allowing for bad reporting or something in the back channel. If the station had somehow learned where Ortiz was and passed it to the police, they would have said something about it. It would have been a real coup, right?"

"Getting rid of Ortiz? Yeah."

"A real loss to the Tups. The station would have said something. The word would have been out. Feeling was running high. They just wouldn't say: 'Oh, by the way, the police got Freddie Ortiz the other day.' They'd be puffed up, be sure that the word slipped out somehow that the station did it. They'd have been tap dancing all over the southern cone."

Oliver nodded. "She asked me whether Pooch—her husband, that is—was working for us. Then, I mean, when the police got Freddie."

"Was he?"

"No. The only point is, she seems to be casting about."

"What about the Brit?"

"Well, there you are. She's after him too."

"But is she asking the Brit if we did it? Or asking him if the Brits did it?"

"I hadn't thought about that. Both, I guess. Say, Diane, how about it? Lemme take you to lunch."

"Thanks, Teddy. I've got my goddamned yogurt. Why accuse the Agency? Is she one of those Latins that thinks the Agency—"

"No, she's not dumb. Mixed-up about the Agency, yes—add to that the Latin need to believe in conspiracies—but not dumb. What takes the thing out of the academic category is that she insists the Tupamaros are out to get me because I rang the bell on Freddie. But then she goes on to say to tell her who else did it if I didn't."

"That's nice of her. Well, look, dummy, someone had to tell her that."

"How about running a quick search on Tupamaros emeritus in Mexico?"

"Emeriti. Be glad to, but why Mexico? They don't have to be in Mexico. They fly in, tuck a bomb under the front seat of your car, and Bob's your uncle."

"Yeah."

"Well, you ought to be taking this personally, Teddy boy, instead of sitting around and rummaging through files with dear old Diane."

"Well, great—where do I start? I mean, who's in touch now? How do we go about investigating—"

Diane stubbed out her cigarette and ran her hands through her hair. "You know the Tupamaros are legal now in Uruguay, pamphleteering, publishing a journal, working within the system. On the other hand, they have refused to renounce violence, in theory, at least." She stared at Oliver for a moment. "Come to think of it, there are a few ex-Tups wandering around in the States. The Bureau is presumably keeping tabs on them," she added, with a quick, artificial smile.

"What can the Bureau do? Anyway, getting violently rubbed out in theory is not what I'm worried about. Why me, Diane?"

"Is that some sort of existential yelp or why do I think they're picking on you?"

"The latter."

"Well, let's see. A: They think you did it to Freddie. B: You didn't do it to Freddie but the CIA did, or if the CIA didn't, never mind, it was the filthy imperialists and you're a good symbolic victim. C: Someone told them you did it to Freddie and that's all they need to know. D: Revive the old spirit, get away from this boring nonviolence, and D sub one: Rally the boys around the flag, get some international help, like the IRA, Libya, so on. E, or maybe it's D sub two: Get media attention by leaking that they knocked off a CIA station chief. It's ideologically okay—the execution, the sentence passed in absentia—the media would love it. Do I keep on?"

"Back to C. Why would someone tell them I did it?"

"God! I feel like a computer. A: To get them to knock you off for him. B: Because he wants to put the blame on the Agency. C: Because he wants to throw suspicion from himself. D: Because he doesn't like you. Know anyone who doesn't like you? E: He's jealous. Maybe you're seeing his girlfriend. His wife? Teddy? F: Maybe you know too much. You know something the rest of us don't know? Finally—and that's what all of this amounts to—cui bono? as we say, we Latin speakers, that is."

"Yeah. Cui bono. That's one of Harley Drew's favorites. Who would benefit?"

"Answer that and you've bought yourself some life insurance. How is old Harley?"

"Old Harley's fine. Getting ready to head for France in the usual leisurely, hippopotamus fashion." Oliver stood up and took out his wallet and looked in it. "I'll get something out of the machine and read what you got, okay?"

Oliver slowly ate a sandwich, a piece of ham and a piece of cold, damp, limp lettuce between two pieces of cold, damp, limp white bread, turning over the papers that Diane had collected on Freddie Ortiz, occasionally brushing a crumb off the paper. It was quiet except for the rustle of papers and the flicking of Diane's cigarette lighter. Once Oliver staged a paroxysm of coughing, as a comment on the cigarette smoke. Then Diane put her hands over her ears, as a comment on the noise he produced in eating an apple. She got up once and was away from her desk for a few minutes before coming back. At the end of an hour Oliver put a piece of paper on her desk. "You're right—there's damn-all in the files. How about that as a reply to Buchanan? He won't learn anything from it, which leaves us even."

She read the paper. "All right. I'll send it down to you. While you were feeding, I went to check the periodicals in the library. There's a man named Michael who has written—"

"Oh, yeah," said Oliver.

"—on the MIR in Chile, on the Montoneros, the FMLN in El Salvador, the *Sendero Luminoso*. He's discovered Latin America, made it his own. Thought I'd seen something. I went to check. The byline on the Peru article said he's doing something on the Tupamaros."

"He would, wouldn't he? Robin Hoods."

"You've read his stuff?"

"Some of it." Diane would not know of the Bureau connection with Dr. Michael, their handling him as a dangle. "Can you keep your eye out for that one?"

"That's the idea, the point being, Ted, that he supposedly will have interviewed some Tupamaros. If you've read him, you know he sets himself up and speaks with immense authority, maybe the only living authority on the subject, whatever it is, as though he personally invented it. But one thing, I think he really does talk to the people he says he's talked to. Never mind the cutesy-wutesy, I'm-so-smart-Washington-is-so-dumb-I'm-above-all-that style."

"Bully for him. In my book, he still gets it wrong." Oliver made a face. "Jesus. In my book—O'Rourke's got me saying it." Oliver got up. "Look. Thanks a lot." He put on his jacket. "What's it like around here, Diane?"

"Oh, Ted." She shook her head. "Talk about continuity. The kids don't understand. In the old days if they put some nincompoop in charge, it didn't matter because we all knew what we were doing and went ahead and did it, no matter what. Now they put— Well, you know, that clotheshorse, Whitney, and now this horse's ass—pardon my French. The kids don't know. They think it's the way it is." She laughed. "Or am I just getting old?"

That afternoon Oliver took the Metro to McPherson Square. At a shop in the National Press Building he bought a set of twelve-point crampons with straps to fit his old hiking boots; ankle gaiters, a light metal ice axe, a balaclava cap, long wool socks, tinted goggles with leather blinders, long underwear, wool gloves with waterproof shells to go over them, a water bottle, and two packets of granola bars.

Oliver was shocked at the size of the bill. He went down the list of items without finding anything he could do without. After paying, he put the bill carefully in his wallet. Depending on how this worked out, he might convince Finance that he should be allowed to charge the purchase to the Agency.

Chapter 17

Oliver walked to the battered coffee table in his office, spread two reports on the table and took a noisy sip of coffee. Enriques's was the first, transcribed and passed on by Drew:

> In the Russian embassy there are clear class distinctions, and here I do not refer simply to matters of rank or privilege, although the upper of the two major classes is usually so favored, but to more subjective distinctions. A friend of mine stood in Red Square outside the Kremlin's Spassky Gate at the end of one working day in June. He watched the civil servants leaving work, those who left on foot, that is—he could not see through the lavender curtains in the black Zíl limousines that whirled out the gate across Red Square with no regard for the passersby. He saw first that their clothes were better than those of the ordinary Soviet citizen one sees on the street, an easy and nearly meaningless observation: one would not expect them to be worse.
>
> It was the faces that captured the attention of our observer. They wore more sensitive expressions than did the Russian tourists lining up at Lenin's tomb that day, the features sharper, the glances more thoughtful, refined by curiosity as well as by contemplation. Their strides were more collected, their figures more erect—in short, a finer lot of beings.

A BLACK LEGEND

My friend did not claim that all members of this upper class had power or were in favor. Nor did he claim that those on top in government were all graceful or refined. Hardly! Look at Khrushchev! Brezhnev!

I use my friend's recollections as a way of loosely placing Gennadi Alexeyev, a member of this upper class, in the embassy on Tacubaya. Perhaps we Latins find a certain sort of Russian more brutish, coarser, more badly-put-together than we should, because of our limited acquaintance and therefore small sympathy for the heavy peasant type of Soviet. Nevertheless, the embassy has a number of this sort that one feels to be here for the rougher, even cruel tasks the regime assigns to its subjects to keep itself in power.

One would like to know what sort of family (or families) produced Gennadi Alexeyev. One cannot assume them to have been artists, superior clerks, officers, or teachers, only because he has about him an air that others in the embassy lack. To assume that he could not have sprung from plain peasant stock would be a denial of the hope for the elevation spiritually, socially, materially—of the oppressed in our own culture.

It is less the physical attributes, the bone structure, the facial features, of Alexeyev that illuminate his character than the superior demeanor that marked those second-level Politburo functionaries that my friend so acutely observed that June evening in Moscow, that is—gentility.

"Nuts," commented Oliver.

Drew had appended a note.

Enrique asked me, before he replied to your question about Alexeyev, if I would mind his referring to certain observations of my own made outside the Kremlin wall some years ago. I readily agreed, as you see. Not long ago I had spoken so to him and my thoughts had impressed him. I think you will find his remarks useful.

"Oh, hell, Harley. A pair of anthropological snobs!" muttered Oliver to himself.

There was a note from Van Schaik:

Name: Gennadi V. Alexeyev.
DPOB: Not known, appears to be 40–45 years old.
Height: 5' 9".
Weight: 175.
Eye Color: Green.
Hair: Straight, dark blond, probably darkened with age from what it was.
Brown mustache, twirled at ends but sometimes droops.
General Appearance: Athletic looking, walks on balls of feet, leans slightly forward. Wears gray suit with white shirt. Often takes off tie, rolls up shirtsleeves. Also wore brown slacks with dark blue sweater one cool evening. Wears "American" or "British" shoes rather than "Argentine" or "Italian" shoes(??). Eyes deepset, rather high in face, a long narrow somewhat bony nose, a wide mouth. Very "Russian-looking," but of the northern "Viking" strain. No epicanthic fold on the lids, says Pooch. Has disciplined look, as though concealing his thoughts by maintaining a "poker face" (Pooch expression). Alexeyev alert, and Pooch noticed that he constantly flicks his eyes from the road ahead to the rearview mirror, which Pooch says shows Alexeyev is an intelligence officer (noting that I do the same thing, so give me high marks for alertness!!)

Pooch has *not* seen the ice axe or any camping or outdoor gear in the dark blue Ford, which Pooch says is very clean. (Does Alexeyev drive more than one car?) But Alexeyev has talked about volcanoes. Says he likes hiking.

Alexeyev is studying Spanish, Pooch thinks, from teacher in their embassy. He likes to practice with Pooch. (Pooch drops his Rio Platense dialect with Alexeyev, he says, just as he does with me. N.B. says my Spanish better than Gennadi's. Bet he tells that to all his agent handlers.) Alexeyev speaks good British-accented English (which, of course, impresses Pooch deeply, putting Gennadi on higher cultural plane than yours truly.)

Pooch introduced Gennadi to Maria Elena and says Gennadi obviously interested in fairer sex. I asked her about him during a language lesson and she said he is "charming—a real Russian." (What makes a Russian "real"? How spot a false one?) Thing is, she said he was going to "prove useful," but would not elaborate on what she meant by that. And that brings me to this, something I'll write up in more detail. Alexeyev has been asking some not-so-subtle questions of Pooch about "his relations with the Americans!!" I think Pooch has been smooth in his answers but he is not happy. I told him that Alexeyev may just assume that as an Uruguayan politician he knew our people. Has asked Pooch about Brits too. But Pooch, who can be a worry wart, thinks either that Alexeyev knows he (Pooch) is in touch with us or that he (Alexeyev) is going to make a pitch, or both. Pooch is very uneasy and making noises about breaking off with Alexeyev, thinking up reasons for not seeing him, etc. Maybe this is a good idea—with Alexeyev knowing both Pooch and wife, he may be moving in too close for our good. I'm pulling more detailed report together but am writing this up to get the physical description etc. to you and need guidance.

Outside Oliver's door Mrs. Pott was speaking to someone. Van Schaik rushed into the room and stopped a short way in, standing, panting, staring at Oliver.

"Well, Nick." Oliver looked at Van Schaik curiously. "I was just reading—"

"Thank God, you're here."

"Well, yeah." Oliver stood up. "What's happened?"

Van Schaik paced across to the window, came back across the rug, and stood again staring at Oliver.

"Sit down," said Oliver.

"Yes, sir."

Oliver walked around behind his desk, turned to look at Van Schaik again and sat down himself. "What's wrong?" he asked.

Van Schaik sat, knees apart, elbows on his thighs, clasping and unclasping his hands, clapping them softly together. He looked at the door, hopped up and went to close it. "Buchanan," he said. "I just saw him with Alexeyev."

"Ivor? With Alexeyev? You sure?"

"Yeah. I'm sure, all right." Van Schaik ran one hand through his hair. "Ivor was walking from the British chancery, over on Lerma, to the metro at Insurgentes. He ducked down there and obviously was going somewhere, you know." Van Schaik sat back in the chair, jammed his hands into his pockets and crossed his legs at the ankles.

"Going somewhere."

"You know." Van Schaik leaned forward again. "Well, so, I decided to follow him."

"You followed Ivor."

Van Schaik ran his hand through his dark reddish hair again. "There was something funny—furtive, sort of."

Oliver leaned back in his chair. "Something furtive. Go on."

"He went two stops, to Chapultepec, and got out. He was in a big hurry, obviously running late. He's always late for tennis. He went up and walked along Reforma by the anthropology museum. Suddenly he ran right across, right through traffic, I mean, crazy. On the other side he stopped and turned to see if anyone was after him—you know—not too obvious, but sloppy too. Then—right away, almost—a car pulled up and I could see him plain as day. Alexeyev, I mean. The timing was something. Ivor just did get there."

"Timing sounds pretty good to me. He see you? Ivor, I mean. Or Alexeyev, for that matter."

"No, I'm sure they didn't. But the point is—"

Oliver held up a hand. "Wait a minute, now. You've never seen Alexeyev—"

"Okay. I know. He was driving a dark blue Ford. I swear it's the same car that Pooch has been in a couple of times now. Dip plates."

"You get the number?"

"No, but dip plates, that's definite."

"Let's get back to—you're sure Ivor didn't see you?"

"No, sir. He didn't see me."

"All right, then. Next question is, Nick: Why follow Ivor, furtive or not?"

"I think the question should be, sir, if I may say so, what Buchanan is doing making a clandestine meeting with Alexeyev."

"Thank you for your suggestion. I'll be getting to that. But, first, where'd you get the idea that we're in Mexico to run operations against the Brits?"

Van Schaik got up and walked back and forth, clasping and unclasping his hands, Oliver watching him. Van Schaik sat back down and looked at Oliver. "Okay. After you went to Washington I saw in the reading file the trace request on Freddie Ortiz you sent to headquarters."

"So?" commented Oliver.

"Well, I knew from that Ivor must be seeing Maria Elena."

"So what? I told you I saw them together that time."

"I know, I know."

"And that's why you followed him?"

Van Schaik sat again, head down, looking at the rug. "Well, in a way. Yeah."

Oliver looked at him for a few moments and said, "Let's hear all of it."

"Okay." Van Schaik looked up at Oliver. "Okay. After tennis the other day I said something casual, like: 'So you know Mrs. Puig?' " Van Schaik looked up at Oliver, who, saying nothing, was shaking his head from side to side. "I know. You told me not to say anything to him. But knowing he knew Pooch, it was a natural—" Van Schaik slapped his hands together and ran one hand through his hair. "I guess I shouldn't have—" He jumped up.

"For the Lord's sake, Nick! Would you sit down?" Oliver himself got up and went over to sit across the coffee table from Van Schaik. "What did Ivor say?"

"Oh, nothing—you know—something witty, offputting, the way he does. I know you told me not to say anything, but I didn't see any harm—"

" 'Obsession' doesn't cover it."

"What do you mean?"

"You and the fair sex."

Van Schaik reddened. "I don't know why you say that. It's perfectly normal. If I didn't feel attracted by a woman as attractive as Maria Elena, then there'd be something wrong—"

"Attractive, yes. And old enough to be your mother."

"No, she's not!" Van Schaik got up again. "No, sir. She's just a little bit more than ten years older than I am. What does age have to do with it, anyway?"

"Well, nothing, for present purposes." Oliver got up, too, to walk behind his desk. "That night, Nick, coming from the airport, you told me—I don't remember exactly—how glad you were to have another chance—"

"Yes, sir. I still am, but—"

"Well, what do you think you're doing with that chance?"

Van Schaik exhaled noisily. "Maybe I don't look too good on this one."

"You can say that again." Oliver leaned against the desk. "It isn't just a matter of appearances either. How about it: you ready to testify, swear in a court of law, it was Alexeyev you saw? Not some buddy of Ivor's in a British Embassy dip vehicle? Someone from our embassy? A Norwegian? A blond Argentine?"

Van Schaik snorted. "Well, a court of law—it won't come to that. Sounds to me as though you're trying to talk me out of what I saw. Alexeyev: a mustache, as Pooch said. That was a meeting, a clandestine meeting."

Oliver went to sit at his desk and picked up a letter opener and gestured with it as he spoke. "First, you sit down and write what you saw in detail, right? Next, I look it over and send it to headquarters with some comment or other—I'll think of something. Back home they'll scratch their heads and send it to London with their comments and then our people in London scratch *their* heads and pass this blivet of yours across to the British. First thing the British wonder what in hell the Yanks are up to now. They sit there, stiff upper lips and all, staring at one another. Nobody has to say it: the bloody Yanks are telling us we got another Philby, another Blake, on our hands."

"Ivor went to Cambridge."

"Oh, for Christ's sake, Nick! Forty or more years after all that."

"Sir, with all respect, I don't think that—"

"In the meantime we are getting frantic queries, from home, from London, from the British. Can you picture the CI people? The questions?"

"Sir, I think you're making too much—"

"The Brits yank Ivor home for interrogation. Perhaps they'll want you there to confront him—"

Van Schaik was sitting with both hands on the coffee table as though he had been told to hold it to the floor. "Sir, may I say something?"

Oliver was silent.

"Given everything you say, it's also clear that Maria Elena and Pooch may be sharing the same place but there's nothing between them. She despises him, you can tell, the way she treats him."

Oliver waved his arms. "Talk about your non sequiturs."

"Not at all. I'm trying to show how—"

"Go right ahead." Oliver took a toothpick from his

drawer and began to chew on it. "I didn't realize we'd finished with the previous subject, but go ahead."

"It's not unconnected. I mean, she suspects Pooch had something to do with Freddie's death. That trace you sent for Ivor. Well, Maria Elena asked me if Pooch was working for us in Uruguay."

Oliver took the toothpick from his mouth. "Go on."

Van Schaik asked Oliver. "Was he?"

Oliver stared at him before speaking. "And if I tell you he was, do you run back and tell Maria Elena?"

Van Schaik turned red.

"You see my problem." Oliver threw the toothpick in the wastebasket, took another one from the drawer, peeled off the paper tube, stopping to read the legend on it. "Haven't been to Bellinghausen's for weeks. Like the way they do *huachinango*." He looked at Van Schaik. "He wasn't, though."

"She thinks he was."

"She thinks a lot of things that aren't true."

Van Schaik was still red. Oliver picked his teeth and stared at him. Finally he said, "You'd better get started on that report. I'll be right here."

Van Schaik was back within the hour with his report. He sat down with fingers drumming on the table next to him. Then he folded his hands, watching Oliver as he read his account of his surveillance of Buchanan. Then he looked away from Oliver. Then he got up and looked at the map of Mexico on the wall. Then he went to stand at the window. He was there when Oliver spoke.

"For the moment, I'm going to leave it the way you have it, not add anything about your motives, which I see you have skillfully avoided exposing." Oliver threw the sheets of paper on his desk. "You know what 'connive' means?"

Van Schaik stared at him without expression. " 'Connive?' Well, it means plan something secretly or plot something. You mean, what I did?"

"No. That's not what it means at all. It means to wink

at something, ignore wrongdoing, become an accessory. What I'm doing. I don't like it a goddamned bit, Nick. I'm doing it because you're promising me right now, telling me that you're not going to mix your personal obsession—oh, yes, that's the word, friend—with the work. Do I have that?''

"I don't think we should sweep this under the rug, that's all."

Oliver put up his hands. "Here you are, a CIA officer. Over here is Ivor, making a meet with Alexeyev—if indeed he did. You might, by the way, give a bit more thought to that meeting than you have so far. You also might consider a couple of alternative explanations for Ivor getting together with Maria Elena. But never mind. Those things are separate, understand? You just damn well remember the difference between duty and your love life, keep your jealous—"

Van Schaik was red. "I resent the way—"

"Don't bother me with that! Did I hear your promise?"

Van Schaik, red in the face, nodded. "Yes, sir."

"Hmm," said Oliver, wondering what the promise was worth now that he had extracted it.

Chapter 18

The atmosphere was no more serene the next morning with Drew.

"I don't 'suspect' her of anything," Oliver was saying. "It's the principle. Why bring her in on everything? You'd think we'd brought her aboard as a consultant." Oliver was facing Drew, who was red-faced with annoyance, planted solidly in the center of the white rug in his blue bathrobe. Without replying, Drew turned toward the door. "Where you going?"

"To change out of this dressing gown," said Drew.

"Not on my account," said Oliver. "We can talk—"

"And to turn off the music."

"Not on my account."

"It is not on your account. I cannot stand chattering with the music on. One or the other."

"What is it, anyway?"

Drew was disappearing through the door. "Surely you know that!" he said, sulkily. "Mozart. Clarinet Concerto in A . . ." Oliver could hear Drew's voice receding but not his words. Paco entered with croissant and coffee.

Oliver had finished one cup of coffee and was pouring himself another when Drew returned. He had been brooding, a disgruntled look still on his face. He wore leather slippers, gray flannels, and a high-necked, camel-colored pullover under his large, blue blazer. He threw a manila envelope on the lacquer table and started right in talking. "I do not wish to discuss it further. It is a supremely private matter," he said, sagging heavily into his armchair.

"I don't want to be rude about this, Harley, but you talked to me about Galina, then Marge, and now Maria Elena, about this supremely private matter. You'll be on a talk show next. I understand your feelings—"

"I seriously question that."

"Come on, Harley. It's an official question too. That's why I'm jumpy about Maria Elena."

Drew put his hand to his face and rubbed his eyes. Keeping his eyes closed, he let the hand fall dramatically. "Very well. I do admit I am much taken with her."

"You mean—taken with who?"

"With whom." Drew's eyes popped open. "With Maria Elena, who else?"

Oliver let himself slowly into the gray armchair. "Go on."

Drew spread his hands. "What more is there to say?"

"Insects spray something called a pheromone to attract the opposite sex, the females bringing in the males. Maria Elena must be shooting it out like an aerosol bomb, surrounded with clouds of the stuff, all of you buzzing in—"

"Very coarse, Ted."

"What about Galina?"

Drew frowned and shifted about in the chair. "I have not decided. It is for that reason that I find the advice of sympathetic persons to be useful." Drew emphasized the word "sympathetic," giving Oliver a peevish look. "Maria Elena is nothing if not simpática. Soliciting her advice came entirely naturally."

"And what does she sympathetically say?"

"See here, Ted. Women have their ways of looking at these things. They're not always the same as ours."

"What's her way, in this case?"

"I have always been fond of you, Ted. But you have a hard side to you that, frankly, can be unattractive."

Oliver said nothing, watching Drew and pulling at his lip.

After a moment Drew continued. "She feels that I should go, go find Galina. That I would never be satisfied—and, who knows? Perhaps she's right." Drew flopped his hands.

"Cui bono, as you would say?"

"That's the side of you I find objectionable. I would be the beneficiary, obviously. It can mean nothing to the good of Maria Elena."

"Yeah. I wasn't thinking of her, exactly. Of the Sovs, rather, to whose benefit it might just be, and you have to wonder why Maria Elena may be pushing a Sov cui bono line. Or I have to—you'll be rushing around Helsinki or maybe Leningrad—"

"You are pulling the taffy entirely too long, Ted. Absurd!"

"I hope so. Let's see what headquarters has to say about the Galina letter. We haven't got their—"

"Yes, yes, Ted, of course, but a measure of tolerance, if you please."

Oliver went back to pulling at his lip.

"Maria Elena has her own incubus, you know," said Drew.

"You mean the brother?"

"Yes. Incubus. An unfortunate word. More precisely, her obsession with identifying those responsible for his death."

"This is National Obsession Week around here."

"The husband is an amiable but, *au fond*, an unsympathetic type. She suspects him. Are you aware of that? Yes? And she suspects us as well. She asked me if her husband had worked for the Agency in Montevideo. I told her I had no idea. She asked what you'd ever said of that to me. I said that you had never divulged anything to me."

"Thanks for sharing this. Next time she wants a full field investigation, let me know, will you?"

"No need for that tone. I could hardly have told you

sooner. It was only yesterday we spoke. She hinted that there are others from whom she can seek the truth if we continue obdurate. Who would that be?"

"I'll give you three guesses who. Whom."

"The Soviets? All the more reason for us to tell the poor woman something. Why leave it all to them? What about asking Washington?"

"I did." Oliver stood up and said: "They don't know. She's playing a dangerous game."

"Melodramatic, now."

"I don't think so. She's way over her head. She has no political judgment, no sense of how the world works. Like a lot of women, it's all emotion."

Drew was immediately pleased. His belly began shaking. He rumbled with laughter, followed by a bout of coughing. Red in the face, he said, "I dare you to repeat that remark to Marge."

"I didn't say 'all women'—"

"Trying to climb out of the hole you dug. Doesn't know—" He tittered. "—women don't know how the world works!" Drew was turning purple between his coughing and his laughing. "I can't believe—" He sputtered.

"The political world—you know what I mean. Listen, if you're going to have a fit, I'm leaving."

Paco came in, glancing at the tears running down Drew's cheeks, to tell Oliver he was wanted on the phone. Oliver followed him to the kitchen. Paco covered the mouthpiece with one hand. "El Gordito. He was trying to reach you at the number you gave him. He's in Amecameca."

"Thanks."

On the phone El Gordito was cagey. "The twenty-eighth," he said.

"The twenty-eighth?" repeated Oliver.

"That morning, early, I'm taking him by Las Cruces to the crater and back. If this weather holds. He wants to get to the very top—to the Pico del Anáhuac proper."

Oliver thought: "What time would you be down?"

"If all goes well, say by fourteen, fifteen hours. Better be there an hour or two before that, just in case."

Oliver returned to the living room. "Anything wrong?" asked Drew, stuffing a silk handkerchief up his sleeve.

"No, no. About those names, now."

"Oh, the Tupamaro names." Drew leaned forward to pick up the envelope and pull out a yellow legal pad. "I took these notes, talking with Enrique."

"Well, all right, but why couldn't he just write it up for you? Why does he always talk at you?"

"What do you mean by that? You've never liked Enrique, have you?"

"It's not dislike—I don't know him. But why can't he write it up? Why does he sit around debriefing himself while you have to sit there scribbling it all down? Surely he's literate."

"Quite literate." Drew looked unhappy. "Those questions about Alexeyev—he was offended. Now this request—"

"Offended!"

"He said it makes him feel like a spy."

"Lord preserve us, Harley!" Oliver stared openmouthed at Drew.

"I'm sorry this had to come up," said Drew.

"Here's a guy working in the propaganda apparat of the Salvador guerrillas—a fine bunch of assassins if ever—"

"The Salvadoran right is—"

"Not only that: Enrique's hot to be a big frog in the political cesspool of San Salvador. He'll take all the help we'll give him, but he's too delicate to give us the names of some Tupamaro cutthroats hiding out in Mexico?"

"Enrique might not agree entirely with your wording. And he did get the names you wanted." Drew sighed. "Let me explain."

"Don't, Harley, I get the picture." Oliver sighed. "Go ahead."

Drew began to read from his notes. "Obando FNU. Lives in Ciudad Satélite with a Mexican mistress. Works for Cuban Embassy as legman." Drew looked up. "Enrique thinks accommodation addresses, that sort of thing. Obando was in Cuba but apparently a misfit—makes him more likable somehow, doesn't it?—and so they let him out on the understanding he would work for them. Low-level stuff. Sendic—the Tupamaro leader—doesn't want him back. Considers him a thug."

"Boy, he must be, then! Where's Enrique get this? I mean, this is good stuff, knowing who these guys are."

"Some of that background information is about eight months old, actually. But Enrique says Obando is still here—he saw him at a barbecue put on by some of the Argentines and Uruguayans here. His source on Obando was a well-known Uruguayan communist who's back in Uruguay now."

"Oh, yeah? I'll be— What else?"

"Enrique knows Obando by sight. He's about forty-five, stocky, dark, balding on top, heavy, black mustache—let's see—I've written down more particulars."

"I can get it from your notes. What else?"

"A younger man named Aquiles Montes de Oca Baggiore. Italian mother, eh?"

"A lot of Uruguayans are part Italian, part Spanish. There're an awful lot of Montes de Ocas too."

"He is a more presentable type than Obando, married to a Mexican pediatrician, works as a technician in a TV studio. The wife has an office in their house in Delegación Azcapotzalco near the Campo Deportivo Reynosa— wherever all that is. Not known to Enrique why he stays in Mexico, maybe because of the wife. Or maybe he can do better for himself here than in Montevideo. Enrique does not know of any political activity by Aquiles but he says he is rabidly anti-U.S.; very much down on the government in Uruguay. Blames us for all the world's troubles. Up to date on events in Uruguay as though he were currently in touch. Physical description: slender, about forty, fair-skinned, dark hair, usually casually but neatly dressed, still plays football—soccer—on weekends. Enrique thinks he must have some political role, being so rabid, so au courant, but doesn't have any idea what it could be." Drew looked up. "That's it."

"Well, I have to do something with that."

Chapter 19

"My treat," said Buchanan.

"In that case, I'll have the squid," said Oliver to the waiter. Ivor Buchanan made a face. "And a beer."

"The canelones," said Buchanan. "And a beer." He handed the menu to the waiter. "What I like is being on the street yet not of it, if you follow me." They were sitting at a table by a wide window looking out on Amberes in the Zona Rosa. A two-man hurdy-gurdy team was operating in front, one khaki-clad ancient turning the handle, the other passing a khaki cap. "In your sidewalk café they're right in amongst you, you know." Buchanan hummed tunelessly. "Any idea what they're playing?"

"Something operatic."

"Mm. You said you have something for me."

Oliver reached in his jacket pocket and handed a typed sheet to Buchanan.

The beers came and Oliver sipped his while Buchanan read.

Buchanan put the paper down. "Not exactly 'forthcoming,' as your politicians like to say. Or is it 'outgoing'?"

"Or 'incoming'?" Oliver shrugged. "You know that Ortiz was the brother of Puig's wife."

"Mm." Buchanan was cool about it. "That has come up."

"I take it you're in touch."

"All quite casual."

"Seem to remember you had no interest in Puig."

"Quite right," said Buchanan.

"As you would say, 'Mm.' What about Puig and the Soviets?"

"Really, old chap. Couldn't care less."

"All right, what about Mrs. Puig and the Soviets?"

Buchanan took a sip of beer. "Well, now. Where's our lunch?" He was humming again, drumming his fingers on the cloth. "Ted, be a good chap, tell me—ah, here they come."

The waiter arrived with the dishes, presenting them with a flourish, warning Buchanan that his plate was hot. The maître d'hotel came over, fishing for compliments.

"*Buen provecho,*" said Oliver to Buchanan.

"Pax vobiscum," said Buchanan.

When the maître d'hotel had left, Buchanan blurted out, "You knew them in Montevideo, I take it."

"Mm."

"No, really. Tell me about them."

"About Puig?"

"Be a good chap. I know about Puig," said Buchanan, putting his beer down and looking at Oliver.

Oliver looked steadily at Buchanan without expression.

Buchanan giggled and grew red.

Oliver put down his knife and fork and stared at Buchanan. "You too?" said Oliver.

Buchanan laughed then. "I don't know what you're talking about." He frowned. "What do you mean by that, me 'too'?"

"She's attractive, no doubt about it."

Buchanan was thinking it all over. "You see a good bit of her in Montevideo?"

"Oh, yes, indeed. I saw a great deal of her. Maria Elena and I were often thrown together."

"Maria Elena. Pretty name, that." Buchanan laughed—really a horrifying simper, thought Oliver, looking at him with disgust. "Actually, she prefers being called 'Marucha.'"

Oliver was struck dumb. Fool that I am, I asked for that. And got it. Damn her! Unable to speak, he addressed himself to his squid.

During the extended silence that followed, Buchanan recovered his dignity. "Does it strike you odd," he asked, in a more formal tone, "that with some twenty million people in the valley of Mexico, we seem, well . . ." Buchanan began.

"Seem to what? What do you mean?" Oliver was enough in control of himself to be merely surly. "Odd that we're struggling for the affections of the Puig family?"

"That's not what I mean, precisely." Buchanan was frowning. "Or, I should say, I don't mean that at all!" he added. "Something from London in the weekly bag yesterday. Appears to have been an unfortunate sighting on your side. Understand why you didn't pass it on to me directly, our trade being what it is. It does seem absurd, however, in this great metropole—one of the world's largest, I daresay—that the two of us may be stepping on each other's toes. London says we should talk about it, see what we can work out on the ground. I take it Washington agrees. Have you heard? No? Good. If it's all the same to you, I'd like to put that little chat off a bit till I've had a chance to think a bit more about it."

"Mm," said Oliver.

"The thing is," said Oliver to Van Schaik, when Van Schaik had finished reading the cable from Washington, "Michael's wanting to see me again just doesn't hang together, after his vilifying me, twisting everything I said, to the Bureau. It doesn't make sense! I don't like it."

"Well, they say he's coming down for some research and he won't be seeing the Soviet, Alexeyev, but while he's here he wants to see you. I don't see what's so—" Van Schaik was scanning the message. "Says he was hasty in his remarks and wants to apologize." Van Schaik shrugged his shoulders and raised his eyebrows.

"All right, but you don't know him. It's not in character. You know what he said about me to the Bureau. He's not—"

"Maybe Slasher exaggerated that—you know, as Drew said. Trying to build a case against you."

"Yeah." That Slasher would use that against him had occurred to Oliver as well. "But they quoted him—I mean, Michael said those things. He's not the apologizing sort either. More your never-apologize-never-excuse type. He's after something—what? What I don't like is his getting away with setting—insisting on—the same meeting arrangements, going back out to La Marquesa again. I mean, who the hell's in charge?"

"Well, you picked La Marquesa in the first place. He thinks you like it out there, or maybe he likes it. Why did you use it anyway?"

"You know. You're not going to put an unknown quantity like Michael in a safehouse. He didn't want to see me in his hotel room. You can't drive in this traffic and have a serious conversation. So I took him out there. There's no one there during the week."

Van Schaik yawned. "Well, gosh. I dunno. If it's such a big deal, why don't you tell 'em you changed the meeting place?"

Oliver was frowning, a thumbnail between two teeth. He shook his head. "They wouldn't. They baby him." He waved his fist. "There's no time. He's in Austin already, on his way here. Okay, it's no big deal. But they're so adamant—say it three different times. You see? Gotta take him to La Marquesa—that's somehow at the center of it."

"Well, your car breaks down, something like that."

"Then we'd never know. Look, Nick, if he weren't doing a piece on the Tupamaros—I'm gonna feel foolish when it's all over but, look, tomorrow. Put on some old clothes. I'll pick you up around, let's say, five."

"Did you say five? You mean in the morning?"

"Yeah. Lemme make a phone call," said Oliver. "Don't go far. I'll confirm that in a minute."

When Van Schaik had left the office, Oliver went to the

safe in his office, pulled out a folder and took it to the phone. The number rang one of the five phones in the cabinet behind Diego's desk.

"Bueno?" came Diego's voice.

"Mercurio here." Diego had picked that name for Oliver to use on that phone. Meaning Mercury, the messenger, it was entirely fitting to their relationship. Did Spanish also have that old English meaning of Mercury, the clever thief? Of Mercury as quicksilver, that elusive, fluid substance so hard to pin down, to capture? Oliver had always to reckon with Diego's latent suspicion of the CIA, with Diego's trust of Oliver as a person struggling with the popular Latin view, the CIA of folklore, of the gutter press.

"Look, old friend, I'd like very much to see you," said Oliver.

"I'm very busy. Is it urgent?"

The tone of Diego's voice was not that of an old friend. Don't take it personally, Oliver told himself—Diego's run ragged in that job.

"I have no way of comparing my priorities with yours. Yes, for me it is urgent."

"Every moment booked this week and a party conference all the weekend in Guadalajara. Perhaps sometime on Thursday—no, not Thursday. Friday, possibly. I'll call you if there's any time." Diego sounded harassed, not at all sympathetic.

"No time today? How about tomorrow?"

"I'll call you about Friday. Now, if you'll excuse me."

Oliver hung up and stared at the map of Mexico on the wall. "Okay, Diego. We'll see about that." He went to open his door. "Nick!" When Van Schaik appeared Oliver said: "Tomorrow morning at five. Early is good. I've gotta make a run out of town afterward."

Chapter 20

Busy day tomorrow, thought Oliver, as he went back to stand at his desk, looking at the pile of papers awaiting him. When he got an appointment with Diego—he was sure he could set that up—he would be spending all that time, wasting all that time, on Maria Elena's Tupamaro bogeymen. Not only throwing the time away but, if not exactly passing the buck to Diego, passing him a headache. And his meeting with the insistent and duplicitous Dr. Michael would be at best strained, acutely irritating. Maria Elena's warnings threw an ominous light on the meeting, on almost everything Oliver thought about at that moment. He would not be taking her forebodings so seriously had not the meeting with Michael suddenly loomed. It was not Oliver's logic but his instincts that were stirred to caution by the coincidence. He was impatient with this: Van Schaik had said nothing, but he must think Oliver to be an old maid with his fussy preparations for the meeting with Michael.

Oliver had not exaggerated to Drew his annoyance with Maria Elena for moving so close to the men in the Mexico City station. She was dominating their thoughts, even their actions. Oliver, still pausing at the side of the desk, staring vacantly at the far wall, gave a decisive nod of his head. They would pack Puig off to Uruguay and damn well see that Maria Elena left with him. Feeling better for that, he sat down and pulled the stack of reading to him.

"There's someone on the phone for you." That was Mrs. Pott. "She didn't say who she was and of course I didn't ask."

It was Maria Elena. Damned if we don't get her on the way with Puig!

"Ted. Come to tea with me."

"Tea! Tea—?" he began to stammer.

"Ted, it's urgent. I must see you."

"Look, Maria Elena—"

"I must see you. I swear I'll never ask you for anything again, but please, just come."

Oliver closed his eyes. "Where?"

"In the courtyard at the place we had lunch."

"When?"

"At four-fifteen. No earlier."

He looked at his watch. "It can hardly be earlier! It's almost four now. I can't possibly—"

"Dear Ted. I'll be waiting."

She hung up.

Once Oliver had overcome the rush of annoyance at this new excess and was sitting in the back of a taxi, he became thoughtful about the summons. Who was it the Lady in Red had lured to his death? John Dillinger. His mind went to others deceived by trust in a woman. Samson and Delilah. Heloise and Abelard—no, she was okay.

Too bad there wasn't another entrance to the Hotel de Cortés. The old rule: avoid the place with only one way in or out. That instructor in training used to say, "If the Alamo had a back door, there'd be no Texas today." Be nice to eyeball that courtyard first. You had to walk right in off the sidewalk through a passage to the courtyard. Just inside was the anteroom where bellboys and chauffeurs stood around gossiping, waiting for the next thing to happen, then the registration desk on the right as you went on through the passage. You couldn't see the courtyard until you were standing in it. There was no way of making a decent assessment of the situation on the sidewalk in front either—there were always cars double parked and men hanging about the narrow door that opened into the hotel.

Oliver told the taxi driver to let him off at the far edge of Alameda Park. He walked through the park and was able to look across at the hotel. He crossed the street in front of the Hacienda building, giving himself space and time to look things over as he walked slowly toward the hotel. The scene was cluttered, a clot of figures in front of the entrance, people walking ahead of Oliver, people walking toward him, and beyond all that was the crisscrossing of traffic where intersections jammed into each other at Reforma and Hidalgo.

It was past four-fifteen. This circling about was useless. Oliver strode up to the men clustered about the entrance to the hotel and they gave way, continuing their talk, hardly looking at him, stepping aside to let him pass. He went quickly through the narrow passage, slowing to edge past a North American couple carrying on resentfully with a nervously patient desk clerk about changing their downstairs room to one on the upper gallery. In the courtyard a waiter nodded to Oliver and Oliver shook his head, putting a hand up toward the waiter, searching the dozen or so tables for Maria Elena.

At a table in the far left corner, half in and half out of sunlight, he saw her gold hair in the sun, and he raised his hand to her, nodded at the waiter and walked around the fountain to join her.

He slowed as he approached. There was a man sitting in shadow to her right. Oliver took four more steps to the chair near Maria Elena and stood behind it, holding it by the top. He looked from the man to Maria Elena. The other man had a drawn expression on his face, and Oliver supposed the taut skin of his own face must show the same shock.

In Spanish, Oliver said, "Why couldn't you have said so? Quickly. What's going on?"

She spoke in English. "Now, don't be rude, Ted. Just sit down." The waiter came to Oliver's side and laid a place for him on the beige cotton tablecloth. Oliver remained standing.

The other man was still leaning forward in his chair, his hands gripping the arms, as though trying to get up. "Maria Elena—" he began.

"Please. Both of you." She turned to the other. "He doesn't like being surprised."

"Neither do I." He had an English accent, all right. He relaxed his grip on the chair arms, folding his hands in front of him, but he still leaned forward in the chair.

Oliver stared at him a moment and then deliberately turned to look carefully around at the other tables, one table after another, staring, to the discomfort of some of their occupants, then to the arcade surrounding the courtyard on three sides, and then to the gallery above them, his eyes stopping for a second on every person he saw. Only after looking back toward the way he had come did he pull out the chair and sit down, pick up the napkin and put it in his lap. He took a deep breath and laid his hands before him on the table. "Is this your meeting?" he asked the man.

"Certainly not."

They both looked at Maria Elena. She tried a small smile and looked down at her hands.

The waiter cleared his throat and asked Oliver, again, what he wanted.

Oliver looked at the teacups of the others. "A margarita," he said.

"And the lady? You, señor? More tea?"

"A margarita," said Gennadi Alexeyev. He sat back in his chair and himself began the same methodical examination of everyone in the courtyard, less crudely than had Oliver, raising his eyes to take in the galleries. Finished with that, he smoothed his mustache with his right forefinger and looked at Maria Elena.

She spoke to him. "You ask about the Americans. This is the only one I know well."

"Hardly typical," he said, looking at Oliver with a

careful expression. While the tightness had gone from his face, he was still not easy.

"I don't say he's typical. But what do you mean? How do you know that he's not typical?" She squinted in the sunlight and shifted her chair into the shade, close to Alexeyev.

"Because he has a picture of me in his files," said Oliver.

Maria Elena looked toward Alexeyev. "Do you?"

He said nothing, still contemplating Oliver.

"Have you a picture of him?" she asked Oliver.

"No, but I know that he's not typical either."

"What is this talk of 'typical'? Is it so important to be typical?" She looked from one to the other.

Neither one spoke, both watching as the waiter carefully handed down the cold, globular glasses to the table, first in front of Alexeyev and then in front of Oliver.

"How do you know him if you don't have a picture?"

Oliver picked up the glass by the stem and held it in front of him, rested his elbow on the table, looking at the crushed ice moving slowly in the glass. The sun was warm on his neck, on his back. What the hell, he thought. "Because he has a brilliant reputation," he said, looking at Maria Elena as he answered her question. She was giving Alexeyev the smile, Oliver saw, that a mother gives a child who is being praised by a teacher.

"Please," said Alexeyev, putting his head on one side. He frowned and took a bare sip of the margarita, pressing his lips together at the sourness, putting the glass back down.

"Not only with his own people but with us," said Oliver, almost reckless now, his eyes back on the glass, talking at it as he kept it in front of him. "He is admired for his accomplishments. He shows a reserve that earns the respect of his colleagues. He doesn't run with the pack. Some are made uncomfortable by this. That seems not to have hurt his career, although it is difficult for an outsider to judge that." Oliver stared into the soft green of the margarita, the frost on the outside melting with the heat from his hand. "There are those who talk behind his back, jealous of him, offended that he holds himself back, that he prefers to go it alone, shows an independent spirit." All right, careful now, don't overdo it. Oliver tipped the glass to his mouth and took a sip of margarita.

"Well," said Maria Elena, frowning at Oliver. "I hope you don't feel like that. I find it admirable."

Alexeyev put his hand over hers. "No, no. What he says is true enough. She is the innocent," he said to Oliver.

Maria Elena narrowed her eyes at Oliver. *There!*

"We discussed that the other day," said Oliver. "It is less her innocence than her refusing to respect the rules."

"You make up your rules as you go along. Why should I follow them? Why should he? He is bold and free, like a—a falcon—a hawk."

"In the high places you find the raven," Oliver commented. "Wiser, far more intelligent than the hawk. But as expert in the air. More—he hovers like a falcon, soars like a hawk, dives like a peregrine. Learns quickly, never forgets."

"*Corvus corax*. We have them, too, you know," said Alexeyev. "That's all very well, but you did not say what the raven feeds on—on, how do you say it?"

"Carrion."

Maria Elena made a face.

"There may be something in that," said Alexeyev. "Hmph." He turned to Maria Elena. "I must go."

"I'm going with you," she said.

Alexeyev signaled the waiter. "Let me," said Oliver. Alexeyev shook his head. "My treat."

That rang a bell. Oliver let the thought drift on off as he watched Alexeyev counting out pesos to the waiter. While Oliver was searching for the next right phrase, Alexeyev spoke. "Do you go now to send off your memorandum of conversation?"

Oliver grinned at him. "You know our regulations as well as I do."

Alexeyev allowed himself the smallest part of a smile. "You mean, by that, 'yes.' " He raised his eyebrows.

Oliver paused before answering, looked into Alexeyev's eyes, green as reported, looking right back at him. "I'm very busy at the moment," said Oliver. "I may not get to it right away." For three, four seconds, their eyes held, until Alexeyev turned to rise, picking Maria Elena's white sweater off her chair, and taking her arm, moved with her across the courtyard. Oliver stood to see Maria Elena looking back over her shoulder at him, and then they disappeared. Oliver kept watching. No one left the courtyard after them. Oliver turned his chair about so that it faced the courtyard and sat down, studying the other faces in the courtyard, slumped in his chair, slowly finishing the margarita.

That night he took Marge to the veranda. "Listen, just in case. Remember what I say."

"What?" she asked, putting her arms about her. "It's cold out here."

"I don't want to talk inside. Look, if anything happens, you have to get to Drew or to Nick and tell them—Drew preferably—"

"What do you mean 'if anything happens'?"

"Nothing, nothing, just listen."

"Why don't you tell Drew yourself?"

"It's something. I can't—look, you know Drew. I can't trust him with this."

"You can't trust Harley?" She was openmouthed.

"Oh, hell, I trust him. But there can't be any talk. I trust him, all right. But he's a gossip. You know."

"Well, tell Nick, then."

"Marge! It's complicated. Please, Marge. Just listen."

"I am listening," she shivered.

"If anything happens, have Drew or Nick—either one—tell the Uruguayan woman to put you in touch with the Russian."

" 'In touch with the Russian.' I hate this sort of thing. What if I get that wrong?"

"The phrasing isn't important."

"Why don't you tell Washington?"

"Look. I can't. Don't make a big thing of it. Do you have it straight?"

"What do I do with the Russian?"

"Oh, that part's simple. Just see if he wants anything."

"Oh, sure, simple! I'm freezing out here, Ted. I'm going in."

Chapter 21

Oliver and Van Schaik rode out the Toluca highway over the pass at Las Cruces, yawning in turn and at times yawning in unison. Oliver drove down the slope toward La Marquesa, toward the road that goes off to the left into the Valle de los Conejos. The morning was turning out overcast, gray, the sun coming up like a dirty tennis ball behind the dark mountains.

"Why so early?" asked Van Schaik. "Oh, that's right. You have to go out of town?"

"Not that so much. Two can play at looking over a meeting site." Heavy mist came fast at them from where it hung in the road at the bottom of the valley. Oliver slowed down and turned on his windshield wipers. "Better if we're not there at the same time they are."

"They?"

"I don't know. Ghosts." The spirits that had showed up at the foot of his bed last night. Oliver had moved lightly into and out of sleep, waiting for the alarm to go off, bothered when he slept by sibylline prophecies he didn't want to think about now.

Oliver turned left into the valley and drove along the road to where he had parked that day with Dr. Michael. "Hell, that stuff's rain," he said, as they came to a stop. "There's coffee in the thermos." No cars came along the stretch of road that ran back toward the highway behind them. There was nothing to be seen through the windshield either. Ahead, the road dipped and twisted so that cars might be hidden where the ribbon of road disappeared in the green swale, popping up thinner farther on, blue-gray in the light rain until it blended with the hanging mist that hid the far end of the valley.

They got out and Oliver said, "You can see someone coming that way, the way we did, for quite a stretch. Up ahead, no. Someone could hide there and watch you come to a stop here. What d'you think: About two minutes for a car to get here if he moves right along?" Oliver squinted his eyes against the light rain and whistled soundlessly.

"Less than that." Van Schaik pulled up his collar. "You saw Ivor yesterday, didn't you?"

"Yeah. Gave him the answer to his trace. Grass is wet," said Oliver. "C'mon over by that tree and we'll go over the layout."

"How'd he take it? Didn't tell him much, did it?"

"Oh, he commented on that, all right."

Van Schaik laughed. "Teach him to be so nosy. Buchanan's really stuck on himself. You can see why people don't like the Brits."

"Well, it's not that we have the answer. We're not playing games with him."

"Sometimes I wonder. She thinks we have the answer. That there's a cover-up."

Oliver stopped to turn and look at Van Schaik. "I know what she thinks. What do you think?" Oliver's expression was cold.

Van Schaik stared right back at him. "I don't know what to think. Sir," he added.

Oliver's anger led him to weakness, a petty rush of early-morning annoyance. "Ivor told me, yesterday, by the way, that Maria Elena likes to be called 'Marucha.' " Oliver kept looking at Van Schaik long enough to see the color drain from his face before turning to walk, leaving clear prints behind him in the crumpled wet grass.

He stopped at the dying, blasted tree where he had stood with Dr. Michael. Patches of gray rock, blackening in patches in the rain, cropped up in the green. Oliver looked around to see Van Schaik coming up behind him, his face white, staring at Oliver but hardly seeing him.

Oliver kept his voice neutral. "All right, Nick. Down that slope. There's a stream at the bottom, that narrow rocky run you can see up that way and farther down there but not right below us." Van Schaik's eyes dully followed where Oliver pointed, Van Schaik's face loose with discouragement. "See? The hill right here falls off so fast into a steep reverse slope that you can't see the bottom. These rocks that stick up out of the ground here—they give some cover—not much. Tactically, this's what we got to work with. Come on, I'll show you. Careful, it's slippery."

Oliver led the way to the brow of the hill where the land fell so steeply that the slope below was barely visible. "You can get down here and you can also bust your ass doing it. Don't try. It's steep and it's wet now and you'll slip. Let's go down around this side, here, where it's more gradual." Van Schaik followed as Oliver walked to the left and skittered down a shallow slope to the rocky stream. Oliver skipped across with Van Schaik following and they worked their way down the stream below the hill they had been standing on. "Now, if you're at the bottom, there—" He pointed across the stream to the sheltered area under the hill. "—no one can see you from the top, up there. But once you cross the stream to where we are, you can be seen—until you get into the shelter of the pines there. Hold it! Hear that?" Oliver stood still, one hand in the air, openmouthed.

Van Schaik, startled, said, "What?"

"Mountain bluebirds. Like ours but blue all over. Come on."

Van Schaik blew out his lips. "Jeez! I thought you'd heard something."

Oliver hopped along from rock to rock, turning from time to time to look back at Van Schaik. He seemed to have gotten over the shock of Oliver's malicious report on Ivor. "You can see the top of our tree up there, and whoever is standing on the brow of the hill can see you."

Oliver bent to go under the heavy branches of the conifers that marched from the stream up the far slope to a distant pine-clad ridge. The rocky ground was uneven, clumps of boulders, pine needles brown on the rocky forest floor. Oliver was pushing damp branches aside, looking around. "Here. This looks pretty good. You see, there's good visibility if you get down—" He crouched in a nest of boulders. "—here, and you're covered pretty well too. Take a look."

Oliver moved to one side and Van Schaik took his place.

"Now, if you look way off down there to the right or even to the left, you might see a car coming down the road, and again, you might not, and if you did see it, it would be pretty damn late in the game."

"Forty-love."

"Right. The thing is, up on the hill you'd see it. I think." Oliver peered through the branches. "And from here you can see someone on the hill but they won't see you. What do you think?"

"I just hope this rain lets up."

"It's nice to have rain for a change, though, isn't it?"

"Depends where you're going to spend the night," said Van Schaik.

Chapter 22

The road into Tarasco from Mexico City was as twisting, as perilous as ever, condemning Oliver to an impatient, stinking grind up hills and around curves behind the diesel fumes of unforgiving buses and trucks. Once past Tarasco, the highway was clear and the road up the mountainside to the hotel itself was paved—in pleasing contrast to the first time Oliver had come there. Outside the gate a dozen cars were parked, rental cars from the airport in Mexico, three license plates from the States.

By the car the mountain cool was jarred by the sun reflecting from the black asphalt. Oliver took off his jacket and threw it over his shoulder, hooking it on one thumb. By the shaded wall the climate improved, brick showing through the adobe, the soft sound of running water coming from behind the wall.

The young woman at the desk on the other side of the gate was on the phone, trying to convince someone, using English—a travel agent from the sound of it—that there were no vacancies to be had around Christmastime: "Completely booked up," she was saying, playing with a pen as she talked. Her black hair was pulled tight in a bun in a failed attempt to give her pretty face a more severe, official look. She glanced up at Oliver and smiled, fluttering a long-fingered hand at the telephone instrument to excuse herself. Oliver went to stand under the delicate arches of the aqueduct that brought water from the mountain stream to the kitchen, to the cottages around the cliffside courtyard, water from the same stream that kept the natural rock pool in the courtyard filled. An overweight woman in a too-tight, red bathing suit was standing at pool edge to admonish the shiny, pink child splashing in the pool. Two of the chairs were occupied. An elderly man was reading a newspaper. A blond woman in a black bikini had her eyes closed, holding a greasy face to the sun. Another chair had towels piled on it. In the dining room a silent couple was having a late breakfast. It was cool where Oliver stood in the shade, drowsy, too, from the sound of the water flowing through the aqueduct a few feet above his head, the sibilant nagging of the mother, the splashing from the pool, the woman on the phone having patiently to say that New Year's, too, was fully booked. It was the post-breakfast quiet time, some guests in their rooms, waiters making the tables ready for lunch.

Oliver heard the woman at the desk hang up and he turned toward her. She stood up as he wished her good morning. "I'm looking for Santiago."

She was surprised but she quickly restored a businesslike expression to her face. She looked into the courtyard. "He's around here somewhere." She had an attractive accent in English. "He might be in the kitchen or in the garden. I don't know—do you know the garden?"

"Is it still worth your life to get there?"

She laughed. "You've been there, have you? There is a footbridge now."

"Thanks. I know the way."

No one paid any attention to Oliver as he walked through the courtyard past the pool. As he reached the narrow footbridge that crossed the chasm separating the garden—out of sight around the edge of the cliff—from the rocky courtyard, he saw Santiago staggering across the footbridge toward him, a basket in either hand, the handles stretched, one full of tomatoes and the other with squash, onions, lettuce, half hidden by a pile of the orange flowers of the zucchini. *Sopa de flor de calabaza* must be on the menu for lunch. Oliver waited.

Santiago was limping toward him, eyes down, talking to himself, the rusty black beret, the wool khaki shirt—could it be the same one?—open at the neck, a day's growth of beard, corduroy trousers, tennis shoes. Santiago looked up and saw Oliver, shouting *"Dios!"* loud enough to stiffen the courtyard. The mother paused in her toweling of the child by the pool, the man put his newspaper down, the woman sunning herself frowned in Oliver's direction. At the nearest cottage a door opened and a head came out.

Setting down the baskets, Santiago seized Oliver in an *abrazo*, spluttering in Castilian. He stood back to look at Oliver, gave him another *abrazo*, stood back again and slapped Oliver on the chest. "So! I thought you'd abandoned us."

"Never."

"You just missed the patrón. He's up in Mexico at the bank."

"Is he? I was not looking for him. I was going by, so I stopped to see you. Why the bank? Are you broke again?"

"No. On the contrary. He says you get money easily if you don't really need it. Also, if you support tourism. He talks about putting in more rooms here. We're turning people away. Good, I say. We have too many now." Santiago frowned at the people in the courtyard. "They're trying to get me to learn to speak English. *Qué va!* In no manner is it the way it was when you were here."

Oliver picked up one of the baskets and they walked through the courtyard to the kitchen. Hotel guests gathering at the desk, waiting for the tour bus to leave, stared at the pair of them. The woman at the desk turned her head from talking to the tourists to smile at Oliver. Santiago limped through the kitchen door and turned to scowl back at where she stood. Santiago spoke under his breath to Oliver. "You see here? She's one of them. Wants to teach me English."

"She's quite nice. I wouldn't mind studying English with her."

"Why would you study English? Oh, you're joking, aren't you?" Santiago grinned and hit Oliver again in the chest. "Anyway, the patrón is interested in her. I have hopes for that. He needs a woman. I've told him so. Children too."

Santiago turned and led the way past the steel counters to a table near the fireplace, setting his basket on the floor. Oliver did the same. A shy-looking girl who had been stealing glances at them turned back to peeling potatoes. "Eva!" said Santiago fiercely. "Speak to the gentleman. He's an old friend of the patrón. And of me."

The girl squeaked out a good morning, blushing.

"You still cooking, Santiago?"

"Who me? Cook? *Qué va!* We have a chef! Isn't that right, Eva?" Eva bleated softly in confirmation, giving Oliver a tentative smile. "A stuck-up, *cachivache* fellow from Ciudad Juarez with a dirty little black mustache, the size of Evita's little eyebrow." Santiago illustrated that by holding up a little finger, his thumb against the first joint. Eva giggled. "When His Highness is not here I am allowed to cook a breakfast, warm up something." He poured two cups of coffee. "Let's go somewhere and talk." As they went from the kitchen. "One of those from the orphanage," he said in too loud a voice, nodding over his shoulder at Eva. "Scared of her shadow. I caught that so-called chef screaming at her yesterday. I told him one more ugly sound out of him and I pitch him over the cliff. He wrinkled his ugly lip at me but he's afraid. He thinks I'm crazy enough to do it." Santiago took Oliver's upper arm, squeezing it and wheezing with laughter. "Sorry he's not here. You could help me put him over. Oh, he speaks English, all right. Does that make the food any better?"

They were sitting on a bench in the shade of the wall. Santiago had gone for more coffee. It had not been necessary to dwell on the complications of Uruguayan politics—Santiago was not interested. He was immediately angry. "What kind of people are these that would want to kill a man like that?"

"You would know the type from Spain."

"You're right. I do. Do you know what I heard? That at the end the Russians were killing the foreign volunteers just to get their passports." Santiago growled quietly. "The fascists were no better, you know." He touched Oliver on the shirt-sleeve. "Listen! Go see Diego. That's what you do."

"I did call him. But he's exceedingly busy."

"*Qué va!* Too busy for you? We'll see about that."

"I don't want to bother him. After all, he's the senior minister of government!"

"Bother him! I'll bother him. Look. We have a telephone here now. I call him whenever I feel like it."

"You really shouldn't, Santiago. He has a lot on his mind."

After greeting Diego, Oliver sat down, holding himself respectfully straight in the Victorian chair across from Diego's desk. Diego sat as straight behind his desk, not looking at Oliver, rearranging the objects on his desktop, the blotter, the paper knife, pushing the pen set two millimeters to the right. Diego was in a dark blue, pinstriped suit, gleaming white shirt, dark red silk necktie with a paisley pattern, the gold stick pin below the knot. The pale, smooth hand he raised to stroke his mustache was steady enough but it did not require the sensitivity of an intelligence officer to appreciate that Diego was annoyed.

Oliver stopped watching Diego's movements, shifting his eyes to the portrait of Benito Juarez above and behind Diego's desk, Juarez stared back at Oliver, looking no more pleased with what he saw than did Diego, who was looking at Oliver, clearing his throat, and speaking. "You have taken advantage of your friendship with my father. He should in no manner be a factor in what is, in essence, an official and confidential relationship between the security elements of two governments. Now, having said that, I ask you: What is it that is so urgent?"

A BLACK LEGEND

The manner was severe, but Oliver took some comfort in Diego using the familiar form of Spanish with him, the style of speech used with close friends. Oliver responded in the same way. "Diego, I pleaded with your father not to bother you."

Diego took a cigarette from the silver box, picked up the gold lighter from the desktop, lighted the cigarette. "I must emphasize, Ted, that I am extremely busy." Oliver saw the tremor in Diego's fingers which was testimony in itself to his being overworked.

"Exactly what I told Santiago. I should not have spoken to him as I did. I regret it deeply. I am fond of your father but I must tell you he is a stubborn man. It didn't occur to me that he would think to intervene in this. I had forgotten that he has free access to a telephone now. If I had only thought—I should have known better."

Diego gave half a laugh, in spite of himself. "All right, Ted. Out with it." He sat back in his chair and let the smoke stream from his nostrils, dark eyes shining at Oliver. He laughed again, tilting his chair, putting his head back, laughing hard now. He brought his chair back down. "How did he look to you?"

"Seemed fine to me. Profoundly annoyed with a chef from Ciudad Juarez."

"Yes. He is convinced the man has a criminal record. He instructed me, of course," Diego sighed, "to make inquiries. Go on."

Without naming Maria Elena—he described her as an uncooperative source who appeared to have reason to believe what she reported to be true—Oliver told of the alleged threat against him from the Tupamaros. He took from his jacket pocket two double-spaced typed pages, one with a paragraph on "Obando, FNU" and the other with information on Aquiles Montes de Oca. "These are the only two Tupamaros, or ex-Tupamaros, whatever, that we know to be in Mexico."

Diego scanned the pages quickly. "Yes, we know of them too. What reason do you have to believe that they mean you harm?"

"I have no proof that these two are connected to the attempt—the reported plan."

"Nor do you"—Diego crushed the cigarette in a porcelain ashtray—"have hard evidence of a plan, plot against you, is that right? I am simply reiterating what you yourself have said."

"No, Diego." Oliver folded his hands and looked back up at the portrait of Juarez. Juarez stuck with Diego: That's a mighty lame story the gringo tells. What does he really want? "This is not a personal matter," said Oliver. "I am reporting an alleged attempt against the life of a government official. Nothing to do with me, personally."

"Yes, yes. I understand. And I am reacting to your report as an official of the host government."

Well, where in the hell does that leave us? Oliver asked himself.

"And so?" asked Diego.

"Well, I was thinking someone could go around to question them. Knock on the door—throw them off balance if they're planning anything. There may be other Tupamaros of whom your people know—maybe in your files—and with them the same thing—an interview."

Diego picked up the papers again and reread them. "Well, I will see that something is done, of course. You can't expect more unless a crime has been committed or unless you can bring me evidence—" Diego waved one hand and then sat forward in his chair, leaning his arms on the desk. "You're sure there's nothing else? Nothing more tangible?"

Diego may not have meant to make Oliver look foolish, panicky, pusillanimous. Damn it: but that was how it came out.

Diego was twirling a letter opener and stabbing lightly at the papers Oliver had brought. "Your drug enforcement people, your congressmen, constantly and publicly attack us for not breaking our own Mexican laws in our struggle against the manufacture and the traffic of drugs that your country consumes in such stupefying quantity.

Yet they are exceedingly tender when it comes to observing the laws of your country. Wouldn't that qualify as a double standard? Of course, by and large, that is the direct concern of your attorney general, not mine. If these two Tupamaros were in Chicago, say, what would you expect the police there to do on this same evidence? "You get my point."

"Yes, dammit. Could not be more clear. I think the Chicago police might send someone around to knock on the door."

"Yes, yes. Another question occurs to me. Does this Tupamaro business have any connection with your previous, uh, disaster? How do you refer to it? The calamity of some months ago that engaged both of us so deeply?"

"No connection at all. This would go back, as I told you, to my time in Uruguay. After the calamity here—that's a nice word for it—we took extreme measures, closed everything down, have had to start all over again."

"So I understood. You are hardly in a position to say anything to me of Soviet activity in Mexico at this time."

"Oh, yes, I am. After getting caught the last time, they will think carefully before contemplating again any interference in your internal affairs."

"So I would assume."

"And I can assure you that they continue to work against the United States from here."

Diego looked at the papers Oliver had given him. "So I would assume." He tossed the letter opener onto the papers. "It is for that reason I am surprised that you allow yourself to be diverted by this Tupamaro business."

Chapter 23

It did rain all night, just as Van Schaik feared it might. Not a hard rain, but persistent. Oliver had the windshield wipers on the intermittent setting. On Dr. Michael's face was the faintly amused look—his settled expression in repose. Oliver wondered whether the facial muscles had become fixed so that, even asleep, a sense of superior disdain ruled his face.

Dr. Michael was so obviously nothing more than a conceited pain in the neck, a harmless, stuck-up, hothouse jackass, that Oliver was prickly with shame over his own foolishness. He owed Van Schaik something, crouched there in those boulders in this rain. Forgive us our debts. You could imagine the steady drip down your neck at your collar from the drooping boughs of the conifers, your knees tightening up so you could hardly stand when you got up to walk around and get warm. All because of an excess of caution. Van Schaik might call it timorous.

Oliver went jumpy, fast, at Michael's remark. "Ah, yes, the place of ambush." They were going through the high pass before starting the run down into the valley to La Marquesa, and Oliver was getting his own back, now, his tour-guide chatter.

"I see you remain resentful," said Michael.

Oliver shook his head. "No, but the way it came down here—"

"If you have had much to do with Bureau people—I

suppose you must have," said Dr. Michael, "it's that they take one so literally, they're so clumsy with the nuances."

"But not given to exaggeration."

"My! How handsome of you to defend them, considering—"

They were coming down the curves into the high valley. Traffic was light on the road, trucks and buses coming at them, mostly, and the occasional car. No one behind. "I don't know about nuances but they seemed to get the names right: García Marquez, Vargas Llosa, Carlos Fuentes."

Dr. Michael squirmed around and adjusted the seat belt so that he half faced Oliver. "A catholic selection, don't you think? But involved, each in his own way. Unlike, say, Borges. I confess you irritated me with your scorn— the man of action's contempt for the mere observer! You shook me, Ted Oliver. And I am in your debt. You will be proud of your pupil. I am, *en fin*, in my own way, involved."

"Well, that's good, I guess, but why are we going back to La Marquesa, Dr. Michael?"

"When you say the word 'doctor,' you put the very faintest sting in it."

Oliver laughed although he was not really amused. "Please don't tell the Bureau."

In the valley there was still no one behind them. Coming at them from the direction of Toluca was a bus, a trailer truck, then another bus, and behind that, a small gray car—he couldn't see beyond that. Oliver slowed down to let the first bus past and then swung left, fast— too fast, for the rear end swerved and the wheel went funny for half a second.

Oliver kept the car moving faster than was safe, looking back to the Toluca highway from which they had turned. His eyes went to the road ahead, to the mirror, to the road, to the mirror.

"What's the matter?" Dr. Michael was watching him.

"Nothing." Oliver's hands were cold on the wheel.

Okay, dammit. Here we go. Through the murk in the rear view mirror Oliver saw a car—looked gray—couldn't tell—everything was gray in the mirror—turning off the highway as though to come on behind them. "Why here, Doctor? Why this place?" Oliver spoke jerkily.

Michael was looking from the road ahead to Oliver, one hand on the dashboard. "Slow down, please." He didn't look happy. "There's no reason—nothing to be—"

Oliver drove faster and when he looked in the mirror again the road was clear but the curve had cut off the view behind. He saw the old tree, there, off to the left, and tapped the brakes again and then again until they were nearly stopped, and here Oliver pulled off the pavement onto the left side of the road. The car lurched unevenly onto soft earth.

Oliver honked the horn—three longs—and hopped out of the driver's seat. Before he could slam the door, Dr. Michael called out in a high voice "Wait! Where you going?"

"Take a leak," announced Oliver, slamming the door. He began walking fast toward the tree. He did want to urinate, actually, but he forgot about that, realizing he had forgotten his raincoat. He half turned toward the car. Michael had rolled down a fogged-up window and was shouting something at Oliver.

The gray car was coming up fast, and Oliver turned and hurried right on past the tree toward the hill. "Here I am!" he shouted. The shout, the movement, took the binding from his muscles, and his body was responding well.

Two of them were piling out of the gray car as it slid to a stop behind Oliver's car. The one in the foreground had popped out of the rear door; heavyset, a black kerchief tied over his face, a smudge of eyebrows, green, wool sweater stretched over a potbelly, his short, thick legs pumping as he ran toward Oliver, one hand held high, coming fast toward Oliver, then frozen in the frame in Oliver's brain. Middle ground; a blurry figure between the two parked cars, running toward Oliver's car, and behind it all, the painted background, a landscape of dark pasture rising to hillside, gray mountains behind. From the next rush of time this was the only picture Oliver later had left in his head.

The *ga-ga-ga* of those exploding rounds—nine millimeter, offhand—echoed over and off the mountains and they got Oliver to running hard. Couldn't stop. Bust your ass here. He bundled head down, arms in, knees drawing up like landing gear—cannonball off the high board—grazing the edge of the hill, pushing the air from his chest with a rough gasp as he wrapped his arms around himself, rolling with it. The next thump down the slope was hard and the air went out of him with a whining wheeze, and then he was rolling around on the bottom. He heard shouting from somewhere and then noise—less sounds than blows on his ears—pounding close by.

"Get back!" Van Schaik shouted. "You're too far out!"

Oliver extended his arms and legs—he had balled up like a wounded spider—and scrambled, fingernails digging in the wet grass, back under the hill, balled up again.

Van Schaik let off another burst. Okay, okay. There was another noise very close. That was his gasping, grabbing air in. He laughed. Jesus. His head was down in the wet and he tasted earth, spitting the grainy stuff from his mouth.

"Ted! You okay?" Van Schaik fired again. Two bursts. Good fingering. "Stay where you are." Three bursts. "Sonofabitch . . . Trying to flank us." Van Schaik gasping too. "You no good, he flanks us."

"Saw two—two of 'em." Couldn't tell whether he said that out loud. Really do have to pee. "There two of 'em!" Someone driving the car. Tell Nick later.

"Ted! Cover you! Now! Run for it!"

Oliver's limbs extended with a jerk; jumping up he slipped, fell, scrambled like a dog on ice, splashed shoe deep through the gushing run turning one ankle on a shining rock, tore through branches, and fell.

Cracks and thuds. Echoes rattling into local infinity.

"Over here! What's that guy—!" Van Schaik was firing to his right. Yelping came from somewhere out of sight. Oliver's ears were ringing. When the buzzing in his head wound down he could hear his own and Van Schaik's heavy breathing, the plopping of rain from the branches.

"You soaked?" Oliver whispered.

"'Sokay. Poncho kept me pretty dry." Van Schaik whispered a laugh. "Oughta see your face!"

"'S my forty-five?"

"Here. 'T hell's happening?"

"Two of them, gray car. Nissan. Regular yellow plate. Maybe driver too. One ran out other side of the car. One on my side, stocky bastard, didn't fool around. Came right for me. Black bandanna over his face."

"Black bandanna down around his neck now," said Van Schaik. "Big, fat mustache. He popped up on top, there—sh! Listen, if they get behind us in these woods, here. He showed up on the right, over there. Laid a couple on him. They hafta cross the creek one side or the other. I don't think they'll come the way you did. Boy!" Van Schaik laughed. "I'll take the right."

Oliver squirmed to where he sat with his back against a boulder, knees apart, the pistol, a round in the chamber, between his knees in his right hand, receiver back, ready to fire. If they knew, began firing blind into the trees—forty-five not worth the powder—Oliver breathed, stopped breathing, mouth open, to listen.

It was quiet except for the dripping.

"What if they got grenades?" whispered Van Schaik from behind him.

"C'mon!" gasped Oliver, panting. "Why'd you think of that?" He looked at his watch. His hands were trembling. He kept looking at his watch because he couldn't seem to remember what he had just seen.

"Hear that?"

"Whuh?"

"Car. Go look?"

"Hell, no. Wait awhile."

They sat in the drip. "Rain's stopped, actually," whispered Van Schaik. "Here." He reached into his musette bag and handed a granola bar to Oliver.

"Thanks." Oliver stretched and chewed it, drymouthed. He took inventory. He'd done something to his right shoulder, his right ankle, ribs on the left side, fingernails full of mud.

"You know Crankshaw?" asked Van Schaik.

"You mean— One I know's British writer."

"Edward. Khrushchev biography fellow. Meant to tell you. Maria Elena says Alexeyev told her he's the guy to read on the Soviet Union."

"He did? Jesus!"

"Yeah. That's what I thought. But how come a Brit?"

Oliver snickered. "Here in the rain doing book reviews. I'm gonna take a look." He was still whispering.

"I'm coming too."

"Okay."

Oliver stood up, staggered stiffly—ribs on the right side hurt too. Crouching, he went to the edge of the woods and stood rigid, still in a tangle of branches. In a moment he splashed across the swollen run, upstream to the right. Van Schaik picked up the musette bag and swung it over one shoulder, close behind Oliver. They were in the bottom of a bowl at streamside and they walked, some ten feet apart, up the slope, weapons ready, until they could peer over the grass toward the road.

"Why does he tell her to read Crankshaw?" asked Van Schaik. "I mean, there're a lot of good American writers on Russia, more recent."

"Well, where'd he get it?"

Oliver's car was sitting quiet and there was no sign of anyone. Across the road, a hundred feet up the gradual slope, there was a clump of pines, and Oliver nodded toward that, the only piece of cover for several hundred yards except for the ditch on the other side of the road.

"Ted." Van Schaik was standing where the gray car had stood, looking at the ground. "Blood." He looked at Oliver, both with gray faces streaked with mud and water. "What say we get the hell out of here?"

"Stay away from the car," said Oliver in a low voice. They must have taken Michael with them, he thought. "I'm crossing the road. Watch those trees up there."

First Oliver crossed the road, feeling naked in the wide-open country. When he nodded, Van Schaik strolled across, holding the Uzi across his chest, Oliver standing with the Colt pistol in his right hand. They looked up and down the road. Van Schaik raised his eyebrows and shrugged. Then they heard the sound of an engine. "Get behind the car," said Oliver. "Don't get in." They scuttled back across the blacktop.

A lopsided truck was chugging into view from their left. There were cattle in the railed-in back of the truck, two men in front. Oliver and Van Schaik stood behind the car, weapons out of sight, heads showing over the top of the car, turning slowly as the truck coasted past them down the slight grade. The man in the passenger seat, dark under his straw sombrero, waved at them. Skinny red steers stood sprawl-legged in the back. One, his head lolling over the rear gate, regarded them with large brown eyes.

"That'd be pretty good, if they'd been in there with the cows," said Van Schaik. "We're standing here with our mouths open. They blow us away."

"Wonder if they took the time to jigger this car somehow."

Van Schaik got down on his knees to look under the car.

"See anything, Nick?"

"No."

"What you looking for?"

"Haven't the slightest idea."

"Hell," said Oliver, taking the car keys from his pocket. "Let's get outta here."

"Oliver! Ted Oliver!" The voice was thin, cross.

"'T hell's that?"

"It's that sonofabitch, Michael."

"Oliver!" Dr. Michael was in sight, slowly walking down from the clump of trees, Oliver's raincoat around his shoulders.

They waited for him by the car. When he was near, Oliver called out, "You alone?"

"Of course I'm alone. What do you think?"

"Get in," said Oliver. "We're getting out of here."

"Let him start the car, why don't you?" Van Schaik was grinning. "Just in case." His hair was wet, matted, his face muddy, mud and pine needles on his poncho.

"Who are you?" Michael was staring at Van Schaik, looking at the Uzi. "They had one of those. Did you— is that theirs?"

"No," said Nick, examining Michael with interest. "That's ours."

"Get in," said Oliver. He got into the driver's seat and put the pistol under his right thigh. Van Schaik climbed in the back. "You'd better put your windows down," said Oliver. "Keep an eye out until we get to the police *caseta*, know where I mean? Intersection Reforma and Constituyentes."

"Yes, sir."

Oliver started the car. It did not blow up. He looked at the bedraggled Dr. Michael. "How many were there?"

"There is some insane mix-up, Oliver."

"No, there was no mix-up, Dr. Michael. We all know that." For a moment Oliver thought the car would not work its way from the soft mud, but the front wheels spun and found the surface of the road. Oliver glanced at Dr. Michael sitting beside him. "How many were there?"

"Those two men. You must have seen them. There was a woman driving."

"That figures. Describe them."

"You must have seen them. I don't know why—"

"Describe them!"

"One with a black kerchief over his face. He ran after you. Why did you run like that? It made them angry."

"That's too bad. Go on."

"When he came back later it had come off. He had a black mustache and he had pulled the kerchief up on his head, so he looked like a pirate. The other was quite nice-looking, slender, brown hair, dark blue polo shirt with the alligator logo, gray slacks, a dark aviator jacket, unzipped. He ran up and pulled the door open, here. He asked where you had gone. He had a gun like that one. And he wore glasses. There was rain on them," added Michael.

"Asked for me by name?"

"No. He said, 'Where is he? Where is he? *Donde 'stá? Donde 'stá*'?"

"And?"

"I said you'd run off, over there. Look. He was waving this submachine gun at me. He seemed very angry."

"Did he know who you were?"

"How do I know? I suppose so. He ordered me to stay in the car and he ran off with the other one."

"But you didn't stay in the car."

"When I heard all that shooting, I went up to those trees."

"Didn't they try to stop you?"

"They weren't there. They were over—"

"How about the woman?"

"I paid no attention to her. Anyway, when the shooting started she backed the car up on the road and turned around."

"Describe the woman."

"I didn't see her. She wore glasses, too, I think."

Oliver kept his eyes on the road, turning to speak loudly to Van Schaik over the sound of the wind blowing in the windows. "Let's keep a good lookout along the road. Especially these blind curves. And then?" he asked Michael.

"The one with the kerchief came back into sight first, from where you all were, over there. He was limping and he shouted something to the woman, and he was looking back over his shoulder, talking, I suppose to the other one. Then the other one, the nice-looking one, appeared and he knelt down beside the one with the kerchief."

"You must have hit him, Nick."

"What happened—when he first came down on the right, looking like he was trying to get into the woods on our flank—I put a couple in the air over his head. But he started running, for the stream, the wrong way, I mean. So I fired at his legs. I wasn't trying to kill him," said Van Schaik. "I wanted him to leave. And he hauled ass."

Oliver looked at Michael. "And?"

"They got in the car and left. Take me to the airport, please."

"They'll be after you now, you know." Oliver was barely able to restrain a glee that revived him. He put a concerned expression on his face. "You'd better find a good place to hide. You've gotten yourself mixed up with a bloodthirsty crowd."

"What do you mean by that?" Michael was startled.

"They'll assume you tipped me off. They wouldn't like that at all. Listen, Michael, you're not going anywhere until we get the whole story," said Oliver. "Then we'll see about the airport."

"Do you think they'll be watching the airport?"

"More likely they'll try to get you in New York."

"They wouldn't, would they? I mean, not in New York. What am I going to do?" In the rearview mirror Van Schaik had a grin of manic joy on his face, his mouth wide open. Oliver gave him a quick wink with his off eye.

Michael missed that as his head turned to give Oliver a petulant look. "If you had not run off like that, they would have no reason to blame me. Why did you do that?"

"Start at the beginning," said Oliver.

Michael said his literary agent was madly excited about doing a book, but they needed a good peg to hang it on. So, here was a chance to do a really lovely piece, based on the Tupamaro interviews but using the interview in

La Marquesa as the centerpiece. Lead with the Tupamaro story—the history bit leading into the death of Freddie Ortiz and that part really dramatically brought out. A sure excerpt in the *Times* magazine—a really dramatic, blockbuster of a piece—exposure of the CIA hand in the death of Ortiz. Then the other Latin political pieces, country by country, bringing it all together with the pièce de résistance, an I-was-a-spy-for-the-FBI sort of thing and with the solution of Freddie's death—the confrontation of Oliver, whatever. You'd expect the *Times* might excerpt that last part too. Maybe that most of all. Then the book.

"Holy—" Van Schaik was leaning forward in the backseat.

"Keep an eye out, Nick. We gotta way to go still," warned Oliver, looking at Van Schaik in the rearview mirror. Van Schaik sat back in the seat, peering ahead as they rounded the curves. Oliver was driving fast, and when he caught up with a red sports car on the road, he stayed right behind it through the ambush area of the high pass. "What was today's scenario?"

"I was informed that two men would meet us here—in La Marquesa—and furnish evidence of your complicity in the death of Ortiz."

"Tupamaros?"

"Of course, who else?" Michael was getting his insolence back, along with his color, the nearer they got to the city. "They were going to confront you with the truth of Freddie Ortiz's betrayal, his murder by the police, and, well, I'd be there to witness it, report it."

"A nice little chat, the four of us. That's all they wanted."

"Absolutely. To get the truth out, published by a prestigious person, so it would be picked up and carried all over."

"Even though I—the CIA—had nothing to do with Freddie's death."

Michael made a face and said nothing.

"Who was arranging this in New York?"

"I'd rather not say."

"Go ahead, say it anyway."

"An official with the Cuban U.N. mission."

"Holy—" That was Van Schaik again, his head almost between Oliver's and Michael's.

"A perfectly nice person. Not at all what you think. Nothing at all like your vivid anti-communist phantasmagoria."

"Does the Bureau know about this?"

Dr. Michael let out an exasperated sigh. "Of course not. And there's no need for you to bring them into it either."

"Get the Uzi out of sight, Nick. I think we're okay now."

"Where are we going?" asked Michael.

"The airport. The sooner you're out of town, the better."

"May I ask Dr. Michael something?" asked Van Schaik as he rolled up the rear windows.

"Yeah. What? Go ahead." Oliver saw Van Schaik, mud still smeared on his face, lean forward to talk to Michael.

"You said Mr. Oliver should not have run away as he did."

"There was no reason for him to do that. It spoiled everything, my trip, the interview, everything."

"Do you really believe that those two were just going to interview Mr. Oliver?"

"I didn't say that—I said that they were going to furnish proof—don't put words in my mouth!"

"When you yourself go to interview someone, do you ordinarily take a submachine gun along?"

"Who is this person?" Michael folded his arms and looked out of the window on his side.

At the airport Van Schaik handed Michael his carry-on bag from the backseat. Michael grabbed it from him and walked away without a word.

Van Schaik was laughing as he climbed in front with Oliver. "He's not really in any danger, is he?"

"I doubt it. The person I worry about is Maria Elena."

Chapter 24

Oliver shouldered through the mid-morning crowds on Calle Londres to the door of the Botica Karina. He paused before opening the door, knowing he would feel out of place inside. As is turned out, at first, the shoppers intent on fingering the blouses and dresses, no one inside the shop noticed him. Generally aware of each other, a male presence was inconsequential if not entirely invisible to the women. Oliver saw the back of Maria Elena. She was standing next to a plump, middle-aged tourist by a full-length mirror. The woman was holding a long yellow Mexican dress embroidered with a design of leaves and flowers. She pressed it against herself, turning from one side to the other, regarding herself in the mirror. Oliver stalked Maria Elena, moving slowly, quietly, from one piece of cover to another, edging sideways closer to the mirror.

As he drew near, Maria Elena turned and Oliver saw her face, white, tired, unaccustomedly stark without makeup. She must have sensed him nearby, for she turned, her eyes widening with the beginning of a smile. She gave him a small nod before turning back to the customer. He could hear her saying, in English, to the woman, "It very much becomes you."

The dress seemed so clearly unsuitable—it would be like a tent on her—that Oliver snorted his private disapproval. He turned to finger dresses on the rack, trying to remember Marge's dress size. Twelve or fourteen: Or was that a glove size? Maria Elena appeared at his side. "I must see you but we can't talk here," she hissed.

"Oh, miss!" A blue-haired woman holding a pink dress on a hanger, showing ingratiating teeth, looked through Oliver to Maria Elena.

"I'm sorry," Maria Elena said, forcing a smile. "I have a customer," she looked over at the plump woman now glaring at Oliver. "But if you'll wait a moment—"

Oliver had grabbed a dress from the rack. "Listen! I have to see you. Now! There's no time."

"Wait outside." She turned with a taut smile to the plump woman. Putting the dress back on the rack, Oliver walked out of the shop, not bothering now with discretion. Oliver paced back and forth in front of the shop until he tired of shuffling his way through the dawdling couples passing both ways past the shop door. He crossed Calle Londres and stood at the curb, out of the way, watching the door of the shop. Maria Elena came out quickly, caught sight of him right away, looked each way for cars, and hurried toward him, moving as she did years ago in Montevideo when they would meet for lunch.

"This is the worst time—what happened to you?"

She put her hand up to touch the red welt on his cheekbone—a scrape from the roll down the hill at La Marquesa—touching the place just as Marge had. He had lied to Marge about it but he told the truth now, to Maria Elena. "It's why I'm here. Your Tupamaros came after me."

She took in a sharp breath. "Are you all right?"

"Sure. Thanks to your warning I was ready for them. It didn't go as they'd planned. But the point is—they may suspect you. That's why I had to see you. You're in danger. The two that—"

"Why me? You are the one. Won't they try again?"

"One was Obando and the other was Montes de Oca. Did you know?"

She shook her head. "Of course not. Where are they?"

"The police have them." Oliver had told Diego of the scuffle at La Marquesa. "The Mexicans will deport them, to Uruguay if they'll have them, maybe to Cuba. But, listen, Maria Elena: with you and Pooch going back to Montevideo—it may not be safe for you there. They'll surely suspect—they'll know that I was prepared. They'll make a report."

"Ted, there is a greater danger than that now—here or in Uruguay." She bit her lip. "I should get back to the shop."

Oliver touched her arm. "Wait. You'll be leaving there soon enough."

"I may not. Oh, Ted. I wish I had never come here. And I don't want to go back to Uruguay with Puig. I still can't stand him. Can you arrange for me to stay here?"

"I don't know how, Maria Elena." And then Oliver told Maria Elena what he had not yet told Marge. "Because of what happened yesterday at La Marquesa with Obando and Montes, I've been ordered home. I was afraid—"

"You too!"

"Yes." He put one hand on her arm. Maria Elena put her warm hand on his and looked up at him. He found himself suddenly short of breath as they looked at each other, unable to speak. Then she gave a small laugh and squeezed his hand.

"Marucha." He was angry. "What are you doing? Van Schaik, Drew, Ivor, Alexeyev." He put his other hand on hers, tucked her arm under his side and began walking. She fell into step with him readily enough, but she had a troubled look on her face.

"I told you," she said, looking down at the sidewalk as she spoke, "that I had to learn the truth about Freddie's death."

"And so you have been chasing after all of them—and for what? Nothing!" He was angry with her for that and even more angry with himself, suddenly appalled by the force of his jealousy.

"No. There you are quite wrong. I know the truth now. And you were right when you told me that I should leave it alone."

He stopped to look at her, for she was very pale. "What is it—what did you learn? How'd you find out?"

"You don't want to know. It's terrible. And I think now you are in even greater danger!"

Oliver shook his head. "Why do you say that?"

"Something Genya said. You see, he has to go back to Moscow. He's been ordered home too."

"Genya! Why? He's hardly been here—"

"Because of me, I think. He says there must have been a leak."

Oliver began walking slowly. "A leak—about you two? Or a leak of some other kind?"

"I don't know. All I know is that I wish I'd never found this out. I don't know that I can live with it." She was crying, and Oliver pulled a handkerchief from his pocket. She saw they were drawing curious glances from passersby and she used his handkerchief to wipe her eyes. "I'm sorry," she said. "That is useless."

"When is he leaving?"

She shook her head. "He has things to do before he can go, and some dreadful men are here."

Of course. Alexeyev would have to make arrangements for the cases he was handling, turn over agents to other KGB officers. "What dreadful men?"

"He said they travel as 'embassy maintenance people' but everyone in the Soviet Embassy knows that is not true. People are nervous but no one says anything. Genya warned me to be watchful, that they have already asked him what I know of Freddie's death. He told them I know nothing, but they may not believe him—here's your handkerchief." She looked around as they walked, trying to smile. "I've never been afraid before, but now I'm beginning to be afraid. He said they are 'dreadful.' If they knew we were talking, you would be in danger too."

"Why?" But he could not help glancing at the people about them on the street.

"Because I know about Freddie now. Department Vee? Do you know what that means?"

Oliver stopped her in mid-pavement, passersby grumbling as they eddied around them. "They call it something else now but the name doesn't matter. A KGB Direct Action team. That's trouble, all right." Oliver was puzzled. "What else did he say?"

"Here is exactly what he told me to look for. One, the leader, is a Russian, thin, tall, long-nosed, very blond, with pale blue eyes set close together—almost white—the eyes are so pale, he said. Another is short, a Ukrainian, so thick in the neck and shoulders he has almost no neck at all, with close-cropped hair, small eyes in a heavy face. The third is dark, quick-moving, not an Armenian—what's the other?"

"Georgian?"

"No, the other." Maria Elena shook her head with impatience.

"Azerbaijani?"

"That's it. They stay in the embassy except when Genya goes out, and then one or two go with him, do the driving. Only one—the dark one—speaks any Spanish. The blond one knows some English." They had walked back down Londres to stop across the street from the boutique. "I'm going back in. I can't help being afraid, Ted. If they find out that he told me—"

"Call me if you need to, if you hear anything."

Chapter 25

Oliver spent the afternoon fumbling halfheartedly through correspondence at the office, leaving notes about what had to be done, advice for his successor, putting off going home and having to tell Marge the news, tidying up loose ends, his heart not in that either. Marge had become fond of Mexico, and the children were adapting well. Oliver dreaded having to tell her of this uprooting so soon after their coming to Mexico.

"It must be hard on Mrs. Oliver, having to leave like this."

"She doesn't know yet, Mrs. Pott. I haven't had the heart to tell her. Only you and I know at the moment." Only you and I and Maria Elena. "I have to go home and tell her. I really don't look forward to it."

"Of course not. It's too bad. I wish there were something—?"

He shook his head.

"I suppose not. But she'll understand, after what happened in La Marquesa—"

"I haven't told her about that, either, Mrs. Pott."

"Of course, that would worry her. What awful people! Deportation is too good for them!"

"Maybe I'll go home early. Not much point hanging around here now, is there?"

"I'm sure your children would enjoy seeing you home early. Let me close up." Mrs. Pott sighed.

Oliver smiled grimly as he glanced at the comprehensive, Soviet program planning document O'Rourke was eager to have in hand before his next report to the director. It had only the one name on it, the one target, Gennadi Alexeyev, the only KGB officer Oliver had identified so far. The Soviet Embassy had been purged of its KGB officers at the same time the CIA station had to be shut down, cleaned out, forced to start all over again, every case of value blown to the Soviets. Of course, Alexeyev, the new KGB resident, was as important as all of the other officers of the Soviet Embassy put together. As KGB resident, he would know each of the KGB cases run out of Mexico—the identities of the agents in the States—real cases, sensitive, not like that jackass, Michael. And given the KGB ascendancy over Red Army Intelligence—the GRU—Alexeyev would probably know the GRU cases too.

Oliver tossed the draft aside. So much for comprehensive planning. Drew had been right, predicting that O'Rourke would find a pretext to get Oliver, the older man—not on the team—out of Mexico, put in one of his own malleable people. The trouble was that the pretext was practically impossible to refute: Oliver could hardly demonstrate that O'Rourke was being underhanded. There had been one assassination attempt against Oliver, and he could not well argue that the Tupamaros would not try again. Oliver would take that chance. The director would not. The director would picture himself under the stare of members of a congressional committee, having to admit that he had left Oliver staked out like a goat in Mexico. Oliver would have had to defang the Tupamaros, make them abandon their plans to kill him, expose them, somehow, if he were to stay in Mexico. Fat chance!

Funny, the coincidence. You had to wonder if Alexeyev had his O'Rourke in the KGB Center on the outskirts of Moscow, using some pretext to bring Alexeyev home— his becoming too attracted to Maria Elena, say. Lord knows, Alexeyev was not alone in that. All of the males in Oliver's circle were sniffing around after her. Oliver smiled, imagining a huffy Drew protesting the vulgarity of that metaphor. Not only vulgar but offensive too. Maria Elena was far too charming for that base thought—good thing Oliver was leaving.

The phone rang. It was Maria Elena.

"Julio phoned. They came to the apartment. Julio was there. Alone, he said, but—"

"Wait. Who came?"

"Those Russian men I told you about. The blond speaks terrible English. The dark one's Spanish is better. I knew Julio was lying. The thin little anthropologist was there, he finally admitted. They thought her to be me, of course. Fools. She's such a pale, washed-out little thing. Julio is a liar but no coward and he told them—"

"But what were they after?"

"Oh, they asked Julio, you see—Genya must have given them the slip, and they're frantic, running all over Mexico looking for him."

"But where would he go?"

"I have no idea."

"You'd better be careful."

"You too. That's why I called."

He told her to let him know if she heard from Alexeyev. After he hung up he stared at the wall. Then he looked at his watch. He blinked once, looked at his calendar, looked again at the date on his watch, jumped to his feet.

"Mrs. Pott?" When she came in he said, "Please do go ahead and lock up for me. That's the trouble with getting shot at; it makes you forgetful."

The children were delighted that he had come home early. Marge was puzzled. Oliver sat on the couch with a child under each arm, thinking, actually, of how to go about telling Marge.

"If you eat a good dinner, I'll read to you."

"*Just So Stories,*" squealed Nancy.

"That's a baby book!" declared her brother. "*Wind*

in the Willows. The part where Mr. Toad steals the car."

"No, where he's a washerwoman," said she, putting forward a quick compromise.

"And then *The Jungle Book*—" The boy overreaching.

"No. I haven't time. *Wind in the Willows*. Those two chapters. Only! I mean it. And I have to change first." He looked at Marge. He put it off again. "I'll be back in a minute."

The climbing clothing, the crampons, and the ice axe, were still in the wrappings from the store in Washington. He rummaged through drawers and the closet for the rest of the clothing he would need. Luckily it was cool enough for him to put on long underwear and wool socks before putting on trousers and lacing his hiking boots. He put the straps on the crampons and adjusted them to the boots. He pulled a day pack from the shelf of the closet, put in his parka, a wool sweater, the crampons, the dark goggles, the wool cap and gloves, the ankle gaiters, and stood looking at the pack, whispering to himself. He took a sleeping bag down from the closet shelf and put it by the pack, along with the ice axe. He clumped to the kitchen in his hiking boots and filled the water bottle from the demijohn. Putting the bottle in the pack, he pulled the gaiters out, threaded the straps under his boots, adjusted the straps, snapped the gaiters tight. Read to the children, get a bite, leave—no, tell Marge, then leave. But not really good, giving the bad news to Marge and then shoving off, just like that, without another word.

He sat with the children, who were full of questions about his climbing clothes. He had to promise he would take them to the volcanoes before they would agree to get into bed. Oliver read the two promised chapters from *Wind in the Willows*, one chapter per child, Nancy becoming fretful because Tom knew many phrases by heart, saying them as Oliver read them. Oliver told him to stop that, looking at his watch, deciding he had the time to read the chapter telling of Mr. Toad's escape.

When he had finished, Tom said thoughtfully: "I think

the part where Mr. Toad is a washerwoman may be my favorite too."

The phone rang and he heard Marge talking to someone. After prayers, requests for drinks of water—honored—and for cookies—refused—good nights, and empty threats from Oliver, he went to the kitchen, put ice in a glass, and poured himself a whiskey. He then regarded it with doubt, knowing alcohol to be the worst sort of indulgence were he actually to be climbing in the morning. Agreeing with himself that it was not a good idea, he took a sip and carried it to the living room.

"The fleeting moment when one book will satisfy them both. It won't last. Nine-going-on-ten—he'll be leaving *Wind in the Willows* just as she's moving into it, begins to appreciate it."

"I hope he never leaves *Wind in the Willows*," said Marge. "May I ask why the costume?"

He had forgotten for the moment that he was in his climbing clothes. "Oh, I'd better put a shirt on. I'm going to run out to Popo. I might go climbing in the morning."

"In the morning! What do you mean? Isn't this a bad time of year?"

"No, not bad. Maybe not the best with the weather so changeable. But it's okay." He peered at his drink, put a finger in to stir the ice into a small whirlpool. He shivered and took a drink, looking past the fireplace to his wife. He was lucky, Oliver told himself. Always had been. "I know how you feel about Popo but, really, there's no place in the world quite like it."

"Why must you go tomorrow?"

"Well, I've got all the gear out."

"That's hardly a reason, Ted."

"No," he admitted with a laugh, "it isn't, is it? All right, then, a hunch. More than that. Maybe one of those rare chances. Nothing ventured—" The doorbell rang.

"Oh, that may be Drew. He called while you were—I meant to tell you. He's bringing a couple by, friends of yours, he said, to say good-bye."

"Friends of mine?"

"He says you know them. They're going back—isn't she the Uruguayan woman you told me to—"

"What in God's—" Oliver hauled himself to his feet and hurried to the door. Van Schaik stood outside.

"What—" began Oliver.

"Have—" began Van Schaik.

They stood looking at each other. Oliver started again. "Well, Nick, what's up?"

"Just thought I'd come by. Mrs. Pott told me the news."

"Shh." Oliver looked behind him. "Haven't had a chance to tell Marge yet."

"Oh," Van Schaik whispered, looking him up and down. "I heard Drew might be bringing the Puigs by and—" He could not go on.

"Yes, I know—Nick, nothing about yesterday at La Marquesa, by the way. Told Marge I slipped when—never mind."

"I see. I won't say anything."

"Okay. Come on in. How about a drink?"

He stood with Van Schaik before the fire, Van Schaik jumpy, Marge making conversation, Oliver stirring the fire, admitting he was pretty damned jumpy himself.

"You'd better put a shirt on, Ted. Perhaps you'd like to change?"

He looked down at his red underwear. While he was putting on a red, wool shirt the doorbell rang and he hurried to the door, tucking the shirt in, buttoning it as he opened the door to find Ivor Buchanan standing one step below him.

"I say! An alpinist. Is it fancy dress?"

"Oh, hi, Ivor." Oliver paused. "Well, come on in."

Buchanan and Van Schaik greeted each other, Buchanan heartily, Van Schaik coldly. Buchanan asked for a bourbon and water. "I do like your American whiskey! I say, thank you, Ted. Do I say it properly? Boor-bun? Cheers!"

Marge laughed. Van Schaik, who had gone to the window to frown at his reflection in the glass, said, "Huh!"

The doorbell rang.

"Jesus," said Oliver under his breath. He was hot with the layer of long underwear under the wool shirt.

Maria Elena and Puig stood outside. Their eyes moved together from his face to his red shirt and on down to his climbing boots.

"Ah, Oliver," said Puig. "Drew's just behind. Perhaps we should wait."

"Aha!" Drew called out on seeing Oliver. He spread his arms and recited in a stentorian voice.

"And from the sky, serene and far,
A voice fell, like a falling star,
     Excelsior!"

"Ha, ha," said Oliver. "Come on in."

Drew was waddling down the hall behind Maria Elena and Puig. Oliver wanted to kick him in the pants. Well, Jesus. Here goes. Oliver presented Maria Elena and Puig to Marge. "I think you know everyone else," he said to them. Only too well, he muttered to himself. Drew and Buchanan introduced themselves to each other. One goddamn happy family. He gulped his drink before setting it down. He'd regret that later, he promised himself.

"Do you want to change?" asked Marge.

"Change! Nothing of the sort," said Drew. "He musn't."

"Slip into tennis togs?" said Buchanan. "What about that, Mr. Drew? Or come back as a champion golfer. A scuba diver in a wet suit?"

"A Neptune, stinking with seaweed and brandishing a trident!" said Drew.

"With a mermaid!" suggested Puig.

The three of them laughed noisily at their wit. Marge joined in. Maria Elena had been biting her lip, glancing at Marge. When they laughed she joined politely, looking from one to the other of them, obviously not having paid attention to all the talk. A somber Van Schaik had come to stand near her and glare at Buchanan.

"We have come to say our good-byes," said Puig.

"Yes," said Maria Elena, studying Marge. "We're leaving for Uruguay."

Van Schaik, his jaw working, went back to staring at the window glass. Oliver moved to stand beside Maria Elena, waiting for his opportunity. She was asking Marge about the children. When Drew came in his courteous way to speak to Marge, Oliver walked Maria Elena away from them.

"Listen," he said out of the side of his mouth. "Don't—she—Marge doesn't know we're leaving—haven't told her yet."

Maria Elena nodded her understanding. "Ted, I want to say again: you were so right—how I wish I had not learned the truth! Now I must live with it." Her mouth was trembling. She bit her lip again, looked away from him, shaking her head from side to side. "I don't want to go back with Puig. But—" She shrugged her shoulders. In a different voice she asked, "Why are you dressed like that?"

"Oh, I'm thinking of going climbing. The volcanoes, you know."

"Oh, no," she said. "I think you better not. Julio!" she called to Puig. He came over to them. "Julio. What is it you said to those people about Popo—Popota? Oh, bother, I can't say it."

Puig laughed. He seemed embarrassed. "Oh, are you telling him about those bad actors?" He looked at Oliver. "I've never had an experience quite like that." His voice dropped as he drew closer, far inside the bounds of North American social distance. "I've never cared for the Russians, you know, but these—"

"Never mind that," Maria Elena interrupted. "What about the volcano?"

"Oh, that." Now Puig looked again at Oliver's climbing garb. "I was joking, trying to get rid of them, I thought I was going to have to throw them out, you know.

All three of them. Particularly nasty piece of work, that blond one."

"Julio!"

"Well, so, I told them: 'Why don't you go look for him at the volcano? Go look at Popo.' The coincidence, bit of a shock seeing you dressed like that!" He laughed uneasily and took a swig of his drink. "Fancy your having the same idea." He left them.

"You see? You can't. What if they are there too?" Maria Elena frowned at Oliver. "You see what a fool Julio is!"

Van Schaik was moving from one group to another, clearly with the intent of making his way to where she was. Oliver turned to present his back to him, not through talking with Maria Elena. Buchanan appeared from the other side. Oliver stepped between him and Maria Elena but Buchanan ducked out of his way.

"Come now, Ted Oliver! You cannot have the lady to yourself!" An angry frown belied the attempted heartiness of his words. Buchanan was staring at Maria Elena as though she were on display, trying to impress her features in his mind forever. Oliver surrendered and turned away. Van Schaik standing mutely, a stricken look on his face as he looked at Maria Elena, had a murderous look for Buchanan.

Drew was talking to Marge but his eyes were on Maria Elena. When Oliver moved toward him he took the opportunity to break off and move at a stately pace toward Maria Elena. At that moment Maria Elena, with the female sense the men lacked, her eyes going to Marge, announced that it was time to leave.

Puig was cordial, taking Oliver by one elbow and leading him aside. "You won't regret this, you chaps," he said. "By Jove"—he had been playing the part of jolly Brit with Buchanan earlier—"you shall come visit. So many friends, Orientales, old times. Maria Elena delighted to be going back. Your wife, Marge. Charming. Might have known."

The three single men began to vie, with transparently

ill temper, to take Maria Elena and Puig home, they having come with Drew. They agreed to Puig's compromise, deciding to meet at Delmonico's for dinner. Puig tried to insist on the Olivers' coming but Oliver pleaded weariness.

When he saw them out, Maria Elena took his hand and squeezed it hard: "Good-bye, Ted." She stood on tiptoe to peck at his cheek. It wasn't proper, ending it like that, but Oliver did not know how to make it right.

Chapter 26

He had eaten and put away most of a pot of black coffee; it was past midnight when Oliver sped through the dark streets of Amecameca, past the shrouded stalls in the market, the one-storied fronts along the way lacking color but clean-lined and sharp-shadowed in the moonlight, the sound of his passing rattling from the narrow way. The road ran straight out of town through blots of shade from the eucalyptus trees, on to the left-hand turn east, the road running straight again from the turn, climbing steadily up the long grade of the lower slope of the mountains. The car shuddered when Oliver forgot the speed bumps by the school beyond the turn. He slowed and sped up again after rumbling over them. The treeless farmland was revealed by the moon, and he could have run between the low adobe buildings of the moonbright pueblito ahead without his lights.

In the rearview mirror he saw the lights of a car hesitating at the turn, a good two or three kilometers behind him now. Oliver sped up, turning off his lights, giving in to caution, maybe to nerves. But why would anyone else be heading this late for the Paso de Cortés? Oliver drove faster, telling himself that he might know the road better than the driver behind him, whether or not the other felt the same prick of urgency that he did.

As the car raced into the shadows of the tall conifers where the road began to climb and twist, Oliver switched the lights on and shifted down for the sharp climbing turns up to the pass, taking the turns with as much dash as he could afford; in the deep shadows, cautious, in the bright straightaways, reckless. No other cars were on the road to slow him, and in twenty minutes he had reached the Paso de Cortés. He paused there to contemplate the sign that directed one left toward Ixtaccíhuatl and right toward Tlamacas and Popocatépetl.

Oliver had always been amused by the signs, posted at regular intervals along Mexican highways, that plead with the Mexican public not to destroy road signs. Was the urge to destroy signs a sullen symptom of resentment of the system? Oliver had a different motive. He drove slowly up to within five feet of the sign and accelerated enough to give the post a sharp crack. The sign disappeared from sight, and Oliver backed the car quickly around. One less aid to navigation. In the open country as he approached timberline he could see the road well enough in the moonlight to switch his lights off again. He began to race around the turns leading to Puerto Tlamacas.

At the top, the striped barrier was across the road. Oliver swore, swerved into the black sand of the parking lot to the left of the road, and hopped out, slamming the car door shut. He snatched his light day pack and ice axe from the back of the car and walked as quickly as he could up the road to the dark *albergue*. The moon was bright on Popo's flanks, a high cloud moving across one quadrant of sky. At the steps to the broad plaza he stopped to listen for the whining of a car climbing the road, for the squeal of brakes at a bad turn. He could hear nothing, and he strode quickly to the door of the *albergue*, jerking at the locked doorknob. He began to pound on the door, adding a few kicks for emphasis.

The door cracked open. It was El Gordito. Oliver slipped in. "Lock the door again," said Oliver. "Is he here?"

El Gordito paused, his eyes darting about, looking at Oliver's clothes, pointing then at his boots. "If you come in, you have to take those off."

"Okay." Oliver put down his gear and sat to unlace his boots, looking up at El Gordito as he did. "He's here, isn't he?"

"You're the one who said it. He told me to tell no one."

"Listen. There's no time to play about. I've got to see him."

El Gordito rubbed his chin. "That wouldn't be to his taste."

"Where is he?"

El Gordito tossed his head over one shoulder. "Back there."

Oliver stared hard at El Gordito, thinking. "There are some people looking for him. They might be coming here. There was a car a couple of miles behind me. I must get to him first."

El Gordito was frowning, hard.

"Let's go!" Oliver got up, strung the boots around his neck by the laces, picked up his pack and ice axe, and took El Gordito's arm. "C'mon, Gordito." He shook the hard-muscled arm. "Let's go."

"He is worried." El Gordito flicked his head behind him. "Three men. One a rubio, very light. The—"

"I know. Maybe they're the ones coming. Understand?" Oliver dropped his hold on El Gordito's arm and they went through another set of doors, turning right to go past the desk of administración. It was cold, the air stale inside. A greasy smell welled from the direction of the café on the left, a sharp whiff of urine came from the lavatory across from administración. El Gordito, padding in tennis shoes, led Oliver up a flight of steps, indicating with a nod of the head a door on the right. "The climbers are all in the dorm. Not there." El Gordito led the way up another short flight of steps past a copper-hooded fireplace in the center of a small lounge. He pushed open a door on the left and led the way into a dark dormitory of empty beds. Moonlight came through the window. Halfway down the dorm a sleeping figure lay wrapped in a blanket on a bare mattress.

El Gordito shook Alexeyev. He sat straight up and clutched at El Gordito, saying something in Russian. He saw Oliver and looked startled. "Why are you here?" He spoke in English.

"Maria Elena told me the three Department Thirteen, Vee, Department Eight—whatever they are these days—went to her apartment today. Pooch—Puig—her husband, told them to try looking for you at the volcanoes."

Alexeyev was sitting up now. "Why would he do that? Did they harm her?"

"No. She wasn't there. I saw her not long ago. She's all right. Listen to me, Alexeyev. When I drove up from Amecameca just now there was another car not far behind me. I wonder—"

El Gordito put a hand up. "Listen! A car coming," he said.

"What did he say?" Alexeyev asked Oliver.

Oliver's heart gave a thump. "A car coming." In his excitement Oliver had spoken in Spanish, and he had to repeat it in English. "A car, he says." By the time he spoke, he and Alexeyev could hear the car too. To El Gordito, Oliver spoke in Spanish. "See what you can see. Don't open for anyone." He went back to English to tell Alexeyev what he had said to El Gordito. "This place is a trap," he added. "We've got to find a way out." He sat down. "To hell with their rules," said Oliver. "I'm not going to be caught here in my stocking feet."

Alexeyev moved quickly across the space between the rows of bunks and switched on a light. Enrique's report on Alexeyev came into Oliver's head. Gentility was a good word for Alexeyev. He had a dignity, a way of bearing himself, a refinement of expression in his face. That face was showing uncertainty just then, staring with narrowed eyes at Oliver, both of them blinking in the sudden light. Oliver, frantically lacing his boots, forgave Alexeyev his suspicion. Alexeyev had been roused from sleep by the CIA station chief—the representative of the main enemy, in KGB terms—who was trying to hustle him into panicky, unthinking action. He would not be rushed. "Now, then, we shall see," Alexeyev was saying.

Oliver stood up to face Alexeyev, wondering how to persuade him to move if the Direct Action team was at the door. If not, fine. They could sit back down and have a chat. Alexeyev's fair, light-boned face was relieved from a crafty narrowness by the wide spacing of the malar bones, an honest span across the cheekbones. That gave him a Russian-enough look. He had a straight nose above a red-brown mustache with its ragged, twisted ends, and under that a strong mouth and chin, gentility joined by a stubborn and insistent look to the tight jaw.

Oliver was older than Alexeyev yet they were not far apart in age, Oliver knew. The frontal baldness, the laced network of fine wrinkles around the eyes, the sag under the chin, were features all more advanced in Oliver. Nothing wrong with Van Schaik, Ivor, Maria Elena, Marge—not a sin, being young. But talking with Drew, say, was so much easier, in a way; so much less to explain. The shared age, despite Alexeyev's suspicion, gave Oliver a rush of confidence.

"I'm going. Better come along." Alexeyev continued to look doubtful as Oliver turned to run down the hall.

"Three of them, all right," said El Gordito. "Going around the parking lot with flashlights."

The plates on Oliver's car—a dead giveaway. Whether or not the Direct Action team had a record of his license number, the diplomatic plate alone would be enough to excite them. Furthermore, his own radiator would be hot, if they had the wit to check it.

Oliver hurried toward the stairs to warn Alexeyev and saw him, parka halfway on, coming down the hall, pack over one shoulder, an ice axe showing over the top. Oliver quickly told him what El Gordito had reported.

"Where is your car?" Oliver asked.

"Just outside," said Alexeyev curtly. They walked together to where El Gordito stood. "Listen, we have to get out of here." Oliver told El Gordito, then translated for Alexeyev. "I'll tell him to slow them down, throw them off the scent."

"Not so fast," said Alexeyev. He took El Gordito by the arm and went to the door. Oliver came behind, breathing heavily. A real waste of time—we gotta get outta here. Alexeyev stood with El Gordito as he cracked the door open and looked from the darkness past the moonlit plaza to the parking area. He whirled around without speaking and gave a curt nod to Oliver. Oliver gave the same quick nod to El Gordito, who pulled the door quietly shut, motioned with his head, and walked quickly toward the café. He pointed to the kitchen, the open space behind and half a flight below the bar. "Get down here. Once they get inside I'll send them to the dormitory where the climbers are and cut off the electricity. There are some twenty people in there." El Gordito's small eyes glittered in anticipation. "The door to the courtyard is in the back, there." He hurried off. In the kitchen the smell of grease was stronger, rancidly blending with the scent of dirty dish towels.

The banging on the door started. They could hear El Gordito rushing back, hissing for them. "They are doing something to the cars. The car they came in is sitting across the road below the barrier. One of them remains there beside it."

Oliver translated for Alexeyev. Oliver gestured with his head toward the kitchen door. The banging on the front door was louder now. Shouting too—unintelligible. Alexeyev nodded vehemently several times, confirming, Oliver assumed, that it was the KGB team. Sleepy voices were rising from the near dormitory, protesting the noise. Oliver looked at his watch. One twenty-five. No one else would be getting up to climb this early.

When El Gordito got around to opening the main door, Oliver and Alexeyev were standing at the door on the other side of the kitchen. Their bodies tensed when they heard footsteps running their way. A voice called out in Russian and the steps hurried back the other way. Oliver could sense Alexeyev relaxing. One of the Russians—that would be the Azerbaijani, according to Maria Elena—was shouting bad Spanish at El Gordito.

"*Mande?*" El Gordito kept saying, pretending not to understand. Perhaps he didn't. When the angry Russian voices echoed farther away in the hall, Oliver and Alexeyev slipped out the kitchen door into the moonlit yard, Oliver closing the door tight behind them. They still could hear shouting inside the *albergue*.

Oliver and Alexeyev looked around the fenced yard, garbage cans stinking in one corner, the water truck parked by the gate. Crouching, they ran quickly out of the yard, going right to pass under the back side of the *albergue* rather than to expose themselves on the plaza in front, where the watcher by the car would see them. Oliver led the way, dropping down the slope into the scattered tall pines just below the lodge, running from one shadow to the next, moving always toward the volcano, away from the lodge. Alexeyev followed, both of them slipping in the sand, feeling vivid in the moonlight, spurred on by the noise of the angry voices inside the lodge above. Oliver kept below and to the left of the usual path, stopping short-breathed after their panicky, tumbling run.

They huddled in the shadow of a pine. A peculiar sound came from Alexeyev above their frenzied breathing, a sobbing. But Alexeyev was laughing. "The scene inside—the idiots will be turning the place upside down! Those poor climbers!"

They they saw a light flood the plaza so that the lodge above them was backlit in silhouette. "Down this slope." Alexeyev was pointing with his head. "There is a road that leads to Puebla."

Oliver quickly nodded. "That's right. But I've been down there. Yes, there is a road, but right below here," he whispered, "there are steep cliffs, rough country. In the dark, it's difficult. Twist your ankle and—and once on the road the country's quite open. They could run us down like animals there. It's a trap, that way. We'd better go up."

"If we go up, we should go by the Ventorrillo, no?" asked Alexeyev. "Do you know the route?"

"Well. But why that way?"

"From the looks of it, there's good cover in the rocks there."

"Have you a weapon?"

"No, have you?"

"No," said Oliver, biting his lip. "What good is cover, then? They can still hunt us down in the rocks when daylight comes. Do you remember the terrain?"

"Yes."

"Well." Oliver let out a deep breath. He was breathing easier after the rest stop. "If you recall, in this moonlight they might see us if we take the path to the right for the Ventorrillo."

Alexeyev nodded in agreement. "What do you suggest, then?"

Any time for further discussion was taken from them. A light was playing about the fenced yard and a figure came out the door to shine the light down the slope in the direction in which they had fled. The man turned to go back inside, shouting something in Russian. Alexeyev jerked his head at Oliver and ran for the next patch of shadows, Oliver casting one glance over his shoulder toward the lodge and then running after Alexeyev. A high mackerel cloud was moving across the moon, and the valley would darken, then go light again, then dark, the oncoming cloud thicker and heavier. The obstacle light at the microwave station high on the pinnacle behind them was glowing red. Oliver glanced when he could at the darkening of the racing moon, a stroke of luck. But the dark made the going that much more difficult in their rushes from one patch of cover to another, so they went tripping over clumps of grass, slowed by having to keep in the low places, lest the moon burst forth like a star shell to reveal them naked in the open. The track to Las Cruces was easy enough to follow by day, an undulating route up to the left, a long traverse south-southeast across Popo's northern flank, through sand, occasional scrambles across nests of rock along the way, and some nasty, steep pitches.

But there was nothing easy about it, when they reached it, dangerously dark when heavier clouds began moving across the face of the moon. At the rocky spots they lurched and swore, taking the occasional nasty fall, feet catching in the crevices. Oliver, rubbing the kneecap he had nicked against a sharp rock, thought of the flashlight he had forgotten to pack. He would not have dared to show it, a beacon on the dark of Popo's slope.

For the first time, as they stopped, Oliver was aware of the cold. Inside, he was sweating, his long underwear wet under the arms, around his waist, soaking in the small of his back. He looked back and whispered, needlessly enough, to Alexeyev. A light was playing on the trail leading up toward El Castillo. As they stood breathing heavily, watching it, another light showed below that, behind them on the Las Cruces route.

"Good," breathed Alexeyev. "They've split up. Let them blunder about."

"Look," said Oliver. "Once we get to Las Cruces they can't see us behind that shoulder until they get there themselves."

"And what then? Lead them up to the crater, around the top of the volcano? And around and around again?" Alexeyev laughed.

"Claustrophobia," said Oliver, his lips pulled back from this teeth in a grin. He shivered. Alexeyev did not understand at first, and Oliver explained.

"But not here in the open, in the mountains."

"I know," said Oliver. "All the same, open or not, we're in a trap. Maybe, when they don't see us, they'll give up."

"Not these lads, Oliver."

"Why are they after you?"

"Because of Marucha. Ordered home, you see. They've got the wind up now."

Oliver took a deep breath, trying to take nourishment from the thin air for his anguished lungs. "We'd better move on."

Chapter 27

Two-and-a-half silent, agonizing hours after that conversation they were at the shoulder before Las Cruces. Miles away and far below them a filmy layer of smog filtered the lights in the valley of Mexico. Oliver knew his sight took in the place—although he could not mark it—where Marge and the children slept. She might be turning now, feeling for him, to be reminded by the empty place in bed that he was not beside her as he should be.

Alexeyev stood looking the other way, at the nearer lights spread like a bright rug below their feet in the valley of Puebla. They had crunched and slid through pockets of snow along the route, but now it was heavy on the ground, hard, melted in the noon sun, refrozen by the night. They clambered up the slope toward the first white cross to the ruined hut, collapsing against a pile of rocks, panting from the exertion, from the effort of dragging oxygen from the thin and selfish air.

"God, what a headache!" said Oliver at last. "Water?" He was pulling a bottle from his pack.

Alexeyev took a swig, nodding his thanks, handing it back.

"Ivor Buchanan," said Oliver.

"Ivor, yes. A continuing—what do you call it?—dialogue. Since my days in London. Jolly patient, Ivor. They don't rush it as you Americans do, Oliver."

"Ted."

"Ah, yes. And Genya. Early in the training we learn

about the Americans and their first names. Nicknames even more desirable."

"Talk about nerves of steel. How did you live with it? One leak and—"

"Ivor told me that you saw us together. A shock, that. Rotten, bad luck. London is angry with Ivor. But inevitably such affairs have a limited life."

Oliver had been ripping with irritation at the corner of a small, tightly sealed packet. "Ah. An aspirin?"

"Thank you. But—together with other reasons for indecision—the U.K.'s too bloody small. Oh, yes, I grant you, the highlands, the Isle of Skye, all that. A Russian stands out. Where do you go to ground? That's the problem." Alexeyev sneezed once from the aspirin. "Now, the truth, if you please. Most important. Did you run Marucha at me?"

"Certainly not! She came to Mexico on her own—"

"I hoped not. It would have been cruel. You avoid thinking of the hurt in these maneuvers when you are the author. When you are instead the object, it pierces the heart. Her coming seemed too inappropriate to be a coincidence. I was instructed to investigate, to see if the plan had been compromised—if you people had sent her. It seemed to me, and so I reported, that indeed she was seeking the truth of her brother's murder. She had been told it was your doing, according to plan, but she had difficulty accepting that." Alexeyev looked carefully into Oliver's eyes. "She remains fond of you, are you aware of that?"

"Umm." Oliver asked instead, "What is this plan?"

"Ah," said Alexeyev. "No harm in telling you now. Plan Ortiz. You see, with the Tupamaros executing you in Mexico, in revenge for the death of the brother, Freddie, another CIA crime is exposed. They can add that in, run through the whole blasted litany again and again."

"Things begin to make sense, then. But how are you involved?"

"Oh, the concept was ours from the beginning. Let me explain. The plan—Plan Ortiz—was excellent—on paper, do you say?—but faulty in that it did not allow for blunders in execution by the Tupamaros."

"They didn't show much flexibility the other day—couldn't seem to adapt to the unusual. Of course, if I had not been prepared—"

"Really! There was a leak, then. A compromise."

"No, I don't think in the way you mean. I can explain but, first, go on, Genya."

"Very well. It was proposed, for fear of their blundering, that our own Direct Action people take care of the matter, pretending that the Tupamaros had 'executed' you, the Tupamaros announcing afterward that you had been 'tried' and found guilty in absentia. All the usual forms observed. It was argued in opposition that there was no precedent whatsoever for the KGB carrying out Direct Action tasks—the wet stuff—on the behalf of a fraternal movement. Not that the Tupamaros are that, exactly. The KGB was simply using them, the plan offering benefits to both—a propaganda coup for the Tupamaros, echoing through the Americas, and further denigration of the CIA for the KGB. In any event, 'hands off' was the decision, reached at Politburo level. Give the Tupamaros the plan. If they can carry it out, good. If they blunder, the KGB hand is not seen." Alexeyev laughed: "And when it came to the moment, they blundered, didn't they?"

"Do you know that they grabbed one of the embassy officers in Montevideo, back in those days, clubbed him in the head, tied him up, threw him in the back of a pickup truck, and hopped in front, driving off, leaving him bleeding in the back. Tough customer. He wasn't having any of that and he squirmed around and managed to hurl himself out of the truck into the road. They drove right off without him."

"Yes, exactly that example was put forward to argue for our people doing the job," said Alexeyev. "And they killed that officer, Mitrione, needlessly, stupidly."

"They claimed he was a CIA officer—or pretended to believe he was."

"We—the KGB—knew he was not, of course. Where are you going?"

"A little reconnaissance, I think," said Oliver, reaching for the rock beside him, hauling himself to his feet. He walked down the knob of Las Cruces to move carefully to the edge of the shoulder that hid the trail they had followed. Oliver turned to see Alexeyev slumped, his eyes closed.

The aspirin had quieted the pounding right behind Oliver's eyes. Heat was leaving his body and the damp places growing cold. So, Ivor had been working away on Alexeyev all along. That's good. Better that than the opposite. He reached the shoulder, peered over carefully, although sure enough he would not be seen, stood looking, took a deep breath, let it out, turning then to walk back to where Alexeyev was dozing. Cool customer. Alexeyev looked up when Oliver came clambering over the rocks, setting shards to rattling against each other.

"How do you feel about starting up again?" Oliver asked.

"About the way you do. See anything?"

"Lights down the trail, a good way back. I think we should try to keep above them."

"Postpone the inevitable—is that how you put it?"

"Well, let's give time a chance, some opportunity. Those may be other climbers. Or others may come along."

"If the weather turns bad, who will be climbing? Those clouds"—Alexeyev was looking up—"are moving in. At home I would say snow." Oliver looked up to see a new cloud mass moving darkly, slowly, but with firmness, coming at them, above them, along Popocatépetl's slope.

"I hope you have crampons," said Oliver. Alexeyev reached into his pack. "It's solid ice above here. In places the black sand blows over it and you think it's safe and it isn't. We have to be careful farther up. Chunks of rock break loose and come bouncing down the glacier."

Oliver had his gloves off and was pulling, cold-fingered, the crampons from his pack. The points stubbornly clung together, and when they came apart, he made a laborious job of untangling the straps. Alexeyev was cursing over his as well.

"How did you get in trouble over Maria Elena?"

"I reported that she was investigating the death of her brother, that the Tupamaros had told her in Montevideo that you were responsible but that she was not sure, came here to see you, to learn the truth. I reported that she was questioning her husband, questioning me and Ivor Buchanan. Panic! The plan would be compromised. I was ordered to break off with her."

Oliver was putting the straps through the eyelets on the crampons with stiff fingers. It was hard to breathe, bent over as he was, shutting the air from his chest, and he leaned back to take a deep breath. "And you did not."

Alexeyev, sitting next to him, was struggling, too, with his. "I kept on seeing her. At that point I could not help myself. Two things happened. The security people found out I was seeing her. And just the other day, I told her the truth about Plan Ortiz. Stupid of me. Once the truth gets out, you see, Oliver, the plan will have to be abandoned."

"Good. Glad to hear it."

"Precisely. Good for you. They can hardly afford to kill you once the plan is exposed. It would even be in their interest to keep you alive. But before then, if they think that Marucha knows, that I have told her, that you know, too, then—" Alexeyev did not finish.

There was no point in telling Alexeyev that he should not have told her. Alexeyev knew that for himself. Much like the effect of altitude, what love does to judgment. Oliver stood up, wiggled his boots to test the tightness of the crampon straps, remembering the agony of having to stop on the steep ice to redo the straps. "Be sure they're tight, Genya. Getting light over there," Oliver added, looking east toward Puebla. He had felt safe, falsely safe, in the dark. Once it was light they would stand out on the ice like a pair of black flies on a white saucer. Oliver took the lead, planting the point of his ice axe in the snow and leaning on it for a weak moment, slightly dizzy on starting.

There were long gaps in their talk as they climbed. Oliver could not tell whether the pauses were one or three or five minutes long between the patches of talk. Nor did he know how long the thoughts in his own head—started by Alexeyev's revelations—how long those thoughts lasted. He went over the thoughts more than once, rotating them in his mind. The mixture of fatigue and altitude were beginning to empty his mind, like pouring water out of a pitcher.

The crampons were a necessity. Where there was no ice to be seen on the surface, it lay in patches under rotten snow. Oliver slipped occasionally even when he stamped the sharp points to grip the steep surface below his boot soles, lifting each foot carefully, a slow climber's pace. He was not dizzy, precisely; if he were required to debrief himself on his condition—lightheaded, rather, to be precise. Precise, indeed!

"Something else: Galina," said Oliver, at one point. "That's nowhere, Genya. Harley Drew won't go in after her. We wouldn't let him even if he would. Only cruel, as you said. If she's alive, why not let her out?"

"Oh, she's alive. I don't arrange these things, Oliver. But you should know they are quite prepared to let her out."

"So, she's one of you?"

Alexeyev stopped, bending tiredly, leaning over his ice axe.

"Not exactly. Not an officer, I mean. An agent. Drew's file was reactivated."

Better I tell Drew she's dead, thought Oliver to himself.

The sea of clouds was flushed a faint pink, the rising sun coming up somewhere beyond and below that flat level of clouds. In the east the frosting-covered peak of Orizaba thrust above the clouds. Off to one side, lower, but nearer them, to their left, the dark peak of Malinche was swimming in the clouds. Clouds were moving fast across Popo's crater now, windborne, not far above their heads, rushing east toward the sun. Oliver and Alexeyev could not be more than five or six hundred meters below the crater—straight-up meters, that is—more meters than that along the hypotenuse, if you had the time it would take to figure that out.

"The department eight people, the Direct Action boys, their specialty is accidents." Alexeyev gave it the British pronunciation. *Speciálity.* "A climbing accident, wouldn't you think?" Alexeyev said this with the detachment of a cold-faced doctor giving a patient the dread diagnosis.

"What is the point of that remark?" Oliver was tiredly angry, Alexeyev's flippancy having sent a cold rush through his body.

"I've been thinking. If something were to happen to you up here, how might they adapt Plan Ortiz to achieve their end?"

Oliver did not like being singled out. "What about you?"

"Oh, they want me home. The matter of Marucha." Then Alexeyev spoke even more slowly, less from fatigue than from deliberation. "That message you sent when you saw Ivor with me. Now, if there were a leak. Or, if not the message itself—any leak. Then they would want me even more urgently. A KGB interrogation discovers the truth in short order. One confesses also to what is not true—whatever the interrogators want."

Oliver had no comment to make on that. For a moment, then, he could not remember who it was he was climbing with, and after he reminded himself that it was Alexeyev, he could not remember what Alexeyev looked like. He could only recall Buchanan's face and he knew that to be incorrect. Oliver pressed the sharp heel of his ice axe into the glacier and paused clumsily to turn to stare at Alexeyev, getting the features pressed back into his memory.

Drops of water on Alexeyev's mustache. You'd think they'd be frozen. He looked past Alexeyev—who was staring back at Oliver—to the crosses, the pile of rocks against which they had sat, leaning on them, the ruined hut, well below them, but disappointingly close in the clear air. Oliver had thought they would be farther above them—that they deserved to be farther after that steady, plodding effort. Time was rolling right along, and time and distance covered were out of sync: effort expended did not come out equally in distance over the ground.

"Know what a snub dodecahedron is?"

"No," said Oliver, thinking he might have invented the question himself, it coming along so soon after he had been puzzling over the length of their hypotenuse.

"Exact description eludes me," said Alexeyev. "Figure in solid geometry, a solid with faces of pentagons, triangles, complex, intricate, containing within itself the dodecahedron, an icosahedron as well. Moscow Center's genius at deception operations was genius at mathematics too. His last effort was suggested by the death of Freddie Ortiz. Plan Ortiz.

"Vladimir Ivanovich began career in Second Chief Directorate, working against foreigners in Moscow. Specialized in tourists, assuming the tourist to be provocateur, saboteur, wrecker. Moscow, a technological maze, every corner an observation post, behind each window surveillance personnel, binoculars, camera, radio. On the street, teams on foot, on the buses, cars and vans, accosting the tourist on the street: 'Have you chewing gum? American cigarettes? T-shirts?' "

"Blackmarket rubles?" added Oliver. "Where does Plan Ortiz—"

"Coming to that. Immense resources devoted to surveillance and entrapment of foreigners, but nothing, Oliver, compared with KGB resources used against Soviet people. Think of KGB counterintelligence abroad as mere geographical extension of KGB at home, Plan Ortiz as an exotic flowering of deception practiced daily on Soviet citizens. Vladimir Ivanovich's talent for deception led him to get his own shop, a free hand inside Department A."

"Covert Action and Deception."

"Exactly. But Vladimir Ivanovich was going quietly mad. Mind you, the work of the Second Chief Directorate itself is an institutional form of paranoia. Everyone a potential spy or wrecker, most of all the foreigner. Translate counterintelligence, security mechanism of city of Moscow to the whole earth. A logical progression, no?

"Brilliant Plan Ortiz comes to Politburo for approval. Heavy political implications. But Vladimir Ivanovich noticeably queer. Colleagues uneasy. He insisting essential if invisible shape of earth not oblate spheroid at all but snub dodecahedron. KGB to be represented with counterintelligence residency at each vertex of the solid—you have a pentagon, four triangles at each extremity. Some eighty additional triangles—"

"I can't comprehend it," said Oliver. They had stopped and were looking back toward Las Cruces. There was no one in sight. The world had a grayness about it, even the ice a dull no-color, subdued. There was an ache behind Oliver's eyes. He fished from his pack a pair of goggles with leather blinders on either side of the dark lenses. "Better put yours on, Genya. Brighter than you think. Snow-blind. Whiteout."

"Good suggestion, Oliver. Vladimir Ivanovich plotted these points on earth's surface, like an early navigator. Popped up in strange places. Atlas Mountains, Himalayas near Everest, Antarctica—proving Antarctica belongs Soviet Union according to him—the Med, Timor Sea, Adriatic off Dubrovnik, Mexico outside San Cristobal de las Casas, your state of Idaho near Moscow, that's why I remember—"

"What about Freddie Ortiz?"

"Mad but brilliant elevation of a nobody, Freddie Ortiz—our dear Marucha's brother, yes—but nobody. Handsome, a small reputation at football—"

"Rugby."

"Rugby. Yet raw material for lasting symbol. Apotheosis of Freddie Ortiz. Ah!" exclaimed Alexeyev, so that Oliver turned to look at him. "Bad luck, Oliver. There's the first of them. Has a radio. He'll be calling the others in."

Oliver's heart had been working hard enough. Now it went faster, skipped a few beats, thumped right along, fast again. He studied the slender figure below, half lit on the one side by the early light from the east. The man wore a down jacket, a navy blue watch cap, blue jeans, running shoes. He was looking up at them, holding a black walkie-talkie by his head. He took the radio from his face and shouted to them, waving.

Alexeyev was regarding the figure below. "He wants us to come down. What do you say, Oliver?"

Chapter 28

The two officers in charge of their respective countries' intelligence work in Mexico leaned on their ice axes, silent, looking down at the man below. He shouted to them again. "I shall not answer him," muttered Alexeyev. The man turned to go back down the trail.

"Wants to be sure the others see him," said Oliver. The man would have been out of sight of the others, who were over the shoulder by Las Cruces.

"Trouble with the radio reception, more likely."

The Vibram soles of Oliver's boots had left their international seal next to Alexeyev's in black sand a thousand feet below. Here, their tracks were punctuated alike by the points of their crampons. Now, standing together, they could have been—from a good distance—a pair of the most dully matter-of-fact flat-voiced North American students, down at spring break to race up another mountain, add it to their list.

The quality of the moment was dreamlike. Watching the man leave, the conversation with Alexeyev seemed natural enough—if one admitted the outlandish—left room for free verse, accepted the logic that led them to be standing so irrationally together. As though, thought Oliver—groping to analyze how he felt—as though he held in his hand an exhilarating flute of champagne, brut, instead of his ice axe, set a draft of it to bubbling in the cortex of his brain, shared a toast with Alexeyev. "By God, Genya, do you know?—I've been thinking just now.

In all my career, in all my life, I've not spent a time quite like this. Our talk. The things I've learned—what you've told me!"

Alexeyev was watching the figure of the man going over the shoulder before he disappeared on the long slope leading back to Tlamacas. He turned to look at Oliver. "Yes, Oliver. I have enjoyed it, too, an experience I shall never forget. Freer than with Ivor, somehow. I shall not forget you nor shall I forget Marucha." As he turned away, looking up the slope above them, he said, "I have much in my mind that the chances of your passing on to anyone else what we have said together today are very small indeed. Well, we had better go on, had we not?"

Alexeyev wanted to explain something—was he talking to Oliver or to himself?—as they labored on the steep slope of the glacier. He spoke of Lenin and the killing off of class enemies—whoever stood in the way, that is—and of Stalin following with his own great crimes. Then he went back to talking of Vladimir Ivanovich, of how he looked at the killings professionally, thought that Lenin had been arbitrary in his killings where Stalin had shown occasional flashes of imagination, if not brilliance, early on, anyway. Stalin did well to have Kirov killed and then to blame Kirov's murder on Stalin's own rivals, arranging thus their deaths too. That had meaning. But the tens of hundreds of thousands of simple farmers—they weren't kulaks, at all—their wives, their children, their livestock, the millions of almost indiscriminate deaths by bullet or by disease in the camps—the shots in the head in the cellars of the old Lubianka—that gave such pleasure to Stalin, with few exceptions all those deaths lacked the redeeming virtue of art, appealing only to sadists, failing in symmetry.

For Vladimir Ivanovich symmetry was the feature of the well-ordered plan: Plan Ortiz, for example. Freddie's death was a windfall, an opportunity that could not be wasted. "Add your death, Oliver—to complete the picture, like bookends, a pair of caryatids supporting a thesis. There's your justice. There you are—Tupamaro peace and justice." Alexeyev gave Oliver a lopsided smile.

"Freddie Ortiz, a martyr now—a new symbol. A new Comandante Ernesto 'Che' Guevara!" Alexeyev turned about to wave his ice axe in the air, as though addressing the mob that might have thronged the slopes below them. "What Horst Wessel was to the Nazis! Hans Beimler, Kommissar, in Spain! In the best tradition, Oliver"—he went back to walking—"of Soviet history, one long tale of deception. History dictated by assassins to propagandists."

"You people study the Trust, I know, the deception that destroyed the first great opposition in the twenties. Familiar because your services were so thoroughly deceived—so completely taken in—so ready to believe, to rush in. Penetration! Manipulation! Deception! Destruction! Have the Western intelligence services no memory? Taken in by the Trust—"

Oliver was not too tired to show irritation. "Genya! We did not exist in the Twenties, how could we—?"

"But your colleagues—it is no secret that the British and the French were swindled by the Trust and at the same time by Sindikat I, Oliver. Then Sindikat II. Anti-Bolshevik opposition was destroyed!"

"But, Genya, we—"

"And again after the Second War the Polish Home Army Inside was destroyed—by the same manipulation of your people as in the Trust and Sindikat. Impossible without your willingness to be deceived, to rush in. No patience! No discretion! We need only sit back and wait. And the British of all peoples should know! The Black Legend."

As Alexeyev turned to him, Oliver saw that Alexeyev's breath was now frozen on his mustache. "The Leyenda Negra," nodded Oliver. "Elizabeth's propaganda against Philip the Second. The tales of Spain's cruelty and savagery, de Las Casas and the Destruction of the Indies—"

"The grand calumny, Oliver! Down to this day! How

Vladimir Ivanovich admired the English for that, Oliver!" In his excitement, Alexeyev raised the gloved hand with his ice axe to gesture. He slipped and fell with a clatter, sliding, grabbing at Oliver's ankles. Oliver threw himself flat, smashing his ice axe into the glacier. Grasping the haft with both hands he lurched to his knees, put a hand out to Alexeyev, turned to sit with his crampons holding him.

"Oughta brought rope," said Oliver.

"The Mexican—what do you call him?"

"Gordito. Means 'Little Fatty.' "

"One day he said you need no rope here."

"Well, you don't ordinarily. Long as you have crampons. Today is different."

"Quite."

Together they struggled to their feet. The three men were working their way up the slope in line abreast, like skirmishers. They slipped often on the thirty-degree slope, bending to grasp at the ice with gloved hands. Their running shoes were not useful but they kept coming on with an athletic way of moving. When the blond leader slipped the other two were rigid, watching him. A moment later the dark one slipped and the leader and the stocky one laughed, mocking him.

Alexeyev had been right about the weather. A gust of wind brought a quick swirl of snow around them. The wind stopped then but the snow fell heavily.

"Could have used this an hour ago," said Oliver.

Alexeyev started to speak but instead he exclaimed loudly in Russian and sat down.

"What is it?" asked Oliver, his brow crinkled, looking from Alexeyev back to the approach of the KGB team.

"I don't know what you call it—" His lips were pulled back over his teeth, his hands grasping one calf.

"A cramp?"

"Yes, yes. Most painful." He bared his teeth and put his head down. "Don't wait. Get along with you."

Oliver would like to think it was altruism. He knew it for fatigue. He could not go on. "I'm staying here."

"Ted. I assure you. You have no chance with these gentry."

"Who's that?" Oliver lifted his goggles.

"The guide, Small Fatty," said Alexeyev. "What is he doing?"

El Gordito was hopping nimbly along the trail near Las Cruces, singing as he came—especially annoying, the singing, thought Oliver, when he himself had barely the breath to talk. El Gordito sang in a loud but not a tuneful voice. He had a coil of rope over one shoulder. He threw the rope down on getting to Las Cruces and sat down on the rock Alexeyev and Oliver had been leaning against earlier. He was putting on crampons, a lot more quickly than Alexeyev and Oliver had, still singing.

Fool! thought Oliver, sitting there singing, the rest of us in a grim, slow motion chase on the icy slopes of Popocatépetl—sky and mountain as dark as death, and the fool sitting there, singing.

The three Russians had stopped to watch El Gordito, and the sound of their voices as they called back and forth to each other drifted up to Oliver's ears. One of the Russians shouted at El Gordito—probably telling him to shut up. Good. Shut up, Gordito.

El Gordito began to climb toward the three Russians. He was quick on the ice, his short legs pumping away, and when he was some twenty feet below them he stopped and held out an arm with the rope on it. The tall blond one—the team leader—was saying something in Russian to the others.

"They're talking about—he said they should use the rope," said Alexeyev. "I wonder—" The blond man turned and began to move down sideways, arms out for balance, toward El Gordito, who came up the slope to meet him, snowflakes beginning to stick to his brown wool hat. Oliver could hear El Gordito's crampons biting at the ice.

When the Russian reached him, El Gordito knotted the rope about the other's waist, tugged at the knot to test it, motioned for the other two to join them. Small sounds were close in the hush of falling snow. It formed an elliptical room, the two groups of men within the tilted oval, Oliver and Alexeyev in the high end, the Soviets and El Gordito below, beyond them all the swirling white walls.

"How did they get around him so quickly? Money, I suppose," said Alexeyev.

El Gordito was putting a knot in the rope around the waist of the third man. "I don't get it," said Oliver.

"They're thanking him," said Alexeyev. "Told him to go. He'd better be going if he knows what's good for him. No witnesses wanted for this next bit."

El Gordito started back down the mountain and the three Russians started up. El Gordito stopped to turn around to call out something Oliver could not hear, shaking his fist in the air, and the short, stocky Russian pulled out a pistol and waved it at El Gordito. The Mexican whirled about and began to clamber quickly down to Las Cruces. The tall, blond leader shouted something to the stocky one and he put the pistol away. El Gordito had stopped just above Las Cruces, nearly hidden at times by the falling snow.

Alexeyev was sitting, nursing his leg with one hand. He had put his goggles up on his forehead to watch the three men come up, half crouching on the steep slope, arms swinging. They moved no more than eight or ten feet apart, the rope that connected them dragging loose on the ice of the slope.

Oliver was standing, watching them advance, holding his ice axe upside down—reversed arms, as though standing in a funeral parade. He had the lanyard of the axe around his right wrist, the point of the haft sharp in his gloved palm, the axe head resting on the toes of his boots. His hands were grasping the haft of the axe, relaxing the grip, tightening again, over and over. Oliver stood firm, his crampons dug in, his knees trembling with fatigue, taking deep, slow breaths to keep his head clear, looking from one to the other of the three men as they came up in line to where Alexeyev sat and Oliver stood.

A BLACK LEGEND

The blond one was walking slowly toward Oliver, cold blue eyes moving from Alexeyev to Oliver and back. He was talking to Alexeyev, his eyes on Oliver. Behind his dark goggles, Oliver's eyes were going from one to the other of the three professionals of department eight, the Direct Action team. The thin one in the watch cap had heavy, dark brows and olive skin—the Azerbaijani. He was examining Oliver with an impersonal stare, a faint curiosity in his eyes. The stocky Ukrainian with the broad face—the one who had pulled the pistol on El Gordito—was standing above the seated Alexeyev, looking down at him—a careful look, showing Alexeyev the respect due a senior officer. He happened to glance over at Oliver at that moment. He had an opaque expression on his face, as detached and clinical as a dentist's assistant.

The blond one spoke to Oliver. Alexeyev translated. "He wants you to take off your crampons, Oliver. Wants your ice axe."

"Oliver," repeated the blond one, giving Alexeyev a half grin.

When Oliver shook his head in a quick negative, the blond one came to stand in front of Oliver, looking at him but talking again to Alexeyev. Suddenly Alexeyev exclaimed, his head snapping back as abruptly as if he had been hit in the face. He moaned, looking up at Oliver, his lips drawn back in pain. "Oliver!" Alexeyev shook his head from side to side. "He says they shot Marucha and Puig last night." Alexeyev was shouting at the blond one in Russian.

The stocky one had an embarrassed look on his face. The blond team leader barked at Alexeyev, made a brutal gesture with one hand. Alexeyev stared back at him with bloodshot eyes, his head still moving from side to side. The blond one had a pistol in his hand and there was a fixed grin on his face as he looked at Oliver. His pale eyes were searching about Oliver's head, as though measuring him. He motioned quickly with the pistol.

Alexeyev called out something in Russian in a high, hoarse voice, and the pale blue eyes flicked to Alexeyev, an impatient frown on the pale face, the lips drawn back, the grin beginning to fade. He must have sensed Oliver's movement but his eyes did not move fast enough to see the head of the axe swinging up from the ground where it had been waiting, poised in Oliver's sudden hands. All the strength left in Oliver's body was in that arc to the flat of the throat beneath that insolent grin. The axe caught the team leader with a loud crunch square below the chin and his head snapped back with Oliver's follow-through, the impact jarring Oliver himself so hard that his wool cap popped off his head.

Alexeyev, sitting, dashed his axe to one side, catching the outside of the knee of the Ukrainian so that it buckled beneath him. He swayed and fell hard on his side to the ice as the blond one's body somersaulted backward through the air. The stocky one's hands were scrabbling at the ice as the rope yanked at his waist, sending him clattering after the other. The dark one still stood for another long second, knees bent for purchase on the ice, feet slipping, fingers reaching to fumble at the knot around his waist. The jerk on the rope pulled a cough from his wide mouth and he went backward through the air, arms flailing.

Above Las Cruces El Gordito ran to one side as the three bodies spun toward him, gathering speed, hurtling down the slope. El Gordito flashed one look behind him, raised his ice axe high, plunged it into the glacier, flopping head down, hanging onto the shaft as Oliver himself had done minutes ago.

One of the forms, plunging ahead of the others, slithered past El Gordito, did a somersault in the air and crashed into the pile of rocks at Las Cruces. Another body was yanked after it to smash into the ruined hut. The rope held tight to pull the cartwheeling third man in an arc so that he swept on past Las Cruces, snapped the whip, his body sliding like a pendulum to hang limp on the ice below Las Cruces.

The first to move was El Gordito. He pulled himself erect and came slowly up the slope to Oliver and Alexeyev. Helping Alexeyev to his feet, he put one of Alexeyev's arms around his neck, Oliver taking the other. Through the falling snow the two of them swayed slowly down past Las Cruces, Alexeyev hopping on one leg between them, starting the long walk back.

Postscript

Gennadi Alexeyev's book, *Black Legends*, is more than an exposure of Plan Ortiz. Alexeyev is not merely criticizing what now can be seen as the weaknesses of that plan. Alexeyev argues that most such plans fall short of success to a greater or a lesser extent. And those that do work through to a conclusion, he argues, are morally insulting, no matter their seeming success.

Alexeyev has separated into categories the various kinds of deception he discusses. He analyzes the reasons for failures, giving examples of incompetence of execution, of misunderstandings of the elegance of plans on the part of those who must carry them out. It is not their fault alone. The originator of the plan himself—sitting in a room far from the arena where the game will be played—does not see that mistakes in execution are as integral to the plan as is the aesthetic design he imagines. That part is a textbook, really, on covert action in general and on the practice of deception in particular.

But that is not the major point Alexeyev wants to make. He goes further. Deception, these tricky plans, these diabolical plots, the false propaganda, the black legends, should fail, deserve to fail, for their successes lead to great harm, not only to the intended victims but to all humanity. Truth is the chief victim and the crime is the distortion of history.

He writes of this evil in one of those long-winded, philosophical, very Russian, passages. You can skip most of that. The factual parts are interesting. Among his examples is the senseless crime committed by the Direct Action team that night in Mexico City.

It was a natural mistake—mistakes usually are, seen in retrospect. When the party left the Olivers for Delmonico's, Puig made some excuse—it didn't fool Maria Elena for a minute—and went off to say farewell to his mistress, the blond graduate student in anthropology, at a bar in Polanco called, appropriately enough, Our Last Goodbye. When Puig came back from the men's room, the blond team leader—he who would die on Popocatépetl a few hours later—began firing. He particularly enjoyed the chase when its culmination awarded him another death. Puig dived under the table, blood streaming from a light scalp wound. Maria Elena may have been correct in saying that the little graduate student did not actually look much like her, but the resemblance was strong enough to cause her death.

The team leader followed instructions, tossing the Browning automatic pistol to the floor by the dying woman. The pistol had been stolen from the car of a CIA officer in Dar Es Salaam two months before. The team leader did not know why it was important that he do this, not having been briefed on Plan Ortiz. All he knew was that day's cable from Moscow ordering these deaths and Oliver's.

Had it been considered worthwhile to go through with the plan, the Federal Judicial Police of Mexico would have been given the evidence that the pistol was a CIA weapon. And had they not revealed this information, it would have been leaked to the friendly press.

Plan Ortiz sputtered out to its messy end but the truth still had to be concealed, the truth that Maria Elena had learned from Alexeyev. The sequence of deaths that began with Freddie Ortiz did not end with the mysterious murder of the graduate student from Kankakee, Illinois, nor with the climbing accident on Popocatépetl that took the lives of three Russian visitors to Mexico who appeared impulsively to have rushed up the dangerous slopes without so much as a guide.

The truth is that Freddie Ortiz, in his time, had become far too popular a revolutionary figure for the Communist Party of Uruguay to tolerate. The zeal that had been admirable when Freddie was a cadre in the party's struggle became reprehensible in the service of Tupamaro adventurism. The elder brother, ever loyal, agreed completely and told the party where Freddie could be found. Thus it was the comandante that led the police quick-reaction team to the farmhouse outside of Montevideo. The party found the police useful at times.

Just two mornings after Oliver, Alexeyev, and El Gordito came slowly through falling snow down the Las Cruces route, the battered body of the elder brother was found in the horse barn at the *estancia*. One of the gauchos heard a disturbance in the horse barn the night before but he had been too full of grappa to go see what is was about. The gauchos all spoke of how strange it was that the elder brother was found in the stall of that stallion. The investigating magistrate listened to what they had to say but he had no reason to call the death anything but an accident—surely no one would commit suicide in that fashion.

Draw a circle with a radius of, say, fifty miles around Missoula, Montana, and you would have Maria Elena and Alexeyev within it. Alexeyev wishes only that they were nearer a good library. The need for research seems endless.

Maria Elena, aka Marucha, is busy with little Freddie. The name on his birth certificate is Charles Frederick Robinson. When he is old enough—even if the danger of reprisal is not past—he will learn that his true name is Frederick Oliver Alexeyev.

Puig had the stallion put down. From the comfortable distance of Montevideo he manages the *estancia* for Maria Elena. His weekend visitors to the *estancia* leave with the impression that it is the ancestral seat of the Puig family.

Dr. Michael's book—"wise and compassionate . . . we ignore his message at our peril . . ." (*New York Times*)—was mentioned for the Pulitzer Prize that year. Friends were indignant that he did not get it. They wrote letters to *The New York Review of Books* complaining of the harsh cultural climate that denied him the prize. The reason for his being passed over, Michael himself said, was that he never was given the final proof of CIA complicity in Freddie Ortiz's death. Dr. Michael exposed the Agency's guilt, but, of course, it isn't quite the same.

Ivor Buchanan, OBE, is engaged to marry a blond woman from Buenos Aires of Anglo-Italian parentage, her accent in English very like Maria Elena's.

Nicholas Van Schaik is on leave without pay from the CIA. His career counselor suggested he spend some time sorting out his priorities. So far, the Agency is still running second.

The Director of the Federal Bureau of Investigation, on turning the information over to the Attorney General for prosecution, announced that "the Soviet espionage base in Mexico has been dealt a crippling blow."

Harley Drew is in the south of France. He has composed "The Galina Suite," a romantically melancholy piece, by no means unintentionally resembling something by Chopin. When not at the piano or in the garden, Drew is the popular dinner partner of cultured widows as far away as Cannes and Nice.

El Gordito bought the *Ionchería* on the main street of Amecameca. Lonchería Las Cruces is a popular spot with climbers going to and coming from the volcanoes. Ted Oliver is often to be seen there.

About the Author

John Horton grew up on the north shore of Chicago and attended Indiana University before joining the U.S. Navy in 1940. From 1946 to 1948 he studied at the University of Chicago, earning a master's degree in International Relations. He served as an operations officer in the Central Intelligence Agency at posts in the Far East, in Latin America, and in Washington, from 1948 to 1975. He returned to government service in 1983-84 as the National Intelligence Officer for Latin America. He and Grace Calhoun, married for forty years, live on the Patuxent River in St. Mary's County, Maryland. They have four children and five grandchildren.